"Just where do you expect me to sleep?"

Luke angled the flat-crowned Stetson low on his head and squinted at her.

"You must find other shelter. It's simply not decent—"

"Decent?" Luke sat up. "Is it decent to ask me to spend the night out in the rain?" He shook his head. "Sorry, lady. I'm quite comfortable just where I am." He leaned back and settled his hat over his face again.

He heard an indignant sniff. In his mind, he could imagine those morning-glory eyes sparkle with outrage. He knew the only thing that kept him from Noelle's tongue lashing was that proper Eastern upbringing of hers. And he'd bet a grubstake that she could really let loose, if she wanted.

Suddenly he wondered what that volatile passion that flared beneath her Goody Two-shoes facade might be like in bed.

His bed…

Dear Reader,

Entertainment. Escape. Fantasy. These three words describe the heart of Harlequin Historicals. If you want compelling, emotional stories by some of the best writers in the field, look no further.

This month, we are delighted with the return of author Jackie Manning, who has ventured beyond her usual English settings for a jaunt to the Wild West in her sparkling new novel, *Silver Hearts*. Since her debut in 1995 with *Embrace the Dawn* written as Jackie Summers, critics have described her books as "captivating," "marvelous" and "five-star reading!" Here, a doctor turned cowboy with a soft spot for women rescues a feisty Eastern miss from the trail, and their paths just keep crossing! Don't miss it!

Be sure to look for *Joe's Wife* by the talented Cheryl St.John. It's an emotional Americana story about a bad boy turned good and his longtime secret crush, now a widow, who proposes a marriage of convenience to him. In *My Lord Protector* by newcomer Deborah Hale, a much older man offers the protection of a temporary marriage to his absent nephew's betrothed—never intending to fall in love with her....

The Bride of Windermere marks the debut book of the talented Margo Maguire. In this tension-filled medieval tale, a well-connected knight has been sent by King Henry V to escort a beautiful and mysterious young lady to court. Intrigue and passion abound from start to finish!

Whatever your tastes in reading, you'll be sure to find a romantic journey back to the past between the covers of a Harlequin Historical®.

Sincerely,

Tracy Farrell, Senior Editor

Please address questions and book requests to:
Harlequin Reader Service
U.S.: 3010 Walden Ave., P.O. Box 1325, Buffalo, NY 14269
Canadian: P.O. Box 609, Fort Erie, Ont. L2A 5X3

Jackie Manning

Silver Hearts

HARLEQUIN®

TORONTO • NEW YORK • LONDON
AMSTERDAM • PARIS • SYDNEY • HAMBURG
STOCKHOLM • ATHENS • TOKYO • MILAN • MADRID
PRAGUE • WARSAW • BUDAPEST • AUCKLAND

ISBN 0-373-29054-3

SILVER HEARTS

Copyright © 1999 by Jackie Manning

This edition published by arrangement with Harlequin Books S.A.

® and TM are trademarks of the publisher. Trademarks indicated with
® are registered in the United States Patent and Trademark Office, the
Canadian Trade Marks Office and in other countries.

Printed in U.S.A.

Books by Jackie Manning

Harlequin Historicals

A Wish for Nicholas #398
Silver Hearts #454

Previously published under the pseudonym Jackie Summers

Harlequin Historicals

Embrace the Dawn #260

JACKIE MANNING

believes in love at first sight. She and her husband, Tom, were married six weeks to the day after they first met and he proposed, many happy years ago. Home is a one-hundred-and-fifty-year-old colonial in Maine where they live with their shih tzu and Aussie terrier. When Jackie isn't writing romances, she's researching and visiting interesting places to write about. She loves to hear from her readers. You can write to her at P.O. Box 1739, Waterville, ME 04963-1739.

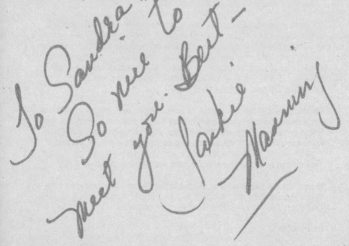

To Sandra —
So nice to
meet you. Best —
Jackie Manning

This book is dedicated to the many readers who hope to someday write a book. Go for your dream, you'll never be sorry. And to my sisters in Romance Writers of America, especially to the New England Chapter, the Maine Chapter and to the future published authors of my critique group.

And, of course, to my darling Tom.

Chapter One

Nevada, 1867

Noelle peered through the prairie schooner's dusty curtains and studied the black speck emerging from the sun-bleached horizon. Hope brought tears to her eyes, despite the reality that the image might be a mirage. She'd known that heartache before.

By habit, her fingers clenched the Hawken rifle. But as the shape loomed larger, the unmistakable rhythm of horse and rider emerged before her eyes. No, the horseman wasn't a fixation of her mind. Mr. Douglas was returning, just as he'd promised.

"Thank You," she prayed, unsure whether to laugh or cry with relief. "Forgive me for doubting You." But when the back wheel of her covered wagon broke down yesterday, and Mr. Douglas had left to find help, both knew that the mission might prove futile. Then later, when she noticed the jug of medicinal whiskey was missing, Noelle wondered if Mr. Douglas had planned to go on without her.

She'd heard tales of trail guides who took advantage

of single women left with all their worldly goods within the cumbersome prairie schooners. But Noelle had faith in Mr. Douglas, and he hadn't failed her.

She laid the rifle down beside her in the wagon, then wiped the trickle of sweat from her temple with her apron. No need for her driver to see that she'd been crying. With shaky fingers, she tucked the stray wisps of blond hair under her poke bonnet. When she looked as presentable as possible, she stuck her head through the curtains to wait for him.

The noon heat caused the green dots of sagebrush and mesquite to shimmer into wavy patterns along the prairie. The endless heat. Thank God she still had half a barrel of water. More than enough to last until they reached Crooked Creek.

She ignored the trickle of sweat running down her spine; her gaze fixed on the advancing horse and rider.

Mr. Douglas's gelding was a chestnut brown, not a grayish tan horse with black mane and tail!

Noelle's heart pounded; her breath caught in her throat. The stranger who was riding toward her wasn't the man she knew and trusted.

For good measure, she pulled out the old spare rifle that Mr. Douglas had brought with them. Two rifles were better than one, even if one was a relic.

Her hands shook while she clutched the powder horn and loaded the old weapon. Willing her fingers to stop trembling, she forced the panic from her mind. With teeth clenched, she laid the spare beside her and grabbed the Hawken, poking the barrel through the crack in the canvas.

The rider was well within her sights.

Dear God, she had never shot a man. But Mr. Douglas had coached her on what to do if the need arose.

She pushed back the images of what terror might have befallen him. If only the wagon wheel hadn't broken…

She could shoot a man if she must.

The rider, dressed in black, brought the horse to a stop. Although Noelle hid inside the wagon, she sensed the man knew, somehow, that he was being watched.

Tall in the saddle, the dangerous-looking stranger studied the wagon. Maybe, she hoped, he'd think the prairie schooner was deserted and leave.

She pressed the walnut stock against her shoulder until it hurt. No, if he thought the wagon abandoned, he might rummage through her goods for anything of value.

"Put down your rifle. I mean you no harm." The man's deep voice rang with authority. He dismounted and ambled toward her. Sunlight glinted off the pistols riding low on his gun belt. She saw with alarm that his right hand hovered close to his holster.

Tall, with a black hat tipped low over his eyes, the man's face remained hidden. She was certain his features were ugly. Only ugly, dangerous men sauntered in that sneaky way.

When he was within twenty feet of the wagon, she yelled. "Stop right there or, I swear, I'll shoot."

He froze. He raised his head. Dark eyes glittered menacingly below the black hat's wide brim. She knew he was deciding how to separate her from her weapon.

"Save your gunpowder. I'm here to help."

Noelle's only answer was the *click click* of the hammer of the Hawken rifle.

"Are you alone?"

"No," she lied. "My men have you covered."

His deeply tanned hand shoved the wide brim from his forehead, revealing an unsmiling, lean and angular face. His dark brown eyes trapped her with their un-blinking stare. The well-defined jaw and chin was hid-den beneath a week's growth of black beard. Her scalp tightened in reaction.

A black eyebrow lifted. "If your men are hiding be-hind your skirts, they're not the sort who'll do you much good." His mouth curled, creasing the dimplelike scar under his cheekbone.

"Get back on your horse or I'll shoot you dead." Noelle's voice held a control she didn't feel.

A tiny smile tugged at the corner of his mouth. "Charitable of you for offering to put me out of my misery." He took a step forward, his dark brown eyes glittered in earnest. "Found a man on the trail. Need to know if he's one of yours."

A well of fear ran through her. "Mr. Douglas?" she cried out before she thought.

The man scuffed the prairie sand with his scarred boots. "Was Mr. Douglas about fifty, sandy grey hair, and did he come to about my shoulders?"

Noelle's breath caught; her heart pounded. "Yes. Is he all right?" she added, hoping to sound less desperate than she felt.

The man took off his hat, the breeze parting his long-ish black hair. "Sorry, miss. He's dead."

The stranger's image blurred with her tears. She bit her lip, forcing back the reality of his words. "Why should I believe you? If he's dead, where's his body?"

The stranger's right hand brushed his gun belt, then slipped behind to pull something from his hip pocket. Noelle tightened the grip on the Hawken. But when the man retrieved a square cloth to wipe his face, she re-alized how tense she felt.

"I covered the body with rocks until he can have a

proper burial. When we get to Crooked Creek, you can give the sheriff the necessary details.'' The man glanced at the sun, high in the cloudless sky. ''We better get a move on. It's a good day's ride.''

He took a step toward her.

''Stay where you are.'' She poked the end of her rifle farther into the sun. ''How do I know you didn't shoot him and aren't planning to shoot me, too?''

''The man wasn't shot. Heart attack, from what I could make out.'' He cocked his head to one side and raised his hands in the air. ''You're holding the rifle, not me. Besides, what would I want with a prairie schooner with a busted wheel?'' He squinted one eye and waited, as if challenging her for an answer, but she gave none.

Finally he said, ''Look, miss. You'd best ride back to town with me. I noticed Indian tracks following your Mr. Douglas's trail back here. Only God knows why the Indians veered from the hunt. Otherwise, they'd have attacked by now.'' He put his hat on, then gathered the reins of his horse.

Tears welled at the corner of her eyes, and she fought down the whimper in her throat. ''All I know is that Mr. Douglas was a decent, God-fearing man, even if he liked a nip or two. All he spoke of was wanting to see the Pacific.''

The stranger shook his head. ''Damn fool greenhorns come out here…'' He paused, then pulled the hat brim low over his eyes. ''Hurry, lady. We're losing valuable daylight.''

''I won't go with you.''

She heard him swear under his breath. ''I'm sorry about your loss, miss. Truly I am. But patience isn't my strong suit. Now gather your water jugs and any whiskey you've got. Hop on back of my horse, and I'll give you a ride into Crooked Creek.''

"You don't understand!" She poked her head out from the canvas opening. "I can't leave the wagon.''

"Pardon?'' He tipped his hat at a rakish angle and studied her. The sunlight bounced off his cheek, and he didn't appear quite so menacing. "We're in big trouble, miss. Those Indians could attack any minute. Now, I'm riding out of here, with or without you. If you stay, you'll end up just like your Mr. Douglas, only—''

"He's not *my* Mr. Douglas. I-I mean, Mr. Douglas is…was my trail guide, not…'' She felt embarrassed to explain anything to this man. "I-I won't leave. You'll have to fix the wagon wheel.''

He glanced at her over his shoulder. "Won't leave? Why the hell not?''

"I'm carrying precious cargo. That's all you need to know.'' She brushed her fingers across her damp collar. "And I'd prefer that you speak to me without profanity, Mister…?

"Savage.''

She sniffed.

His mouth curled, revealing the dimpled scar. "Luke Savage.''

"I'm Noelle Bellencourt. I'd be obliged if you'd fix the wagon, then guide me into Crooked Creek. I'll pay you most handsomely.''

His black eyebrows rose, and wary dark eyes appraised her. "Miss, I've been on the trail for six straight days. All I want is a bloody steak, a bottle of rye whiskey and a bed with a…'' He paused, as though weighing his words. "Real sheets,'' he added without looking at her.

She felt her cheeks warm, aware that he'd meant a

woman—a painted-hussy woman that she'd heard about. She delicately cleared her throat. At least he'd been enough of a gentleman not to say so.

"I'll more than pay you what it's worth, Mr. Savage."

"I'd help you without payment, if I could. But it's a matter of life or death that I make Crooked Creek by Friday noon. Now put down that rifle and gather your things. We're losing time we don't have."

Noelle raised her rifle. "It's you who does not understand, Mr. Savage. You're not leaving without me *and* the wagon." Her voice held strong. "I'm a good shot, but even if I wasn't, at this range I couldn't miss shooting your head off."

His deeply tanned face showed no sign of her threat as he studied her. "Where you heading, anyway?"

"My uncle, Marcel Bellencourt, lives in Crooked Creek. He's a very wealthy silver miner who struck it rich during the fifties. He'll reward you for your trouble, Mr. Savage."

Luke scratched his week's growth of black beard. "Funny. I know all the folks in Crooked Creek. Never heard of a Marcel Bellencourt, rich or poor." He eyed her in that suspicious way that made her uneasy. "Sure it's Crooked Creek where your uncle lives?"

"Of course. My family received Uncle Marcel's letters from there since he arrived in Nevada. When my father died, my uncle asked me to make my home with him." Noelle felt a warm blush rise to her cheeks. She hadn't told a fib, exactly. But what difference did it make if Luke Savage thought her uncle's request had been recent rather than a general understanding? Her father made her promise that if something were to happen, she should go West to live with Uncle Marcel. All that mattered now was that she persuade Luke Savage to help her.

Luke scratched his head and frowned at the broken wheel. His deep sigh spoke louder than words. "That wheel's busted up good, miss. I'll take you to town, then you can find your uncle and have him come out here with another rig."

He sighed again. "You've no proper tools to fix a wheel. Didn't your Mr. Douglas tell you that?"

"I've brought my possessions all the way from New York City. I've traveled the last three and a half months by steamboat, railroad and wagon train, and I'm not giving up this close to Crooked Creek, Mr. Savage."

"Miss, I don't want to scare you, but Indian pony tracks were all over the area where I found your trail driver." He brushed his hat with his hand, waiting for her reaction.

She raised her chin a notch.

"If those Indians meet up with you, they won't just take your clothing and rifle like they did your trail guide."

Noelle gasped. "Took his clothing?" Her stomach almost turned with revulsion.

"Can you describe the clothing Mr. Douglas was wearing the last time you saw him, miss?"

Noelle steadied herself. "A b-brown leather vest, grey trousers and shirt. A g-gold pocket watch and ch-chain…" Her voice broke.

"I'm truly sorry about your guide, Miss."

She felt her throat constrict with tears, but she fought back with anger. "If these Indians are as beastly as you say, then you'd better hurry and fix the wagon wheel."

"You're either the most stubborn woman or—"

"I'll fix you something to eat while you're working."

"I tell you, I can't fix the damn thing!"

"Please, there's no need to yell or swear in my presence, Mr. Savage."

"All right, all right." He mumbled something unintelligible under his breath.

She felt grateful that he thought to spare her.

"I noticed a stand of cottonwoods over that yonder ridge." He tipped his head in the direction of a high rise covered with sagebrush. "Maybe I can cut a few trees, run one over the wagon's front and under the rear axle, then maybe we can walk the wagon into town. Got a saw or an ax?"

Relief and hope swelled within her. "Yes, mister..." She swallowed back the lump in her throat. "There's an ax in the trail box."

"I'll get it."

Her relief was short-lived when she remembered the stories told by the emigrants in the wagon trains loading at Leavenworth. Many guides took advantage of the lone women who drove rigs. After taking their money, the guides would break from the caravans, deserting the helpless women after only a few miles.

But Luke had ridden out of his way to backtrack Mr. Douglas's tracks to the wagon.... Luke Savage was no gentleman, but she felt she could trust him. There was something about the way he looked at her when she reacted to the news of Mr. Douglas's death.

When Luke returned with the ax, he tied it to the horse. "Best you come with me to the ridge in case Indians come. Bring the oxen, too."

She jumped down from the wagon and began unhitching the animals while Luke slipped the handles of the water jugs over the pommel. Luke's horse fidgeted back and forth, kicking clouds of dust into the air. When

Noelle had unfastened the oxen's yoke and hooked on their leads, Luke motioned her toward his horse.

"I'll help you mount."

She glanced up in suspicion. "What if you're only saying that you'll fix the wheel so I'll leave with you? Why should I trust you?"

He lifted the brim of his hat up a notch. His dark brown eyes glittered with speculation and something else that caused a fluttery feeling in the pit of her stomach.

The buckskin whinnied impatiently. Luke grabbed the oxen's leads, then mounted his horse. Staring down at her, he said, "Miss, I'm the only ace you got up your sleeve. Get on the horse, 'cause I'm leaving. If you decide to come, bring the rifle. You'll be the lookout while I chop down those trees."

Reluctantly, Noelle grabbed her rifle. He was right; she had no choice. She took his hand, but averted her gaze as she swung up behind him.

She heard him mumble under his breath. She didn't have to see Luke's solemn face to imagine his begrudging expression as he wheeled the massive buckskin in the direction of the high ridge.

Luke lifted the ax sideways and swung the final blow that brought the quivering young cottonwood crashing to the ground. The rush of air provided a fleeting respite from the oppressive heat. He inhaled the fresh wood smell while he mopped a bandanna across his brow.

This log and the one he'd previously cut would be enough to fix the wagon. It had taken him nearly an hour, he reckoned—time he didn't have.

The buckskin shied nervously, its eyes huge.

"I know, Deuce. I sense 'em, too." Luke glanced at

the spreading cottonwood about a hundred feet away where Noelle sat on a limb, rifle in hand, her gaze scanning the sun-baked range like a hawk. She turned toward him, then shook her head.

Luke nodded, but he doubted that Noelle would know what to look for. He had explained about the telltale dust funnels announcing unseen riders, but if the Indians had seen them ride over here, they could sneak up along the ridge without warning.

One thing was certain, the Indians were out there.

Luke swore again as he hitched one log to each of the oxen, bracing the load to drag behind the animals. He wiped the sweat trickling down his chest.

North and east, the flat, shimmering prairie would be too open for Indians to attack. But the west ridge, dotted with tall mesquite and sagebrush, would easily provide cover to hide the Indians and their ponies.

"I'm a damn fool to get caught up in this," he muttered to his horse. "Beneath all her bluster, she's a real greenhorn." He shook his head, recalling how her hands had trembled while she held that old weapon on him.

Luke led the oxen to the thick shade of the cottonwood tree where Noelle perched on a massive limb, rifle in her lap.

"What's in that long crate that you guard like a she-cat with a new litter?" he asked, adjusting the oxen's load.

"A gift for my Uncle Marcel," she said, her eyes fixed on the green-dotted prairie.

"If he's as rich as you say, why wouldn't he have the goods shipped with an armed guard of men, instead of a—"

Noelle lifted her chin. "It's none of your concern, Mr. Savage."

Damn right it wasn't. He swore under his breath. What he should be concerned about is how he'd make up the time to get to Crooked Creek by Friday noon. Lady luck had turned against him, and there was no sign that she might change her fickle mind.

Luke's thoughts returned to Noelle Bellencourt. He knew women as well as he knew not to draw to an inside straight. Better, in fact. And he'd bet all the poker chips in the Silver Hearts Saloon that Noelle didn't have a rich uncle waiting for her. But whatever her story, once she saw Crooked Creek, Nevada, she'd turn tail and head back East.

At the sound of his footsteps, Noelle turned toward him.

"When we get to town, you're on your own," Luke said. "If we walk all night, we'll reach Crooked Creek by morning."

"Why do we have to?"

"Because I've got to stop Blackjack from hopping the noon stage to 'Frisco. That slippery rascal isn't getting away from me this time."

"Blackjack?"

"My business partner, or I should say, *was.*" Luke mopped his face, then knotted the bandanna loosely around his neck. "Cheated me out of a string of gambling concessions. He knows I'm on his trail, but he'd never dream I'm this close." Luke smiled as he thought of the surprised look on Blackjack's face when he saw Luke, waiting for him with the sheriff.

"What type of business are you in, Mister Savage?"

He grinned. "Gambling, Miss. I'm the best poker player in all of Nevada."

Noelle's face paled. "And this…Blackjack? Is that his profession, too?"

"That, among others. But after I'm through with him, Blackjack will be shuffling his next deck in jail."

Luke strode to the logs tied to the oxen. Satisfied, he moved toward the horse. The buckskin shied uneasily.

"Did you hear something?" Noelle asked uneasily.

"Yeah." Luke felt it, too. It was as if someone were watching them. He'd had the feeling ever since he found Douglas's body.

"Think it's just the wind." Luke hoped she'd believe him. "If Indians are out there, the open country affords no chance for ambush. We're safe for the time being," he added, hoping to reassure her. No sense having a hysterical woman on his hands.

He helped Noelle mount the horse, then walked beside her, leading the oxen as they lumbered along, handling the cottonwood logs easily.

Luke's thoughts strayed back to the lone prairie schooner, stranded like a wounded white dove, and the woman riding beside him.

Before they reached the top of the ridge, a rifle shot, coming in the direction of the prairie schooner, cracked the silence.

Luke's horse whinnied, then reared. Before he could reach Noelle, she had slackened the reins, leaned her weight forward, and grabbed Deuce's mane to keep from falling.

Grateful that she'd had the sense to control the buckskin, Luke secured the oxen's reins to a mesquite bush, then mounted the horse behind Noelle. He grabbed the reins, then kicked his heels into the animal's sides, charging the horse over the rise in the direction of the wagon.

Chapter Two

Ayeee! Hoop hoop hoop! Ayee! Coo-wigh!

Anger and fear raged within Noelle, but fury won out as she listened to the rising shrieks behind her wagon. Several spotted ponies stood nearby. A tall, lanky Indian, dressed only in a buckskin breech clout and knee-high leggings stood, reloading a rifle. His head shot up when she and Luke galloped within sight.

In a lightning-fast motion, Noelle positioned her rifle, ready to take aim.

"Don't shoot!" Luke yelled in her ear. "That's Little Henry, the chief's son." Luke pointed to the lanky Indian, who by now had grabbed the rifle and ducked behind the wagon to warn the others.

"I don't care if he's President Andrew Johnson!" Rancor sharpened her voice. "He's attacking my wagon!"

Although she was breathless with rage, she didn't resist when Luke took the Hawken from her.

He drew the six-shooter from his holster and shot into the air; the acrid smell of black powder was everywhere. A stockier Indian, a few years younger than the first, jumped from the wagon bench and staggered to his knees. He hesitated, shaking his head as though dazed.

Noelle gasped, her blue eyes wide. Her small hand flew to her mouth as she stared. Luke glanced at the brown leather vest and gray shirt the savage wore. From Noelle's stifled cry, he knew the garments must have belonged to Mr. Douglas.

Luke stopped the horse a safe distance from the wagon. After he dismounted, he gave Noelle a stern glance. "Stay on the horse," he commanded, not trusting her to remain out of the fray. "Don't aim, but keep your rifle handy."

Renewed anger lit her eyes, but she nodded. Her teeth clenched as her wide-eyed gaze returned to the stocky Indian bent over on the ground.

Another Indian, wearing a black cowboy hat, stuck his head from the front of the prairie schooner. He shook his fist, then shouted a blood-curdling scream as he tossed an earthenware jug into the air. The bottle bounced along the sand, finally breaking in two.

Whiskey! Luke swore under his breath. Damn the luck. Even peaceful Indians, when drunk, were unpredictable.

Luke strode cautiously toward the chief's son. "Little Henry," he said in the native tongue of the Paiute. "Take your braves and go peacefully."

The dark eyes studied Luke for a long moment, appraising the man and the situation.

Luke noticed the gold watch fob and chain dangling from Little Henry's left braid. No doubt the chief's son took what he deemed the most valuable of their booty. Luke also knew that Douglas's horse must be tethered nearby.

"Tell your father, Captain Henry, that the yellow-haired woman sends her compliments to him, and wishes to give the horse you found, which belongs to the lady, as a gift for raising such a fine son as yourself.''

Little Henry's almond eyes lit with surprise, then he glanced back at Noelle, who waited anxiously on Luke's horse. When he gazed back at Luke, his expression, wiser than his eighteen years, held a question. ''You will tell my father of this happening?''

Luke took his time answering. He knew that a lengthy spell was required to show Little Henry that his question was considered serious. Luke stared into the deep-set eyes of the brave who would one day become chief of the Paiute Nation.

Little Henry had showed good sense in waiting to search the wagon after Noelle and Luke had left. Besides, Luke understood the young brave's need to prove himself. When the Indian found Douglas dead, with his chestnut alone on the prairie, Little Henry knew a horse was the highest honor to give his father.

''I have given your question great thought.'' Luke spoke the words solemnly. ''I find no reason to speak to your father of this happening. If you leave peacefully with your braves and do not bother us again, I believe the matter should be forgotten.''

Little Henry began to untie the watch fob when Luke stopped him. ''No. That is yours. A gift to you from the yellow-haired woman.''

Without any sign of emotion, Little Henry strode to the dazed Indian, still stooped over in the sand. He helped the brave onto a pony. Without a word, Little Henry leaped onto his pony, the other braves following his example. Amid the ponies' whinnies, they rode off, yellow dust kicking up at their hooves.

Before Luke could stop her, Noelle slid from the saddle and dashed toward the prairie schooner.

"Let me go inside first! There may be others," Luke shouted, racing after her. Before he reached the wagon, he heard her cry out.

Noelle shuddered a gasp and stared at the shambles inside the wagon. "Oh, my God!" She rushed to the splintered crate leaning on its side.

Those savages had touched her mother's things. A jolt of revulsion raged so violently inside her that she thought she might be sick. She touched the china cabinet, its fragile door still swaying from the broken hinge. Delft earthenware, once her mother's pride and joy, was reduced to a heap of blue-and-white shards, littering the shelves.

Noelle shook her head, refusing to give in to the threatening tears. The clamor of Indians' taunts and galloping ponies' hooves still rang in her head as she stared at the wooden crates and wicker cartons ripped open, mounds of clothing scattered everywhere.

Behind her, the wagon's floorboards creaked. She jumped, expecting to see another...

Luke's long shadow appeared across the bleached canvas sides as he stepped inside the wagon. She let out a muffled cry of relief.

Luke's jaw tightened as he glanced about. "They've gone. No need to be afraid."

"What if they come back?"

"No. The chief, Captain Henry, is a friend of mine. Little Henry will know that to do so will dishonor his father as well as himself."

"Those *friends* of yours were wearing Mr. Douglas's clothing. How do you know that they didn't surprise my guide and frighten him to death?"

Luke picked up a broken teacup, turning the delicate china in his hands. "Because I know."

"How can you be sure?"

"Because the cadaver showed no signs of fright. Death came from a massive heart attack, brought on by extreme exertion—"

"You're not a doctor. How do you know—?"

"I was once, miss." Luke regretted the words as soon as he saw Noelle's eyes widen with surprise. He saw the questions forming in her mind.

How he knew those questions. Those questions had kept him awake more nights than he could remember.

"But I'm a gambler now. Not much difference between gambling and doctoring, really." He grinned, trying to make light of something that he'd refused to think about any more. Damn, what was there about this woman that brought the past back like the deep ache of an old wound?

"It's nothing I want to talk about, so forget I mentioned it." He placed the broken cup fragments upon an overturned crate.

He turned his back on her as he stepped to the rear opening. "Maybe you should file a report about the Indians at the sheriff's office, Miss," he suggested over his shoulder. "What you do is none of my business."

"B-but…you're a witness." She shouted after him. "My witness. Just look what those fiends did." Noelle's hands trembled when she bent to pick up a black leather-bound book. "My Mother's Bible," she cried. Her eyelids closed as she caressed the gilt-edged tome to her chest. "I can still smell those savages."

Luke turned back and leaned inside the wagon. "Most of that is whiskey smell." He glanced around. "Any more whiskey in the wagon?"

"No. The only jug I had was for medicinal purposes. Mr. Douglas took it with him when he left to get help." No need to tell Luke that Mr. Douglas hadn't asked her permission.

"Recognize the empty crock jug...broken, on the ground outside the wagon?"

She glanced out the front of the wagon, then darted back inside. "Y-yes, it's the same jug."

"The Indians probably found the jug where they found Douglas's body. Drank the whiskey while they staggered along Douglas's backtracks." Luke stroked the dark stubble along his jaw. "That's why it took so much time for them to get here."

"What do you mean?"

"The whiskey. They drank the liquor first, then came looking for more." Luke's mouth quirked. "That whiskey might have saved your life, miss. You're one lucky lady."

"Mr. Douglas is dead. I'm stranded with a broken wheel a day's ride from Crooked Creek. And you're telling me I should be thankful for a jug of whiskey, Mr. Savage?"

His smile faded, and she regretted her words immediately. He was only trying to make her feel better.

"I'm sorry. I didn't mean to sound cross." A rush of gratitude welled within her. "I appreciate your kindness. You came to help, and I'm indebted to you. I don't know what might have happened if you decided not to follow Mr. Douglas's tracks."

"What's in these boxes that's so valuable?" Luke asked, as though purposely changing the subject. His dark gaze raked across the carelessly thrown floral gowns, red and black petticoats, black beaded jacket and a man's formal top hat.

Noelle rose, then straightened the small trunk containing her father's handmade props that he had used in his magic act. Shaking it gently, she felt relieved when nothing inside rattled. She forced a weak smile and glanced around the wagon. "My belongings are of little worldly value, but priceless to me and my uncle Marcel. It was my father's dying wish that I deliver what was left of their magic act. How could I refuse?"

Luke shuffled his feet uneasily. "Maybe some of it's salvageable." He straightened a squat wooden box from its side. The crush of broken glass made him wince.

Noelle squeezed her eyes shut. The mingled scent of rosemary, oregano and peppermint told her that the herb cabinet had fallen, her precious herb jars smashed.

"What's this?" Luke asked, peering into the largest crate of her father's.

Noelle glanced at the padded lid, ripped from the long wooden box. "Father's mirror!" She dashed beside Luke, forcing herself to be brave enough to view the damage. "My father and Marcel used the looking glass for their most famous act—the disappearing man."

Luke's brow furrowed. "The disappearing man?"

"Yes," she answered. "Thank God, the mirror's not broken." She studied the mirror carefully, her pale, serious expression staring back at her. Luke stood behind her, unwrapping the stiff packing. She was immediately aware of how large he was. Broad shoulders, powerful forearms. Her blond head barely reached the middle of his chest.

She felt Luke's warm hand when he placed it on her shoulder. "I'll help you straighten this mess later." He turned and his dark gaze met her blue eyes in the glass. For a moment, she thought his dark brown eyes might

stare through her. He was so very attractive, in an uncivilized rugged way. His thick, wavy black hair framed
his sun-bronzed face. Far away, the straight black fans
of lashes gave a piercing look to his expression. But up
close, Noelle saw the soft, mahogany velvet of his eyes,
like warm, rich coffee.

The heat from his hand felt strangely comforting, and
she made no move to remove it. For a moment, she
thought of how consoling it might be to lay her head
upon his chest and cry.

The shocking idea jarred her back to reality. No
doubt, it was the sudden brush with danger, the loss of
her possessions and the death of Mr. Douglas that beck-
oned such a foolish idea.

She turned from the mirror to meet Luke's darkening
gaze. He removed his hand, then averted his eyes.
"While it's still daylight, I must fetch the oxen."

"I'll go with you."

Fifteen minutes later, Luke found the oxen, still tied
with their loads, grazing peacefully on needle grass.
With a sigh of relief, he waved an okay sign to Noelle,
who waited in the distance. She glanced around cautiously, then followed with the buckskin while Luke led
the beasts, dragging their load, back to the wagon.

"Fix something to eat while I water the animals,"
Luke said when they returned to the wagon.

Noelle wiped her palms on her apron, then climbed
into the wagon. She blinked away any trace of emotion
as she made a path through the shambles of her worldly
goods to prepare their meal.

By the time Luke had returned, the campfire was
crackling, and the aroma of strong coffee filled the air.

Noelle glanced up from tending the fire to watch as
Luke hung the empty pail on the water barrel. A wel-

coming sense of relief flowed through her as she realized Luke could repair the wagon wheel. Soon, she'd be with her uncle.

Noelle's gaze lingered along the sparse knots of prairie grass while she fed the cattle chips to the fire. She'd purchased the bag full of animal droppings from a passing Conestoga wagon over a month ago. Survival had forced Noelle to quickly forget any squeamishness at using dung as fuel. In fact, she was proud of all she'd accomplished—more than she would have thought possible—since leaving New York City.

Her mouth felt as dry as the endless dust. What might have become of her if Luke Savage hadn't arrived? But he was here, and he'd promised to see her safely to Crooked Creek. Yes, she was very lucky, indeed.

Beside the wagon, Luke balanced the half-empty coffee mug on a rock while he shimmied the cottonwood bolts into place. Try as he might, he couldn't get the thought of Noelle Bellencourt out of his mind. But the harder he tried, the more those startling blue eyes made him want to take her in his arms and protect her.

Damn, he wanted to do more than that, if he was honest. But women like Noelle spelled trouble, in any language, and he was too smart to get caught up with the likes of her, again.

Once had been enough for a lifetime.

Noelle looked nothing like his fiancée, Alice. But the Eastern manner of speaking and thinking were the same. Luke shook his head at the comparison. Alice had wed his best friend while Luke had been in the war. At the time, Luke thought he'd never get over the betrayal, but now, he realized that if he had married Alice, he would have been miserable to be part of that Philadelphia social circle.

It takes a special breed of fool to be enticed by a woman, regardless of how alluring. And damn, he was no fool.

Luke propped up the side of the wagon where the broken wheel had been. Greenhorns. They come out West, their wagons full of wares, their heads full of dreams, only to find their hopes busted like a broken wheel at the end of the trail.

He swore under his breath. Why was he thinking about Noelle? His mind should be on Blackjack and getting his money back, not on a greenhorn woman who'd be on the next stage back to New York when she first set her eyes on Crooked Creek.

"Supper's ready, Mr. Savage."

His stomach growled. The tantalizing aroma of pan-fried biscuits and something else he couldn't quite identify nearly drove him crazy. He grimaced.

He dismissed his wayward thoughts as he took the tin plate of fragrant baked beans and biscuits she offered, and sat upon a flat rock a few yards from the campfire. Never had beans and biscuits smelled so delicious.

"More coffee, Mr. Savage?"

He shoved his hat back from his forehead. "Yes, miss," he said with a jaw stuffed with biscuit. He watched the feminine curve of her hip as she leaned forward, pouring the dark brew into the cup. Where had she learned to cook like that? What else might she have learned about how to please a man?

He frowned, totally disgusted with himself for his inability to ignore her.

She smiled as she returned to the plate she had dished

up for herself. Before she lifted a spoon, she bent her head and said a few words under her breath.

Luke felt like a heathen. But he recalled a time, not so long ago, when blessings, manners and polite talk had been a part of his life. He scraped the last of his beans with a spoon. He'd prefer feeling like a heathen than remembering the past.

He soaked up the bean juices with the ragged edge of the biscuit. Manners, be damned. West of the Mississippi, manners could get you killed if you took your mind off your six-shooter for long. No room for fancy manners in Indian country, Miss Noelle Bellencourt.

"Mighty tasty," he said instead. "Last time I had biscuits that melted in my mouth was in Philadelphia when—" His voice halted, as though he had divulged a great secret.

"You're from Philadelphia?" Surprise lit her blue eyes.

He nodded.

"Is that where you had your doctor's practice?"

"It's not polite to ask questions of strangers," he answered. He saw her cheeks color, and he felt ashamed for his rude remark. Yet if he admitted that he'd begun his practice in Philadelphia, she'd only ply him with more questions that he wasn't ready to answer. He took a swig from his coffee mug.

"Your voice doesn't sound as though you're from Philadelphia," she said after a few minutes.

Luke reached for the last biscuit, broke it in two and popped half into his cheek. "Best to talk like the locals. That way, you don't go bringing attention to yourself." He washed the mouthful down with more coffee.

"Are you hiding something from your past?" Her eyes brimmed with questions.

"Nope. Trying to forget." He sensed her growing inquisitiveness. In the lengthening silence, he wondered if she could control her curiosity. After a long time, he discovered that her strong will had won out.

"So, what will you do if you can't find your uncle?" Luke asked, despite his refusal to get involved.

She lifted her head and stared at him as if the idea never crossed her mind. "I thought you said it was impolite to ask questions of strangers." Her mouth tilted into a smug little grin.

"Of course I'll find him," she volunteered anyway.

"Marcel Bellencourt. Never heard the name, miss. Where's this silver mine of his suppose to be?"

"I'm not certain. I do know that he owns a grand house with a small army of servants." She laughed, and for the first time, he realized how very pretty she was. He wished he hadn't noticed.

"I've written to the lawyer in town, telling him of my arrival."

"Mike O'Shea?"

"Yes, do you know him?"

Luke nodded. O'Shea was a good enough lawyer for fixing miners' quarrels, but he didn't have the experience for much else. No need to tell her that, Luke decided.

"Mister O'Shea will escort me to my uncle." She smiled again in that confident way that often worried him.

Luke ran his fingers across his chin. "You know, miss. It's not unheard of for a man to work the mines for years, then not strike color—"

"Strike color?"

"It means not to find gold or silver."

She nodded, intent on his every word.

"Not strike color," Luke continued, "but write to his family back East, and with a gut full of the Silver Hearts Saloon's finest whiskey, compose a boastful yarn or two."

Her chin lifted defensively. "What are you suggesting, Mr. Savage? Hundreds, no thousands of men and women have struck it rich in Nevada. Are you insinuating that my uncle is lying?"

Damn, she and her uncle were none of his business. "Didn't mean any disrespect, miss." Luke scratched his beard as he glanced at her. No sense adding his abject speculation to what she's already been through today.

"Sounds like you've got this all figured out." Luke gave her what he hoped was an encouraging smile. He stood up and drained the last of his coffee. "We'll leave as soon as I finish fixing the wagon. In the meantime, why don't you pack away your gear and throw out all the broken crockery." He glanced up at the growing clouds in the west. "We might be in for a storm."

Luke put the cup on the empty tin plate. "Before nightfall tomorrow, you'll be safe with your uncle, God willing."

The thought brought a soft glow to her face. She smiled and leaned back against the buckboard. "My uncle is all the family I have left," she said wistfully.

A ripple of uneasiness coursed over Luke. He'd wager all of the money Blackjack owed him that Marcel Bellencourt wasn't a wealthy miner living in Crooked Creek. But there wasn't anything he could say to a woman as stubborn as Noelle. She'd have to learn from her mistakes, like all the other tenderfeet. But she sure made a doozie of a mistake when she decided to come West.

Luke cleared his throat. "Miss, I'm afraid you'll have

to part with some of your things. The wagon should be relieved of as much weight as possible. That mirror of yours is heavy and cumbersome—"

"No!" She looked as shocked as if he'd asked to kiss her.

He groaned. "Besides the mirror, those trunks and boxes—"

"Mr. Savage?" she said, her eyes glittered with determination. "I'll walk alongside the wagon, but what I have left that's intact remains aboard."

"Miss, that cottonwood dragging along the ground isn't as strong as a wheel. The stretch of dust up ahead has no trees, in case another wheel breaks—"

"We'll just have to chance it."

Luke swore under his breath as he pulled his hat low on his head. No need wasting a man's breath on a stubborn woman. "Then help me shift the load to the side of the wagon with the two good wheels."

"A fine idea, Mr. Savage."

Noelle smiled in such a heartfelt way that he almost forgot his anger. He mumbled to himself as he stepped up on the trail box and pushed one of the trunks to the opposite side of the wagon.

Damn, Luke thought. Why couldn't he have just kept on riding?

Noelle listened to the slow, steady pounding of Luke's makeshift hammer while she dried the last frying pan and tied down the equipment with ropes.

Tomorrow. How she dreamed of the day she would finally arrive in Crooked Creek. But after the tragic experience with poor Mr. Douglas, then Little Henry and his band, she felt nothing but relief to finally end the long, perilous journey.

This rugged country was full of wild, savage encounters, and she prayed she'd seen the last of them. She stole a glance at Luke Savage.

Wild, larger than life, almost as savage as his name.

No, she decided, after a thoughtful pause. Beneath his rough exterior, Luke Savage could be dangerous, she was certain. But he held to the Code of the West. She felt safe with him. She sensed he was a decent, good man, despite a certain reluctance.

The man was fascinating. Beneath the rough manners were intelligence, keen insight and strong hands that had once had held a scalpel. She sensed that he was hiding something. A dark past, no doubt. *I wonder how he came by that dimpled scar below his cheekbone?* A knife fight, no doubt.

Noelle bit her lip. She stood motionless, her arms clasped over her midriff as she watched him work. His large, steady hands drew the timbers into place. He then began lashing the log to each axle. A few minutes later, Luke tested the log by applying his weight to it between the wagon and where it touched the ground some ten feet behind the wagon bed.

Luke Savage was a genius. Self-consciously, she straightened the folds of her apron. Her gaze met his. "Please forgive my earlier bad manners. I was quite rude. I hope you accept my sincere thanks."

He lifted a dark brow. "You're not under your uncle's roof, yet, miss. Best hold your thanks until we get there."

A flash of her earlier pique ignited. Why couldn't he say, you're welcome, instead of adding another dose of his cynicism?

"You should be more optimistic, Mr. Savage. Those

who dwell on the misfortunes of the world often receive what they expect."

"That's because the pessimists are so busy helping the optimists out of one fix after another." His dark eyes glittered with amusement. "You're just lucky this pessimist happened along when I did."

She couldn't help but smile when she saw the teasing light in his eyes. "I don't believe you're as cynical as you pretend, Mr. Savage. After all, you've fixed the wagon wheel, my load is intact, and we'll be in Crooked Creek by tomorrow night."

He strode to the oxen. "We've got to be there by tomorrow noon. Night will be too late if I'm going to catch Blackjack."

"But we can't travel that fast—"

"It's a fifteen-mile walk to town from here, Miss. If we leave now, we'll have ample time before the afternoon stage leaves Crooked Creek." A muscle in his cheek twitched.

"I won't have my oxen driven into the ground because you have to meet a stagecoach." Noelle straightened her shoulders and tilted her chin. "You said yourself, without a fourth wheel, the animals will have to pull harder. They can't plod that far without resting."

"You're forgetting the Indians. The sooner we get to town, the safer we are."

Her eyes glittered with disbelief. "I've heard that Indians don't attack at night."

"Some do."

She said nothing while she ran her fingers along the curly foreheads of the oxen. By the way they closed their eyes and stretched their necks in pleasure, Luke guessed the beasts were used to the attention.

"Miss Bellencourt, if you care so much for the animals, remember that they're food on the hoof to anybody who decides to shoot them." He felt guilty as the horrifying reaction reflected on her face.

"We'll get a few miles behind us before dark. After we rest a few hours, we'll start up before dawn. It won't be too much for the beasts, I promise." Luke felt relieved when the tight mask of worry faded from her face.

Luke's spurs jangled as he walked to his horse, but before he put his boot in the stirrup, he paused. "What the hell is this?" He yanked out the white linen cloth from under the buckskin's saddle and held it at arm's length like it might bite.

"That's a tallow cloth." Noelle bustled around the wagon. "It's prevents animals' hides from chafing during long rides."

Luke frowned. "Tallow cloth?" He scratched his beard.

"Yes, Mr. Savage. I wrap them around my oxen's necks under their yoke. Once your horse becomes accustomed to it, you'll never want to be without one. It's very simple to make. Just a linen square dipped in melted tallow."

He took a deep breath. "Miss, I hardly think…" He paused, as though considering. He muttered under his breath and tucked the cloth back under the saddle blanket where he found it. He remained silent while he mounted the horse, then cut out for the expanse of prairie grass outside the wagon's circle.

Noelle watched him leave, then quickly scanned the low rise of sand and mesquite for any sign of movement. Despite the early evening beauty, she knew that wolves, coyotes, snakes and scorpions were there along with Paiutes and desperadoes.

Luke was right. The sooner they left here, the better.

Chapter Three

Darkness came suddenly, along with a driving rain. By the time Luke had finished gathering grass for the oxen, he couldn't see one boot-length in front of him. Exhausted, hungry and soaked to the skin, he unsaddled his horse, untied his bedroll, then ran to shelter beneath the wagon.

Luke spread the buffalo hide in the dry space under the wagon when Noelle appeared. She grabbed the coal oil lantern, hooked on the trail box and carried the lamp inside the wagon. A few minutes later, a flickering glow slanted through the floorboards above his head.

Over the wind and rain, he heard her while she readied for bed. She must be near dead from exhaustion, he thought, remembering how she endured the storm without complaint.

After positioning the horse blanket on top of the buffalo skin, Luke laid down and rested his head on the horse's saddle. "I'm right within a holler if you need something, miss."

The bustling noise above his head stopped.

"You can't sleep beneath my wagon." Her words

barely carried above the storm. "It's simply not…proper."

"Just where *do* you expect me to sleep?"

Noelle climbed down from the back of the wagon and leaned toward him. The wind and rain plastered the loose hair from around her face, but she made no move to pull it back. "I-I would think you'd be gentlemanly and find a dry spot under a bush, or something." She flicked her hand in a pointless gesture.

Luke angled the flat-crowned Stetson low on his head and squinted back at her. "Not this gentlemanly cowboy!"

"You must find other shelter. It's simply not decent—"

"Decent?" Luke sat up. "Is it decent to ask me to spend the night out in the rain?" He shook his head. "Sorry, lady. I'm quite comfortable just where I am." He leaned back and settled his hat over his face, again.

He heard an indignant sniff. In his mind, he could imagine those morning glory eyes sparkle with outrage. He knew the only thing that kept him from Noelle's tongue-lashing was that proper Eastern upbringing of hers. And he'd bet a grubstake that she could really let loose, if she wanted.

Suddenly, he wondered what that volatile passion that flared beneath her Goody Two-shoes facade might be like in bed.

His bed.

Relieved that she couldn't see how quickly she affected him, Luke rolled over on his back and pulled the brim of his hat over his eyes. Through the cracks between the floorboards, he could see her, if he was so low-down rotten as to take advantage of the situation.

He grinned, wondering when she'd notice, and notice she would.

He heard the clatter of her bootsteps above his head, then the wagon jarred as she jumped from the tailgate. He muttered to himself as he lifted his hat and saw her leaning down, staring at him.

"Get out from under there, or so help me, I'll shoot you."

Luke sat up and stared at her. A shawl covered her head, and she aimed that antique of a rifle on him.

"Is this how you thank me for fixing your wagon?" He scowled back at her. In the lantern's glow, he noticed a wide black smudge extending from her left eyebrow to her chin. Noelle must have gotten soot on her hands when she touched the blackened campfire rods, then wiped her face.

As self-righteous as a new preacher in a town full of sinners, Noelle studied him, her one blackened eyebrow lifted with superiority. He couldn't help but grin.

Noelle motioned with the rifle barrel. "And what's so amusing?"

Luke forced his most practiced poker face. "Tell me, Miss Bellencourt. How does one tell a refined city lady like yourself that she has soot all over her face?"

Noelle relaxed the rifle. "I beg your pardon!"

Luke smiled. "My my, little lady. The last time I saw a face like yours was at a minstrel show in Kansas City."

She moved the weapon to one side and glanced at her hands. She gasped, and Luke knew that she finally realized that her face was covered with soot.

"You don't look like a cactus blossom, yourself." Noelle lifted her smudged chin in that defiant way that was becoming all too familiar.

Luke scratched his three-day growth of beard and shook his head. "Won't argue with you there, Miss." He shot her a side glance.

As serious as a preacher scrubbing away the devil's footprints, Noelle furiously wiped her face with her drenched apron, all to no avail. The sight of her jaw clenched in steely pursuit as she wiped at the black circles, which now spread across her nose and cheeks, caused Luke to chuckle.

"You're despicable!"

"I-I'm sorry, but—" A round of helpless laughter overtook him. "I'm not laughing at you, it's just that I can't remember when I've been so damned tired, so damned wet and so damned miserable." He gasped before laughing again. "Go ahead, Sunshine. Shoot and put me out of my misery." Another fit of hilarity overtook him.

Noelle's mouth tilted with a hint of a smile. "I guess I do look rather…disheveled."

"Rath-er." He pronounced the word in two exaggerated syllables, then fell back, laughing.

Noelle's smile deepened. "I've never been so utterly miserable, myself." Her lips parted, revealing perfect, pearl white teeth. She laughed, and the light tinkling sound reminded him of his summers during the family picnics along the Delaware River. The image gave him a start. He hadn't thought of his childhood since his brother, Chad, died.

"Good night, Mr. Savage." Noelle retreated inside the wagon.

Jarred for a moment, Luke muttered, "G'night."

After Noelle had washed and prepared for bed, she listened to the rain pounding the canvas ceiling above her head. She eyed the covering warily. This was the first rain she'd endured since Nebraska, while she and Mr. Douglas traveled with the main wagon train over six weeks ago. What would she do if the priceless objects she had brought all the way from New York became ruined with water?

As though to assure herself that her things were safe, Noelle opened the creaky lid and peeked inside the metal trunk. Cocooned in paper lay the blue satin gown and feathered bonnet that she planned to wear when she finally met her uncle. How she wanted him to be proud of her.

Despite all the upsetting events, ending with Mr. Douglas's death, she knew that her troubles would be over once she found her uncle. *Tomorrow*. She would have a family again.

Noelle hummed softly as she covered the hat with paper and straightened the blue satin hair ribbons before closing the trunk lid.

If only she could wash her hair, but she knew better than to waste precious water with such frivolity.

Raindrops hammered a steady rhythm as she towel-dried her wet hair. Suddenly, she had an idea. Noelle rose, wrapped a blanket around herself and stepped from the shelter of the wagon into the storm.

Luke's hat lifted from his face when he heard her steps on the tailgate. "Where are you headed?"

"I'm going to collect rainwater."

He raised his head and watched her. "Why?"

She sniffed. "I need to wash my hair, if it's any of your business."

Luke shoved his hat over his face and laid back. "No need to gussy yourself up for me, miss. You look as pretty as a filly."

She knew he was teasing, and she refused to take the

bait. "I care nothing for what you think," she huffed, but she knew that wasn't true. As if to validate the lie, she added, "My uncle would expect a Bellencourt to arrive looking respectable, Mr. Savage. *I* shall not let these primitive surroundings affect my personal standards, but I wouldn't expect someone with your sensibilities, or lack of them, to understand."

Luke watched her unhook several enamel wash basins from the side of the tail box and place them along the ground. "We've got another hard day of travel ahead of us, lady. You're going to get all dusty again. You can clean up at the public bathhouse in Crooked Creek. Only costs a nickel."

"Good night, Mr. Savage."

Luke knew he had been dismissed. Well, let her get gussied up for whomever she thought would be waiting for her in Crooked Creek. For once, she wasn't bothering him.

He rolled over and tried to go back to sleep, but the ping of the rain pelting the metal washbasins echoed above the storm like rifle shots.

"Jeezzo, woman! What other kind of torture will you think up next?"

Noelle chuckled as she slipped inside the thin bedroll and blew out the lantern. Outside, the wind and rain droned like a coyote howling at the moon. Despite the storm's fury, she felt safe and protected, thanks to the disquieting man who slept beneath her wagon.

Noelle bolted up from her bedroll, wide awake. She glanced about. Thunder rolled. Lightning flashed, then another clap of thunder boomed. The wagon creaked against the wind. Brushing the loose tendrils from her face, she laid back against the makeshift pillow. Would the rain prevent them from reaching Crooked Creek by tomorrow? If so, would Luke go on ahead without her?

Another crack of lightning lit the sky, then earsplitting thunder. Suddenly, Noelle remembered the basins of rainwater. A gift from heaven.

Wrapping the shawl about her shoulders, Noelle braced for the storm. Wind tore at her as she wedged her way to the ground. As quietly as she could, Noelle crept to the enameled pans. Delighted to find them almost full, she lugged each container back inside the wagon.

Excitement rushed through her as she realized this was her first preparation for the most important event in her life since her father died. Of course, deciding to leave New York City had been the most important decision, but finally to meet her uncle—the only relative she had. Yes, it was decidedly the most important event.

Noelle carefully poured the precious essence of lilac into the cold water. The fragrance always restored her spirits with happy memories. She smiled as the sweet floral essence filled her lungs. She felt as if she were ten years old, hand in hand with her mother, strolling Central Park after attending Noelle's father's Saturday matinee performance at the Niboli Theater. How her mother had loved the hedge of blooming lilacs along the park.

A sudden sadness wrenched her as she remembered her mother's tearful surprise when Noelle purchased the essence of lilac for her mother's birthday. Noelle had tutored students in Latin and mathematics to earn the extra money. She knew the perfume was extravagant, but that was why she bought the gift. She knew her mother would never lavish something so expensive on herself.

Noelle blinked back the sting of tears. The smell of lilacs also reminded Noelle of her own wish. Someday, she'd have a house and garden, just like the one her mother had always wanted. But Noelle would have her dream, unlike her mother, who had no choice but to settle for the rented rooms above Harrison's Saloon where Noelle and her parents lived.

Noelle put the thought from her mind as she poured the soft water over her head. Then, she soaped her long hair, enjoying the simple luxury. When she'd finished, she carefully squeezed the thick, white lather from her coils of hair before dipping her head into the rinse bucket. The rainwater felt silky to her fingers. Definitely a gift from heaven.

Soap stung her eyes. She muffled a cry as she squeezed her eyes shut while carefully feeling in the darkness for the towel she had carefully laid on top of the trunk. Suddenly, the water bucket tipped and a whoosh of water spilled into her lap. She forced her eyes open.

"What the hell!" Luke yelled, coughing and sputtering below the prairie schooner.

Oh, no! Noelle felt her way in the darkness for the lantern. She reached on the top shelf for the Mason jar filled with matches. "I-I'm so sorry, Mr. Savage," she offered. Her eyes stung with soap as she forced herself to see. "I-I tried not to disturb you—"

"Disturb me? Jeez, woman! You just drowned me."

Her fingers shook as she lit the lantern. "I-I'm so sorry, Mr. Savage." She winced at the thought of him beneath the wagon, jarred from sleep by the deluge of water between the floorboards of the wagon.

She crouched down beside the sputtering lantern,

moving clothing and boxes out of the way of the spilled water.

Suddenly the curtain jerked back and Luke stood, glaring at her. Black hair streamed down his face, his shirt and vest were splotched with white suds, his leather pants and boots glistened with dampness, and essence of lilac permeated the air.

"Mercy!" Her hand shot to her mouth as she took in the sight of him.

"Where'd you think the water was going to go?" Luke's breath caught in his throat at the sight of her. His anger vanished, replaced by a feeling like a boot kick to the stomach. In the soft yellow lantern light, Noelle bent over the spilled water bucket. The neckline of her gown dipped provocatively over one shoulder. He caught sight of the dark cleft between her breasts.

Cursing himself for the effect she had on him, Luke tried not to look at the wet-stained bosom where a long tangle of hair, the color of saltwater toffee, fell over one shoulder.

"I'm so sorry," she repeated, jumping to her feet. Her nipples were hard beneath the thin, wet nightgown. Suddenly aware of her appearance, she grabbed her shawl and pulled it modestly around her. Unfortunately, the gesture did nothing to halt his imagination of how she would look, naked beneath him.

She rose to her feet, clutching a thick towel. Before he could say anything, she took a step toward him and daubed his wet shirt and vest with the cloth.

"I-I'll do that," Luke managed to growl, yanking the towel from her. Their fingers touched, and he felt as if he'd been struck by the lightning streaking outside the wagon.

Noelle released the towel as if it were a hot branding

fork. She stepped back, suddenly self-conscious for touching him. "I-I didn't mean—" Her cheeks flamed with embarrassment. "I-I'm so sorry." She stroked her wet hair, as though she didn't know what to do with her hands. He wondered if she could possibly feel the same way as he did.

Of course she didn't. She was a proper New York bluestocking, and she trusted him, damn his soul. She had no idea what low-down thoughts were going through his mind faster than a Nevada jackrabbit.

He forced his gaze away, but in his mind, he could still see the way her breasts strained against the drenched, sheer cotton nightgown. "I'll dry myself off with the horse blanket." He chanced a darting glance at her. "Here, you need this worse than I do," he said, tossing the towel back at her.

Noelle shivered, catching the towel. For the first time, Luke realized that she might take a chill. He took off his jacket and dropped it over her shoulders.

"Dry your hair and change into warm clothes. I'll bring you some whiskey to chase that chill."

"Whiskey?" Her chin lifted a notch. "Amelia Bloomer says that liquor is the devil's own hell's broth. Look what trouble those poor Indian braves encountered after drinking Mr. Douglas's whiskey, besides—"

"Who the hell is Amelia Bloomer?"

She sniffed. "Amelia Bloomer is the publisher of *Lily,* a very respected ladies' periodical—"

"You're in Nevada, Little Miss Sunshine, not New York City. Here, whiskey is medicine, among other things." He turned and shot out of the wagon while he still could. He swore, then put on his hat while he trudged to his saddlebags. He reached inside, pulled out the bottle of whiskey and gulped a generous swig himself. Noelle's shadow was silhouetted against the schooner's stretched canvas, reminding him of her every feminine curve, much to his consternation.

Damn, what did he ever do to deserve this temptation? He swallowed, then strode back toward the tailgate. He could force himself to be a gentlemen for one more day. But once they reached Crooked Creek, that lady was on her own, Uncle Marcel or no Uncle Marcel.

"I said I don't drink spirits."

He pulled out the cork and handed the jug to her. "This might be the only thing that will keep you from catching a fever. Just how far will we get if you get sick, huh? Now, take a swig. You won't go to hell—I promise."

She shot him a reproachful glance. "Very well, I'll take one taste if you promise to quit pestering me." She closed her eyes, held her nose with two fingers, then took a mouthful and swallowed.

Her eyelids flew open, and she gave a choked cough.

Nick grabbed the bottle from her before she dropped it. "That wasn't so bad, was it? I bet ol' Amelia Bloomer couldn't have belted one down any better."

Noelle managed a scathing glare before she coughed again. Finally, she inhaled a deep gasp of breath.

Nick grinned. "Now get out of those wet clothes. When you're dressed, blow out the lantern. G'night Miss Bellencourt."

Noelle heard him climb down the back of the wagon. The whiskey burned a path straight to her belly, and already she felt flushed from the experience. Or was it Luke Savage?

What was she feeling? She wasn't afraid of him, of that she was certain. Luke was nothing like the men who would frequent Harrison's tavern late at night, ogling her when she came home from the theater. Maybe that was it. She had never met anyone quite like him.

Her pulse quickened when she recalled how Luke had stared at her. Soaked to the skin, he was justifiably angry. But she recognized the dark and mysterious way that his eyes brightened when his gaze raked over her.

Desire.

She'd admit that it was desire that stirred her being when he grabbed her waist, earlier. When she began to touch his leather vest, she felt him tense beneath her touch, and in that fleeting moment...

Nonsense. What she felt was appreciation, nothing more. She was grateful to him, and Uncle Marcel would repay his services once they arrived in Crooked Creek. Then she could forget Luke.

And they would arrive safely, thanks to Luke. Yes, it was gratitude she felt and nothing else.

She removed her wet garments and put on a high-necked cotton nightgown. After blowing out the lantern, she turned her bedroll over, then curled up to sleep. "Pleasant dreams, Mr. Savage."

Luke's low mumbling from beneath the wagon renewed her feeling of safety. She closed her eyes, content.

"Come on, Sunshine, time to wake up!"

Noelle opened one eyelid and peered into the darkness. A few inches from her, Luke leaned on one elbow and smiled down at her. He lay on a rumpled bedroll, the horse blanket hugging his shoulders.

Noelle jerked her head up. "Wh-what are you doing in my wagon?"

Luke's mouth tipped slightly. "I was sleeping. What did you think?"

She gasped, unable to hide her astonishment. "I didn't give you permission to—"

"No sense asking for something you can't get," Luke drawled. "Besides, only a fool would sleep in a mud hole if there's a dry space available." He stretched lazily. "C'mon. The storm has stopped. I noticed you've got dry kindling under the wagon. You make the fire, I'll be back in a while."

Noelle clasped her shawl in front of her and pointed to the closed curtains at the rear. "Now that you're awake, get out!"

Luke raked back the hair from his face. "Jeezzo, woman! Are you always this snappish in the morning?"

"Out!" She grabbed his bedroll and blanket, tossing them after him. His deep chuckle made her cheeks burn.

After he left, Noelle took a deep breath, then tried to calm herself. But his words plagued her mind: *Only a fool would sleep in a mud hole if there's a dry space available.*

She sighed. What he had said made a logical sense, so very much like Luke. After all, his gear was soaked because of her—although it had been an accident. And with all that he'd done for her, how could she begrudge him a dry place to sleep?

She peered out the back of the wagon. Early dawn hugged the prairie in a stretch of deep violet shadow.

"Mr. Savage?" she called into the stillness.

Only the buckskin's answering whinny disturbed the silence. The horse was tethered to the side of the wagon. Perhaps Luke had gone to fetch the oxen. When he returned, she'd apologize for her testy words.

By the time Noelle had finished dressing, Luke hadn't

returned. The unbidden thought that something might have happened to him flashed through her mind.

Tossing her shawl around her shoulders, Noelle grabbed the rifle and set out to look for him. Even a man as invincible as Luke Savage was vulnerable to wild animals and Indians, although he probably didn't think so.

Her shoes sucked in the mud as she strode through the prairie, her eyes becoming accustomed to the half light. Although it should be easy to follow his steps in the wet sand, it was still too dark to see them. The storm rumbled in the distance; the moon hid behind low clouds.

Mesquite and sage hung heavy with last night's rain, splattering her skirts with droplets as she strode past. She moved along the swaying shadows of brush, while visions of crouching sharp-fanged beasts or Indians with raised tomahawks intruded on her logic. Her heart began to pound. Had a pack of wolves or bandits sneaked up on Luke when he'd untied the oxen?

No, she would have heard something. Then where was Luke? Maybe he was disgusted with her earlier bad temper and felt she needed to be taught a lesson.

No. He wouldn't deliberately cause her to worry. The idea surprised her, and the thought made her realize that not only could she trust him, but she knew he'd protect her, even with his life.

The thought gave her pause. Luke Savage was basically a decent man, despite the darker side of him that she'd rather not know about. Gambling—the social ill of the lowest kind. But she sensed he'd do her no harm, and for that, she'd be eternally grateful.

A coyote howled in the distance. She trembled, pulling the shawl tighter about herself. Maybe she should have started a fire before she went to look for Luke. Without a campfire to keep away wild animals, the coyotes, hungry and smelling the oxen, were a threat.

The wind picked up, cool and damp with the smell of sage. Noelle sidestepped a large tumbleweed rolling toward her, safely avoiding its sharp prickers.

So, where was Luke? The fine hairs on her forearms tingled. She took a deep breath, willing herself to keep a calm head as Luke would do.

Suddenly, a whiff of something dreadfully familiar drifted on the wind. Her head lifted toward the scent of death. Since her journey West, she had smelled its presence more times than she cared to remember.

Bracing herself, she picked her way slowly toward the source of the stench. The area of the prairie grew open, flat and sparse of grass. After a few minutes, she hesitated, wondering if she should wander so far from camp. She glanced over her shoulder, astonished at how far she'd walked. She should return to the wagon. Then after sunrise, she would return to pursue her curiosity. Besides, maybe Luke had come back and was searching for her.

Before Noelle had time to turn around, she heard a whisper of movement beneath the wide branches of a mesquite bush. She wheeled around to see a hunched figure in the shadows. Her mouth went dry. She raised the rifle to take aim, while juggling the lamp. Her fingers shook on the trigger as she drew the object into her sights.

"Luke? Is that you?" she called out, hopefully. The only answer was the rustling of branches as the dark shape crept closer.

"Luke?" Her voice rose to an unrecognizable pitch. Her mouth filled with the metallic taste of fear.

A feeble cry shattered the stillness as a wobbly-legged calf staggered toward her. Noelle gasped with relief. She lowered the rifle and the lantern, her heart racing like a runaway mare.

Not more than a few weeks old, she'd guess. She'd witnessed many cattle births while she traveled with the wagon train.

Where was its mother? Then Noelle saw the silent, dark heap of an animal, obviously the calf's mother, lying nearby. Her throat tightened with the harsh reality of life.

"Come here, precious," she whispered to the orphaned calf. She knelt beside the furry animal. She rubbed the calf's velvety white face, and checked the animal's rib cage for broken bones. She winced at the frail little body, but the animal appeared not to be injured.

"Wait until Uncle Luke sees you," Noelle said, smiling. She set the lantern on the ground and slung the rifle over her shoulder. When she gathered the calf in her arms, she was surprised at how tame the calf appeared to be. Poor thing. Probably too weak from hunger and thirst to protest.

"You won't have to worry about those bad coyotes any more," she whispered.

Its saucer-size brown eyes gazed up at her with such innocence, that Noelle felt her throat strain with unshed tears. She hugged the calf and strode purposely in the direction of the wagon.

When she arrived at the camp, the horse whinnied, but there was no sign of Luke. Her worry returned. Although she wanted to search for him, she decided she'd wait until the sun rose. By then, she wouldn't need the light, but she wouldn't forget to retrieve the lantern where she left it in the prairie. She put the rifle down near the wagon.

The calf uttered a weak, mooing sound. She patted its head while she thought. It would be dawn within the hour. If Luke wasn't back by then, she'd follow his tracks to see where he'd gone.

The calf nuzzled against her warmth, and she rubbed her fingers across the pink nose. The animal grabbed her finger, sucking hard. Noelle felt a pang of sympathy for the starving animal. She felt inside its mouth; a row of teeth protruded along the lower gum, but the upper gum was bare. She picked up the calf and placed it down inside the wagon, then she rummaged through the sparse food supplies. The only suitable food she had was canned milk and cornmeal.

She jumped down from the wagon and opened the trail box, but nothing she found would provide a container to give the calf a drink. The buckskin whinnied nervously, pawing the ground, as though jittery that its master hadn't returned.

Noelle glanced toward the horse, then noticed Luke's leather gloves shoved under the ties on the saddle. She took one of the large gloves and tried it on her right hand.

Yes, this would do nicely. She smiled as she strode to the water barrel. First, she'd poke a hole in the finger, then fill the glove with milk mixed with water. At least it would provide the calf with immediate nourishment until she made a gruel out of cornmeal. When they were on the trail and into better pasture conditions, she'd cut needle grass for the poor little thing.

With a knife, she poked a small hole in the fingertip of the sturdy leather. She winced at what Luke might say. But when she arrived in Crooked Creek, she'd ask

Uncle Marcel to advance her enough money to purchase a pair of gloves for Luke from her first week's wages.

Luke's long strides gained ground as he strode in the direction of the prairie schooner. Coffee. Black and hot. Sizzling bacon and a pile of feathery flapjacks as only Hoot, the cook at the Crooked Creek's café can make 'em. Luke groaned at the tempting images in his mind as his stomach growled louder than a grizzly.

If only Luke had kept riding instead of following the dead man's tracks back to Noelle's wagon. By now, he'd be waking up beside Jubilee at the Silver Hearts Saloon, well rested, with all of his needs deeply sated.

Instead, he'd have one more day of walking through prairie, back to town, leading a team pulling a busted wagon, with nothing to quiet his appetite but beef jerky. He swore as he shoved the binoculars back in the case and looped the strap around his neck.

Appetite, hell. What bothered him wouldn't be satisfied by food, damn him. Noelle Bellencourt was a hindrance he couldn't afford. Yet she ignited a flame in him that grew each time he saw her.

He swallowed, remembering how she'd looked when he crawled into the wagon, drenched from last night's storm. He'd made the mistake to steal a glance at her after he'd fashioned a makeshift bed from his saddlebags and blanket.

Her flaxen blond head nestled against the pillow of blankets where she lay, asleep. Even in the darkness, he'd been able to see her lovely face, framed in the white lace of her nightgown, like an angel in repose.

He'd tried not to stare, but damn, he couldn't help himself. The memory brought an unbidden rush of feelings, feelings he didn't want to feel. Women like Noelle

Bellencourt came with a high price. Marriage. Home. Children.

He drew a deep breath. She needed a responsible man to take care of her, and she wouldn't find him in a rough mining town like Crooked Creek. She'd learn that lesson sooner or later, and he didn't want to be around when she did.

Early streaks of sunlight began to appear along the hilly horizon. The chimney of a lantern glimmered in the sun. Luke's eyes narrowed as he strode toward the familiar object. When he recognized it as Noelle's lantern, his mind raced. *What the hell had she been doing this far from the wagon? And where was she now?*

Luke charged toward the prairie schooner. Deuce tossed his head, nickering a welcome as the animal sensed his master approach the camp. Before Luke reached the unlit wagon and tore open the curtains, he heard Noelle's humming from inside the wagon.

Relief, as monumental as he'd ever felt, coursed through him. When he returned his rifle into the saddle scabbard, he realized his hands were shaking. He took a calming breath, while he scratched along Deuce's neck. The sweet sounds of Noelle's voice drifted on the sage-scented air, and he could hardly keep himself from running inside, holding her to be sure she was all right.

What are you doing, Savage? He took another deep breath, but nothing seemed to burn the image and the resulting thoughts from his mind. He forced himself to face her.

"Miss Bellencourt. I'm back," he called before climbing onto the tailgate and peeking inside.

Noelle glanced up from her place in the center of the wagon. In her lap was a calf, not much bigger than a large dog. She was spooning a thin, yellow liquid down the animal's throat.

"Jeezzo, woman—"

Noelle's smile faded, and she stiffened. "I found him while I was searching for you. His mother had died." She frowned. "And where have you been? I was worried to death."

"I've been out checking the trail ahead."

"Why didn't you take your horse?"

"Too noisy."

"How could you see in the dark?"

"I was looking for campfires." Luke studied the scrawny calf. "Besides, I can see in the dark as well as an animal."

Her brows lifted in skepticism. "Did you see any Indians?"

"Indians are too smart to leave signs. We can only guess that they're out there. I did see a campfire up ahead, about three hours away. With any luck, they'll be gone by the time we get there."

"Do you think they're friendly?"

"Prepare for the worst." He glanced toward her. "We've got to be on our way. Let the calf go."

"What do you mean, let him go?"

Luke sighed. "We can't take the calf. It'll slow us down. Most of the grass around here is pale green. That means alkali. We'll have all we can handle to keep the team away from the bad grass, without having to play nursemaid to a calf."

Luke jumped down from the wagon and strode toward the oxen.

Noelle shot her head out the rear curtains.

"Mr. Savage, may I remind you that this is my wagon and my calf."

"The calf or me, Miss Bellencourt." Luke's long-legged stride didn't falter. "It's your call."

Chapter Four

*U*nreasonable, pigheaded, mule of a man! The words remained unspoken, because Noelle refused to give him the satisfaction of arguing. Besides, she knew Luke was right. The calf *would* slow them down.

The calf scratched its curly head against her arm. She couldn't help but smile at the little creature. *There must be a way to convince Luke to take the calf.*

She raked her fingers along the top of its chin as she thought. "Pay no attention to your bad-mannered Uncle Luke. He has a great deal on his mind. But rest assured, little one. You'll not be left behind as a meal for the coyotes."

The calf licked her hand with its raspish tongue, and Noelle smiled. Finding the calf was a good omen. A good omen for Luke, as well.

By the time Luke returned to the wagon from scouting ahead on the trail, Noelle sat primly on the driver's bench, the oxen were hitched and waiting, and the calf was nowhere in sight.

Luke tied his horse to the back of the rig, then strolled to the driver's seat. Grabbing the reins of the oxen, he glanced at the woman beside him. "Came to your senses, I see."

The poke bonnet she wore hid her expression, but he didn't miss the challenging lift of her chin in response. Luke knew better than to think she'd give up easily on the idea of bringing the calf. He paused, waiting for her reply.

Finally she met his gaze. "We're losing daylight, Mr. Savage. I thought you were in a hurry—" A long raspy bleat from inside the wagon interrupted her.

Luke jumped up and dashed inside the rig for the calf. But Noelle grabbed the calf only moments before and clutched the bewildered animal to her bosom.

Noelle's blue eyes glittered defiantly. "Don't you dare touch him."

"Jeezzo, woman! Don't you know that you can't hold that animal all day? And if you leave him in a moving wagon, he'll fall and break his neck. Use the sense God gave you and think of the animal."

Her stubborn glare was her only answer.

Luke swore, then took a deep breath. "Be reasonable, woman. Give him to me, and I'll put him out of his misery. He won't feel a thing."

Noelle's eyes rounded in horror. The calf shifted awkwardly within her grip. She moved to the back of the wagon, coaxing the animal to her, then grabbed the spindly-legged critter in her arms as she climbed down.

Luke watched as Noelle marched around the prairie schooner, the calf in her arms, and strode in front of Luke as she made her way along the trail. Wind swished the calico skirts about her ankles as she balanced the calf in her arms.

"You won't last five minutes," Luke yelled. Angry

with himself as much as with her, Luke snapped up the oxen's reins and urged the team after her.

The wagon creaked and swayed with the load. Luke held his breath to see if the cottonwood log would hold fast as it dragged in place of the rear wheel. He sighed with momentary relief. So far, so good.

Within minutes, Luke and the team caught up to Noelle and the calf. She stepped aside to let him pass, her determined blue gaze focused straight ahead.

Damn, she was an ironclad female! He'd laugh if the situation wasn't so dangerous. "We're beginning a stretch of alkali desert with water unfit to drink," he yelled at her. "Grass unfit to eat that only teases the animals. If we break down, we'll be forced to leave the wagon and strike out on foot through country fraught with Paiutes, desperadoes and greenhorns who are so frightened they'll shoot first and think later."

Her only answer was a quickened pace. He grumbled to himself. "Of course if those culprits were to come upon a woman…" He paused, hoping his words had finally found their mark.

Instead, she clutched the critter as a she-bear clutches its cub. Noelle's poke bonnet pointed straight in the air as she marched past the prairie schooner, with the calf mooing plaintively from her arms.

"Okay, lady. It's your choice."

Luke urged the team to a slow, steady gait along the slope of desert that spread before them. A few minutes later, he stole a backward glance. The calf's head bobbed as Noelle began to struggle with her load. Her jaunty march had slowed to a dragging shuffle. Beneath Noelle's loose gown, he could imagine her knees almost buckling with the weight of the calf. But he knew Noelle wouldn't give up until she dropped. "You've been warned, lady. Don't call to me for help. I've got a stage to catch.''

Luke clenched his jaw, determined to be as stubborn as she was.

When he had traveled several more miles, Luke drew the team to a stop. He glanced over his shoulder briefly and felt relieved to see that now the calf ambled beside her. Luke shook his head as he watched Noelle force one foot in front of the other, trail dust from the wagon covering both her and the calf. Damn if he didn't admire her determination. He'd never met any woman who would have put up with what she had without complaint.

The sun and dust beat through the thin calico of Noelle's travel-worn gown and apron. Loose hair from beneath her sunbonnet flew across her face. It didn't matter. Each painful step brought her closer to meeting her uncle. To see the surprised and happy expression on his face when he saw her was worth every sacrifice.

What if Uncle Marcel had married since his last letter over a year ago? Perhaps she might have a new aunt and maybe even a little niece or nephew. The idea almost brought tears of joy to her eyes. Yes, she was tired, but she'd walk through fire to be part of a family again.

Ahead, she noticed that Luke Savage had stopped to rest the team. He leaned against the wagon, drinking from the water barrel and smoking a cigarette. His broad shoulders contrasted attractively with his slim hips and long tapered legs. She felt a frisson of feminine response, chastising herself immediately. She averted her glance to the calf, wobbling along beside her. She would refuse to rest; she would take his offer of water, but nothing else.

''Don't move!''

Noelle glanced at Luke, who stood about twenty feet from where she walked. He aimed his six-shooter at the calf.

"Whatever are you…?"

"Don't take another step, I said." Luke stood as still as the mountain range, aiming his gun at the calf ambling at her side.

"No!," she cried. "No, don't—!"

The shot rang out, echoing along the far hills. She froze, afraid to look. She forced her eyes open and glanced at the calf. Within two feet of the animal lay the largest rattlesnake—a sidewinder—she had ever seen. Shot dead.

She hugged the calf, then gazed up at Luke as he sauntered toward her. She swallowed the dry dust in her throat. "I—I thought…" She swallowed the words.

"I know what you thought." He slid the revolver into his holster. "I think this is the time when you tell me how Uncle Marcel will reward me most generously." His deep brown eyes glittered with amusement as his fingers slid over his dimpled scar.

She wiped her face with her apron. Lack of sleep, heat and fatigue made her dizzy. A flush of self-consciousness tore at her senses. She lifted the calf in her arms, refusing to give him up.

"You win." Luke spat the words as he strode beside her. "Give me the runt."

She glanced at him suspiciously.

He scowled. "Don't look at me like that. I won't hurt the critter." He shot her an arched look. "Besides, I've changed my mind. If the animal makes it to town alive, you can sell it. The extra money will help pay your fare back to New York where you belong."

Noelle pulled back. "I'm not a quitter, Mr. Savage."

"That's nice." He took a long drag on his cigarette, then tossed it to the ground, grinding the butt in the sand with the heel of his boot. "But this land makes quitters out of a lot of strong people. If your uncle isn't waiting for you in town, you'll have little choice but to head back where you came from."

Noelle shot him a fueled look, but she said nothing. He watched her climb onto the driver's seat and pick up the reins.

Within the next few minutes, Luke had unhitched Deuce from the back of the wagon and mounted the horse, placing the calf across his lap. The grating bleat was its only protest.

Luke watched as Noelle straightened the reins, then settled back against the seat. She turned to give him an appreciative smile. "You're a decent, kind human being, Mr. Savage."

I'm a sucker for a pretty face, he thought irritably. Damn, you'd think he'd know better after what he'd been through with women. "Let's move out," he said instead.

With one hand, Luke balanced the calf across his lap while he pulled out the gloves he kept tucked beneath his saddle. Pulling on the right glove, Luke glanced down to see his trigger finger poking out of a hole in the leather.

"What the…?"

The critter lifted its head and bleated. In a heartbeat, the calf grabbed Luke's trigger finger and sucked. Luke stared, then glared at Noelle. He didn't need the sticky dampness inside his glove as further evidence to know that he was wearing the calf's nursing mitt.

Noelle's chuckle further irritated him.

"Don't tell me." His words shot back. "I assume

you'll be asking Uncle Marcel to buy me a new pair of gloves.''

"Mr. Savage," she said, purring the words. "You've been so very kind that my uncle will reward you with a new suit, as well." She pursed her lips and stroked her chin as she studied his travel-worn outfit. "Maybe a new hat, neck scarf and boots—"

"No need, Sunshine, but thanks." Luke shoved his hat down over his face and led Deuce into a slow walk. *Does she think she can buy her way to whatever she wants?*

Damn, he really didn't want to know what she thought. All he knew was that because of Noelle, he'd arrive in Crooked Creek carrying a bony animal in his arms, which stunk worse than he did. He only hoped he could sneak into town without anyone seeing his trigger finger sticking out of the calf's nursing glove, and his clothes reeking of lilacs.

Little Miss Sunshine, on the other hand, would arrive fresh as all springtime, her shiny curls bouncing beneath a sprightly new bonnet. She'd probably wear that blue silk gown that he'd noticed after Little Henry and the other two Indians had rummaged through her trunks.

Luke's gaze wandered across the muddy trail that sprawled ahead of them. *Proves that women like Noelle Bellencourt could take care of themselves. Besides, it was none of his business what happened to her.*

But Blackjack on the other hand...

A corner of Luke's mouth lifted into a smile. *If Blackjack was planning to make that 'Frisco stage to-day, the old man would be waking up just about now, yawning and scratching, never dreaming that by nightfall, he'd be staring out of prison bars.*

And with a little luck, Luke might make it to town

in time to surprise Blackjack before he embarked on the stage. Yeah, with just a little luck.

About ten-thirty, Luke guessed, gauging the distance of the sun from the horizon. He'd taken the driver's seat while Noelle had busied herself, preparing for her arrival to meet her uncle at Crooked Creek.

The sun-faded wooden buildings spread along both sides of the main street of Crooked Creek like miniature wooden blocks he and his brother had played with as children.

The curtains behind him swished open and Noelle came to take the reins from him. He glanced at her. Noelle, dressed in the blue silk gown, looked more lovely that he'd imagined. Freshly scrubbed, radiant with excitement, Noelle smiled at him, as though waiting for him to notice.

Their gloves touched when he handed the reins to her. "Changed your frock, I see," he said, wishing immediately that he hadn't mentioned that he'd noticed. He kept his eyes on the trail, feeling more flustered than when he was ten years old and forced to attend his first dancing class in Philadelphia.

Luke stepped from the wagon onto his horse in one fluid movement. He knew Noelle was watching him. Probably she was irritated that he didn't tell her how pretty she looked in her blue dress that matched the color of her eyes.

Seated on his mount, Luke leaned over and picked up the calf from behind the seat. The calf appeared at ease as it laid across Luke's lap. Within minutes, it curled its head back around to the pommel and went to sleep.

"Thanks to you, Mr. Savage, we have survived," Noelle said. He felt her appreciative gaze upon him.

"Yeah."

"My uncle will want to meet you, Mr. Savage. Where will you be staying, if I may ask?"

He pulled out a bag of tobacco, then rolled a cigarette paper with one hand. He didn't have to see her to visualize her my-uncle-will-make-everything-all-right look on her face.

"Silver Hearts Saloon."

He heard her slight intake of breath.

"Oh."

They rode in silence, listening to the creaking and jostling of the wagon and the steady braying of the oxen.

"There's the jail," he said, pointing to a one-story, adobe building. Luke's back straightened as he glanced around for any sign of the waiting stage. "I'll drop you off at the lawyer's office above the bank building, then I'll take your rig over to Shep's Livery Stable where your uncle can pick it up."

"I'm much obliged to you, Mr. Savage. I don't want to think what might have happened to me if you hadn't come along."

The smell of lilacs still wafted from his clothing. His perfectly fitting gloves were ruined, and as soon as he yanked Blackjack off the stage and saw that the scoundrel was safely behind bars, Luke planned to head for the public bath. He'd need to soak a month to get the dust from his bones. "My pleasure, miss."

He gazed at her. The blue silk *did* match her morning glory blue eyes. With that perky bonnet with the jaunty feather curling above her heart-shaped face, Noelle would captivate the lawyer, Mike O'Shea, at first sight.

Among the widows, prospectors' wives and hookers in Crooked Creek, there weren't any single women like Noelle Bellencourt. Yeah, O'Shea would be dazzled, all right.

Luke took a deep breath. Her hands, holding the team's reins, were clad in delicate sprigged muslin gloves. He hadn't seen such stylish clothing since he'd left Philadelphia.

Suddenly Noelle's eyes widened. "Isn't that the stage you were waiting for?"

Luke tore his gaze from her and stared as the San Francisco stage tore through the main street and angled off in a northwesterly direction.

"Hell's bells!" Luke's horse circled around. "Here," he yelled, dropping the calf into her lap.

"But I—" Noelle's mouth opened to protest, but by the time she grabbed onto the calf and pulled him onto her lap, Luke had already kicked his horse into a gallop and taken off after the stage.

Noelle stopped the team, then settled the calf behind her inside the wagon. The calf leaned heavily against her back. She watched Luke and the buckskin shorten the distance between him and the stage.

"Come little one," she said finally, picking up the reins. "Let's find Uncle Marcel."

Luke's single shot brought the stage to a halt. The driver's smile of recognition widened. "Whoa, Luke. What's the matter?"

Luke slid from his horse and grabbed the stage door. "Don't mean to delay you for long, folks," he said, tipping his hat to the astonished faces staring from the windows, "but I'm only—" Luke opened the door, and in those first few seconds, disbelief filled his thoughts. "Where the heck is Blackjack?"

Willie Hanson, the stagecoach driver jumped down from the driver's bench. "Blackjack? You haven't heard?"

"Heard what?"

"Dammit, Luke. I hate to be the one to tell ya, but your partner went to his justly reward."

Luke leaned on the open stage door, his boot on the step. "Justly reward? You saying Blackjack died?"

Willie touched his hat brim. "Three days ago, Luke. I—I thought you knew."

"No, I've been at Lake's Crossing the past two weeks." He turned back to Willie. "How'd it happen?"

Willie shook his head. "Ol' Blackjack was headin' back along the Truckee River when he must have hit a bump, or his horse got scared by a rattler. His rig toppled into the river and he drowned." Willie removed his hat and stared at his shoes. "Just after the big rain, and the river was swollen by the flash flood." He shook his head. "Terrible shock."

"Yeah." Luke had never thought of Blackjack as being capable of dying. "Did I miss the funeral?"

Willie shook his head. "Never found the body, but his coat and that black top hat he always wore were snagged on a branch alongside the river. Figured the body is long gone to China by now."

Luke knew a rat when he smelled one. "Are you telling me they never found Blackjack's body?"

Willie squinted, frowning. "Can't have a body if it rushed along a ragin' river, too, can we?"

"How do you know that Blackjack didn't stage the accident to make us think he drowned?"

"Why'd he do that?"

Luke mounted his horse and turned toward town. "Never mind, Willie. Sorry I held you up for nothing." He waved, then headed back to town.

Luke knew what he'd do. He'd file criminal charges against his old partner, whether he was dead or alive. But deep in his soul, Luke sensed that Blackjack was somewhere, alive and well. "Not for long, partner. I'll track you down until you pay me back every dollar that you've cheated me."

By the time Luke reached the sheriff's office, he was grinning. "Just like Blackjack to think he could outsmart the townsfolk. But when I find him, he'll sure as hell wish he were dead."

Ten minutes later, as Luke stepped up to Sheriff Wade's office, Noelle Bellencourt and the town's only lawyer, Mike O'Shea, were coming out the door.

"Mr. Savage, the most awful thing has happened." Noelle's face was pale and from O'Shea's protective hand upon Noelle's elbow, Luke knew he had been correct about the lawyer's reaction to her.

"I've had a bit of bad news, myself," Luke said. Focusing back to her, he asked, "Didn't your Uncle Marcel arrive yet?"

Tears sprung to her eyes. "Oh, Mr. Savage. My uncle is dead."

"Dead?"

Just then, Sheriff Wade stepped outside into the sunlight. "Terrible thing, Luke. Who'd ever think that Blackjack would end up being flushed along the Truckee River."

Luke and Noelle turned to stare at Sheriff Wade.

"Noelle's Uncle Marcel?" Luke asked.

"And Luke's partner, Blackjack?" Noelle's voice was barely a whisper.

"One and the same." Sheriff Wade glanced at the lawyer.

"It's true, Luke." Mike O'Shea pulled out a clean linen handkerchief and handed it to Noelle. "I've got his last will and testament in my office. My client's legal name was Marcel Jacques Bellencourt."

Noelle's chin quivered, her fingers tightened around the white handkerchief in her hand. "Mr. O'Shea said that my uncle had called himself by the last name of Bell. And he went by his middle name." She swallowed. "I think I'd like to see his home now, please." Her eyes blinked back tears.

"Come this way, Miss Bellencourt. It's—" Mike O'Shea exchanged glances with Luke. "It might be better if I found you a place to stay with one of the widows in town."

Noelle shook her head. "No. If the house is good enough for my uncle, it's good enough for me."

Luke already knew what she had in store. "O'Shea, why don't you let me show her Uncle Marcel's *home,* since I'm going right by there, myself."

Luke took Noelle's arm and eased her from the lawyer's grasp.

O'Shea flared. "As her legal representative, I think the lady should come with me."

Luke's only answer was a smile as he led Noelle across the dusty main street and past the half-dozen saloons and dance halls that crowded the main drag of town.

Mike O'Shea glared at Luke as he raced to catch up with them. Noelle's mouth pressed into a firm determined line, her gaze straight ahead. Luke grinned. Damn, he could hardly wait to see the look on her face when she saw the Silver Hearts Saloon.

Chapter Five

Ike's tinkling piano rendition of "Oh, Susanna" blared from inside the swinging doors of the Silver Hearts Saloon.

Luke stopped, then swept his arm toward the sign above the establishment. "Miss Bellencourt, may I present your kindly uncle's abode."

O'Shea grabbed her sleeve. "Don't go in there, Miss—"

"I'll take care of the lady, O'Shea," Luke said, removing the lawyer's hand from her arm. "Why don't you go back to your office and file some claims or something?"

O'Shea glared at Luke like a man who'd just had his claim jumped. "I think the lady should have something to say about that." He craned his head around Luke's broad shoulder to peer at Noelle. "I'm certain your uncle would have wished me to act as your protector, Miss Bellencourt," he said, his left hand straightening his bow tie.

Noelle gave him a proud little smile. "Thank you, Mr. O'Shea, but I'll be quite all right."

That's what you think, Luke mused, though he didn't

want to say anything to scare her. Damn, but she needed a solid dose of the grim reality of what life was like in Crooked Creek, and the sooner she found out, the sooner she'd be on the next eastbound stage.

"Very well. I'll be in my office, across the street, if you need anything, Miss Bellencourt." O'Shea's smile faded as soon as Noelle turned away, then he shot Luke a murderous look.

Luke chuckled back at him. Noelle pushed through the swinging doors and hurried inside the saloon. Luke dashed after her, his hand at her waist, half expecting her to swoon.

He led her past the men at the bar, who doffed their hats and shuffled their feet self-consciously, their drinks forgotten as they gaped in openmouthed surprise at the lovely young woman by Luke's side.

Curly, the bartender, leaned his large torso upon the bar, his thick arms braced as he stared openly. His bald head reflected the golden lamplight from the kerosene lanterns along the wall.

At the piano, Ike's fingers didn't lift from the yellowed ivories. His brown hair, parted in the middle, slicked flat against his head. "Glad t' see ya, Luke!" he yelled, over the rollicking chorus of "Marching Through Georgia."

Only Noelle's faintly blushed porcelain skin gave hint to her emotions as Luke ushered her farther into the saloon's dim interior. Frankly, he was surprised at her staunch composure.

A faint commotion stirred at the top of the stairs. "Luke, darlin'!" Jubilee drawled. The tall, red-haired woman, dressed in a low-cut green taffeta gown, scurried down the steps and dashed around the green baize-covered tables of poker-playing cowboys toward Luke.

"Yoo-hoo, Luke," hollered Marigold and Iris, the remaining dance hall girls, who waved from the second-floor landing. A feminine curiosity Luke recognized all too well, spread across their faces as they watched Jubilee and Noelle eye each other warily.

"I've missed you," Jubilee said, purring the words into his ear. She angled her hip against him in a shimmer of green taffeta. He tried to ease her away but not before she kissed him hard on the mouth.

He pulled back, and Jubilee's green eyes slanted at Noelle, who lifted her head and sniffed. Her shoulders drew back, and she hid any further emotion behind carefully schooled features.

"Who's she?" Jubilee asked finally, jutting her hip in that female territorial gesture that Luke knew usually meant trouble.

A hush fell over the room as though every ear were tuned for Luke's response.

Luke cleared his throat. "Everyone," he said, his gaze appraising the crowd. "Let me introduce Miss Noelle Bellencourt, Blackjack's niece and the new owner of the Silver Hearts Saloon." He smiled lazily and winked at Noelle.

"New owner?" Jubilee spit out the words. "Since when?"

"Since Blackjack's untimely death," Luke said matter-of-factly. Moving toward Noelle, he said, "Let me show you around," he said, as he steered Noelle away from the red-haired woman.

Jubilee pursed out her lip and glowered at Luke, but he ignored her. With his hand on Noelle's waist, he guided her toward the side door of Blackjack's office.

"Just one moment!" Noelle stopped and turned toward the crowd. In a clear voice she said, "I'm certain you were as devastated to hear of my uncle's death as I was. Perhaps more so, because…'' She paused, and Luke wondered if she might break down in tears.

''…Because you knew him,'' she continued, her head high. ''…Which was something I never had the privilege of doing.'' She spoke the words with an eloquence of sincerity.

''My uncle's death has been a bit of a shock, so if you will please bear with me.'' She paused, then glanced at Luke. When their eyes met, he looked into those glorious blue depths. An overpowering urge came over him to wrap his arms around her and protect her from the disappointment and uncertainty that he knew she was feeling. But Noelle's gaze was unflinching and asked no quarter.

''I'm closing this…place,'' Noelle continued, ''until further notice.''

The assemblage broke into shouting and yelling. Everyone was talking at once. Noelle clapped her hands, to no avail. Stepping up on a chair, she clapped her hands again. ''Please! Everyone, Please!''

A gunshot rang out, silencing the room. Ike stood beside the piano, a smoking revolver in his hand. ''Shut up and let the little lady talk!''

Noelle's eyes were the size of saucers as she stared at the tall lanky man. ''Th-thank you, Mr.…?''

''Ike, miss. Just call me Ike.'' He smiled, revealing several missing teeth, which added to his charm. His Adam's apple bobbed up and down and his long face blushed the color of red poker chips.

Noelle smiled graciously at him. ''Mr. Ike, and all of my uncle's employees, please line up along the bar. I wish to speak with you. Everyone else, please leave in an orderly fashion.''

Instead of the exodus, which Noelle had obviously expected, no one moved. Finally, Luke pushed back his black Stetson and held up his hand. "You heard the lady. Everybody except Ike, Iris, Marigold, Jubilee and Curly. Out!"

The grumbling and swearing continued as the men reluctantly surged forward and filed past. As Luke watched them stream outside, he wondered what Noelle was now going to do. Damn, he had to hand it to her. Although she was as stubborn as Blackjack, Noelle handled herself with a grace and style that was truly her own.

Luke stood at the end of the line while Noelle paced back and forth in front of the crew. When the saloon had emptied, she folded her arms and assessed the three dance hall girls and the two men as though she were a calvary sergeant with new recruits.

"First, my wagon needs to be unloaded, and the oxen taken to the livery stable and tended to," Noelle said. "If we all pitch in, we should be finished by sundown."

Jubilee stepped forward. "I'm not one of your fancy servants from back East, lady. If you want a pack mule, buy one from a prospector. I'm not doin' your dirty work."

Noelle glanced at Luke, who leaned lazily against the bar. He reached for a cloth bag of tobacco from his vest pocket, and focused his attention on rolling his cigarette.

Noelle glared at him, then back at Jubilee. "Suit yourself. I noticed plenty of other saloons in town where you can obviously seek employment...for whatever it is you do."

Jubilee thrust her hands upon her hips and glared defiantly. "Luke? Are you going to let her talk to me like that?'' Jubilee's question held more at stake than her job, Luke knew.

He struck a match on the sole of his boot, then lit his cigarette. Smoke drifted around him. ''Looks like the choice is yours, Jube.''

She flared back, then indignantly grabbed her ruffled skirts and stormed out of the saloon. Marigold and Iris stared at each other, then proceeded to follow Jubilee through the swinging doors.

Luke leaned back against the bar and pulled another drag on his cigarette. ''Well, Sunshine. Looks like your crew is thinning fast.''

''An' good riddance,'' Curly said, giving the swinging doors a disgruntled look. ''I've been your uncle's bartender since he first opened those doors, miss. I'll not desert his niece in her time of sorrow.''

Noelle smiled with relief. ''Thank you, Mr. Curly.''

Curly's round face blushed scarlet.

''Me, too, Miss Noelle.'' Ike's thumbs twined around his suspenders. ''You can count on me in your hour of need.''

''Thank you, both.'' Her smile faded. ''I don't know what my plans are—''

''Her plans will be to get on the next eastbound stage,'' Luke said, stepping forward. ''And no sense unpacking her rig. She can sell her goods right from inside the prairie schooner. She's got a team of oxen and a calf, to boot.''

Noelle's blue eyes flashed fire. ''See here, Mr. Savage—''

''Sit down, Luke.'' Curly shouted. ''You're not her keeper.''

Ike moved beside Curly. ''Yeah, Luke. Who says that you know what's best for the little lady?''

Dammit! Why was he playing her protector? He'd known that Noelle was trouble the minute she started to brag about her rich uncle. "You're right, gentlemen," Luke said. "Besides, I can see that Miss Bellencourt is more than qualified to take care of herself."

She threw Luke a warring glance. "I'm not a quitter, gentlemen. My plan was to live with my uncle and to seek employment in his business." She took a deep breath. "I have no wish to return East, regardless of what Luke Savage would like me to do.

"But I'll need a place to sleep for the night, so while I go upstairs and ready myself a room, I'll leave you gentlemen to carry the large crates from my wagon. Stack them in front of the bar for the time being."

"Yes, Miss," Curly and Ike said in unison. Both men dashed for the door, then raced toward the wagon.

"You're forgetting me, Miss Noelle." Luke lazily tossed his hat on the table. "The name's Luke Savage, and I'm your new partner."

She blinked. "My what?"

"I own the gambling concession at the Silver Hearts Saloon, and although you'd like to close the place, legally, you can't. You have no say about the gambling tables."

Damned, if he didn't enjoy the look of surprised outrage spreading across her face. "That's right, Sunshine. Just you and me and the Silver Hearts Saloon."

"I don't believe you!"

"I'm sure your lawyer friend, Mike O'Shea, would love to explain it to you." Luke grinned through a cloud of cigarette smoke. "And another thing. You owe me two hundred dollars. That's the money Black…er, I mean your dear Uncle Marcel cheated from me by selling me a gambling concession at Lake's Crossing—one your departed uncle didn't own.''

Luke watched her steady herself on the back of a chair, and a flicker of weakness threatened to dissolve his stand. Damn! He only wanted her to realize that Crooked Creek was no place for a lady.

''You're a low-down, loathsome creature, Mr. Savage. I don't believe a word of what you're telling me.''

''Oh, yes you do. And when the truth of your situation finally dawns on you, remember who told you so. In the meantime, I'll haul your rig to the livery stable. I'll see that the oxen and that critter you're so fond of are watered and fed.'' He picked up his hat. ''I'll check at the stage depot for when the next eastbound stage will be leaving, too. So long, miss.''

Noelle watched as he strode purposefully through the swinging doors. For a moment, all she could do was stare after him. Then she forced herself to turn and confront the cavernous room, now silent and empty.

Oh, Uncle Marcel. I don't know why Luke Savage despises you so, but I do believe that you never could have done the things he's accused you of doing.

She shook her head and made her way to the curving staircase. Halfway up, she paused to sit down upon a step. Closing her eyes, she rubbed her temples, recalling the shock of the sheriff's words when he told her of Uncle Marcel's fatal accident.

Still stunned, she felt as though she'd been thrust into a never-ending nightmare. All her hopes had blown away into dust. Was Luke Savage right? Should she sell her wagonload of furnishings and return to New York City?

She would think later. It was too soon to make any

permanent decisions. After she'd bathed and slept, then she would decide what to do.

She grabbed the banister and forced herself to her feet. By sheer will, she steeled herself to climb the stairs. First, she had work to do. She would prepare one of the rooms above the saloon for herself. Without money to pay for a decent hotel—if Crooked Creek had a respectable hotel—she had no choice but to remain here. After all, if the Silver Hearts Saloon was good enough for Uncle Marcel, it would be good enough for her, too.

Noelle had only been asleep for what seemed like a few minutes when she sat bolt upright in bed. Whooping and hollering noises in the street below shook the glass in the bedroom window. She slipped on a robe over her nightgown and peered outside.

Several riders, obviously drunk with the devil's broth, were firing pistols and yelling blasphemies up and down the dusty street. Music from the numerous saloons and dance halls blended into a cacophony from Hades.

Noelle crept beneath the sheets and hugged her pillow. She felt numb inside. If only she could cry, maybe she would feel better. Maybe later, when she could feel again.

Dear God, after all this, she was still living above a tavern, just as she and her parents had lived above Harrison's Saloon in New York City. The untimely death of Uncle Marcel, the vision of her new life in a new land—all destroyed. What was left for her to do?

She closed her eyelids, but sleep eluded her. Finally, she went downstairs. Maybe if she walked around, it might relax her enough for sleep.

Half lit by moonlight streaming from the shuttered

windows along the street, the saloon loomed as forsaken as before. Noelle stood beside the cartons she had lovingly packed before starting the long journey West. The boxes had originally been shipped at great expense by her parents on their first ocean voyage to America from Belgium, before she was born.

Noelle rubbed the familiar wooden containers she remembered from childhood. In her parents' tiny apartment, her mother had sewn cotton scarves together to cover the boxes and used them as benches. Noelle smiled as she recalled the many happy hours she had spent, as a child, playing with her dolls atop these crates.

Gently, Noelle lifted one lid. Inside, brightly colored silk squares cushioned the wooden props that her father had hand-crafted for his magic act—the Great Bellencourt.

What fond memories these objects would have given Uncle Marcel. What stories he might have told her about when he and her father had first performed the act on their European tour.

Her insides wrenched with an incredible emptiness. "Papa, what should I do?" She moved to the long narrow box containing the rectangular mirror. Luckily, the glass had survived the Indian's attack on the prairie schooner. She rubbed a small circle within the veil of dust covering the mirror's surface. Her blue eyes—the same shade as her father's—gazed back at her.

How his eyes could sparkle with determination, blaze with outrage, and warm with laughter. She smiled, remembering.

Oh, what would her parents have done in her situation?

She must have a plan. One thing she could count

on—Luke Savage would face her in the morning and expect to hear what she decided to do.

How she hated the bossy way he ordered her about! She'd not allow him to bullyrag her, especially in front of her uncle's employees. *Her employees,* she corrected, with a tug of pride.

Luke Savage. Her business partner. Her heart pounded at the very idea. Oh, how she'd relish proving to him that she wasn't a tenderfoot. But how?

From the wooden crate, Noelle carefully unfolded each silken square on top of another, recalling the way her father packed away the material after each performance. Childhood memories enveloped her. She noticed the tiny stain of red paint in one corner of the yellow scarf. She was reminded of when she was seven. Without asking, she had opened her father's box of props and found the irresistible silks and artificial flowers he had used in the hat trick.

Later, when her father found her wearing full makeup, dressed in his black tuxedo jacket and trousers with his top hat askew her blond curls, he had called Mama to come and see. Together, they watched her pull the colored silks from the tall black hat, laughing as the youngest Bellencourt performed her first bit of magic.

How proud they were of her. She smiled as the memory warmed her soul. All that remained of that happy incident was the red stain of theatrical paint she had spilled on the yellow square.

Noelle covered the box with the wooden slats and bent the fasteners in place. With their unconditional love, her parents had taught her that she could accomplish anything she chose to do in this new land of opportunity. "Hardship is the great educator, Noelle.

Never bow down to adversity, but learn from it and be strengthened by it.''

From a round, squat box, Noelle pulled out her father's black top hat. Holding the shiny silk hat made her feel close to him. She placed it atop her head, then twirled his black shiny wand. Her reflection in the dusty mirror surprised her. For a moment, her eyes—so like her father's—beneath the black hat rim gave her a start.

The youngest Bellencourt.

The idea came to her like a bolt of lightning. Could she possibly resurrect her father's routine and perform the acts in the saloon?

She knelt down on the floor amid the circle of boxes, excitement pounding in her veins. What other choices did she have? Nothing was left for her in New York City. She was penniless except for what she owned in the prairie schooner. At least she had her uncle's saloon. He had left it to her in his will—he had wanted her to have it. Besides, how would she ever know she could make it in this new land unless she tried?

Luke was wrong about Uncle Marcel. Maybe her uncle had exaggerated to the family what his life was like in Nevada. But he was a Bellencourt. He did what he had to. Nothing could keep her down, either.

She had Ike and Curly. She'd teach them how to assist her with the act. Would Luke also help her?

No, she decided. Luke was a gambler. A sporting man who didn't want to get involved with anything except cards and games of chance. He had already told her that she was on her own. Besides, a gambler was *always* a gambler. But how she'd love to see Luke Savage's face when she proved she could take care of herself. She'd love to erase his smug, know-it-all expression with one of genuine admiration.

"Jeezzo, woman. Don't you ever sleep?"

Noelle whirled around to see Luke's broad-shouldered figure leaning against the doorjamb of Uncle Marcel's office. From his unbuttoned shirt and rumpled hair, she could see that he had been sleeping. "What are you doing here?" she asked.

Chapter Six

"I live here." Luke stretched, rubbing the back of his neck. "Although I've never slept on your uncle's bumpy old sofa before." He kneaded the small of his back and grimaced.

"Well, you don't live here anymore." Noelle tightened the belt of her robe and dashed into the office. "You said nothing of staying here."

The remark raised Luke's eyebrows. "I thought you'd gone through enough for one day. I figured if I mentioned that I have a room upstairs whenever I'm in town, you'd act just about how you're behaving now." He grabbed the quilt stretched across the sofa and hooked it over his shoulder. "I wanted you to get a good night's rest."

She whirled to face him. "A room upstairs?" She sniffed. "Jubilee's, no doubt."

He laughed out loud as he lit the kerosene lamp on the desk, yet Noelle noticed he didn't deny it. She remembered the curious wrench in her stomach when that red-haired woman possessively staked her claim on Luke by kissing him so blatantly in front of everyone.

Miss Parson had warned her students about such

women, but Noelle had seen enough of them along the streets in front of the burlesque theaters where her father had finally found work to know of their plight. Her mother had said such women should be pitied, yet Noelle couldn't help feeling pleased when Luke hadn't given in to that Jezebel's advances, or whatever her name was.

Noelle took a seat on the sofa, then noticed the sheet slanted across the velvet cushion. A blush rose to her cheeks as she realized she was sitting on Luke's bed. She steeled her jaw and glanced the other way. She wouldn't let him think he could make her feel uncomfortable.

He took a seat across from her. She averted her gaze to the corner cabinet where Luke's black cowboy hat angled from a rack on the table.

"Mr. Savage," she said, grabbing his hat and handing it to him. "From now on, please keep your personal things behind the bar."

Luke glanced at the hat rack, then stepped in front of the table, as though shielding it from her.

"What are you doing?" Noelle eyed him warily, then stepped around the side of the cabinet. In the lamplight, Noelle noticed that instead of a hat rack, Luke had hung his hat on a white marble statue of a...

Noelle blinked. The figure of a nude man and woman embracing in a kiss! She gasped, touching the polished stone in disbelief. "Mercy! Is this your idea of a joke?"

Luke's dark eyes glittered with teasing. "It's your uncle's idea of art."

"Art?" Noelle glanced back at the white shiny figures, their arms and legs tangled with desire. "Art?"

"*Ode To Love,* Blackjack called it. Won it in a poker

game when he was in 'Frisco." His grin broadened as her disbelief increased. "He was real proud of it, too."

"I don't believe it!"

"Now, Sunshine, I'd expect a city girl like you to know all about art."

"I do, but…" Noelle ignored the hot blush on her cheeks. She hastily placed the objectionable statue on the floor behind the cabinet.

"But what?" he asked, his eyes twinkling.

Her tongue felt as if it were tied into a knot. "Oh, never mind." She got to her feet. "You can't sleep here tonight. Surely there must be someplace you can stay."

"That's not a friendly way to speak to your new partner." Luke leaned forward and pulled a flask from his hip pocket. "Think a little drink might relax you and make you sleepy?"

"Mr. Savage, I've told you before what I think of men who ply women with whiskey."

He gave her a knowing smile. "The devil's hell broth, I believe your Miss Bloomer called it." He reached for the two glasses from the silver tray on top of her uncle's bookcase. "A shot of booze isn't plying you with whiskey, Miss. I think we both could do with a belt."

"I have an early day ahead of me, Mr. Savage. If you'll excuse me, I'll bid you good-night."

"A right busy day, too." He sat on the arm of the sofa. "I checked with the ticket officer at the stage depot. The next coach East arrives day after next. Nine in the morning. I told Shep at the livery stable that you'll be selling your rig and animals. He said he'd pass the word around and collect any offers. You can look over the bids, tomorrow."

Her fists tightened inside the pockets of her robe. Her blue eyes flashed fire. "You had no right to do that."

"Watered and took care of the oxen. Critter, too. He's in a stall next to the owner's mule. Calf thinks ol' Sally is his mother. Settled right in for the time being."

"Thank you for that, Mr.—"

"Out here, only tenderfeet call their business partners *Mister.*" He smiled at the frown she gave him at the word *tenderfeet*.

She tucked her hands under the lapels of her robe. "Give me time, and I'll prove to you I'm not a tenderfoot."

He sighed. "There's nothing to be ashamed of for being a tenderfoot. But you need to face facts. Tomorrow, you should talk to Mike O'Shea about selling your interest in the saloon." He saw a flicker of steely determination brighten those eyes, and he knew she was getting ready to tell him some half-baked idea that he really didn't want to hear.

"Thank you just the same for your advice, but I'll not need Mr. O'Shea's help, either. I've decided to remain in Crooked Creek."

Luke straightened up. "But you just said—"

"No, *you* said, Mr. Savage. I plan to make some changes in the saloon, then reopen in a few weeks."

"What kind of changes?"

She smiled in that certain way that he knew meant trouble. "Cleaning, painting, adding a few touches."

"Just like a woman to go changing things that don't need changing." Luke got to his feet. "You can't close down my gambling tables." He tilted his hat lower on his forehead. "Fussy up the place all you want, but the poker playing starts tomorrow evening and goes through until closing time."

"You don't seem to understand, Mr. Savage. My uncle left the building to me, and if you persist with your mule orneriness, then you and your cohorts can play poker in the street for all I care."

"You better care, lady. It's my rental of the gambling concessions that line your pockets. Without that money, you have no income."

"Very well, then. But the bar will remain closed. No alcoholic beverages allowed."

"The bar will remained closed except for when the men are gambling." His brows lifted when she started to object. "Remember, you get half the profits."

The fiery lights of battle raged within her eyes. Her pulse quickened in the soft hollow of her throat. He couldn't help but grin. Damn, in that high-necked, prim white nightgown peeking out from the wrap of her robe, she looked sweeter than a prairie primrose. With her wheat-colored hair hanging in a thick curtain of soft waves down her back, he was reminded of the night in the wagon—the night she had washed her hair.

"Very well," she conceded. "The bar will remain open only during the gambling hours."

"Deal."

She stared at him, her cheeks flushed with anger, her pink lips turned down like a petulant child.

But she was no child. Her full breasts rose and fell with each annoyed breath. He remembered how her nipples had budded when her wet hair hung down past her shoulders, and he wondered if the tips of her breasts were firm buds now.

Damn, why hadn't he thought to remove that damn statue of Blackjack's? How her eyes widened in shock at the sight of the clinging lovers; her fingers had drifted over the polished, cold stone. But she wasn't cold.

Beneath that ladylike exterior, Luke knew, dwelt a passionate woman. Again, the question of what she'd be like in his bed brought him crashing back to reality. He should just go pay a visit to Jube as she'd invited him to, and rid himself of this torture.

But Jubilee Kincaid no longer held any desire for him since he'd first seen Noelle .

"What must I do to convince you I'm not going to fold like a tent from a traveling medicine show?" Noelle took a steadying breath. "I'm here in Crooked Creek to stay."

Despite her words, she looked as delicate as bone china. "You're not safe alone in the saloon. I'll stay here tonight and protect you."

She huffed with laughter. "You? Protect me? From what?"

"I think it's time I show you."

Luke reached for her, and he heard her breath catch in her throat. Then took her in his arms and moved his face toward hers. Her feathered lashes beat against his cheek as his lips took hers. Finally the fluttering lashes stilled as he deepened the kiss.

He felt the stiffness melt from her as she leaned into him. Her hands slowly pressed against his chest as she raised up on tiptoe until her fingers curled behind his head. All innocence, she started a fire in him that nearly took his breath away.

Please, don't, she thought to say, but, again, her unspoken plea was covered by his lips. His tongue, with the exhilarating taste of brandy, explored the sensitive reaches of her mouth. She felt his hands shift, the sash at her waist loosen, then her wrapper swing freely about her hips. She drew back and stared at him.

Lamplight from the desk threw fiery casts against his

sun-burnished face, accentuating his dimpled scar beneath his cheekbone. Rumpled, unshaven, his dark maleness contrasted sharply against his white, open-necked, ruffled gambler's shirt. Heat unfurled into a deep yearning as their eyes met. She wanted him to kiss her again, wanted to be drawn closer, wanting with a dangerous need that ached within her.

He pressed her closer; the sweet moan he heard further ignited his desire. What was there about this woman that so drove him to distraction?

He had only meant to warn her, to frighten her into the reality that she didn't belong here, alone and unprotected. But it was Luke who heard the siren's song—he was treading in uncharted waters with an innocent like Noelle. And behind that guileless innocent face was a passionate woman who came with a steep price—marriage.

What the hell was he doing? His insides twisted with guilt. With all the determination he had, Luke forced himself to pull her arms down to his chest, but he held her small hands in his.

"This is no place for a woman like you, Noelle." His voice was hoarse with desire. He felt her uneven breath feather his face. He should release her, but he couldn't. Not just yet. She was goodness, purity, all the things he didn't deserve. She was marriage, home and family. All the things he didn't want.

He gazed into her confused eyes, and the look of desire that he saw gave him the strength to release her.

She stared up at him, confused. Her face glowed with the burn of his rough beard. Her full lips parted slightly, an unanswered question on her lips. *Why?* her eyes asked, and he didn't have the answer.

"Meet me at the livery tomorrow morning." He

couldn't hide the huskiness in his voice. "I'll help catalogue your things for sale."

Her breath came in uneven spurts. "For the last time..." her voice was low and breathy "...I'm not leaving Nevada. Instead, I've decided to do a little gambling of my own."

Luke waited, frustration building within him. "What do you mean by that?"

"I think the saloon could use a different type of entertainment. One suitable for the family." His gasp of surprise brought a twinkle to her eyes. "I shall resurrect the family act that my uncle Marcel and my father made famous in Europe." Her eyes held a faraway look. "I'm going to be the Great Bellencourt—the famed illusionist." She dropped into an exaggerated curtsy.

"Who?"

"I believe you heard me, Mr. Savage." Her mouth tipped up with confidence. "Pleasant dreams, Mr. Savage."

Before Luke had a chance to speak, Noelle turned from the room and headed for the staircase.

Jeezzo! There was no mistaking what she'd said. Luke unscrewed the whiskey cap and gulped the few remaining swigs from the pint. Damn Blackjack! This was all his fault.

For the rest of the night Noelle tossed and turned, sleep eluding her. All she could think of was Luke's kiss and the wild and hungry look in his dark gaze before he took her into his arms. Some mysterious message in those smouldering eyes fascinated her, warned her that she was going to be kissed. Although she had wanted to resist, needed to resist, she couldn't stop herself. She'd wanted to be held, needed to be touched by this disturbing man who bewildered her so.

Noelle sat up and placed a hand across her flushed forehead. What was the matter with her? She pushed the damp tendrils from her face and drew an unsteady breath. She was understandably distraught over Uncle Marcel's untimely death. She wasn't herself, that was it.

Yet she could still imagine the feel of Luke's hard chest against hers, the taste of his lips and the smell of his manly scent. Mercy! She must get a hold of herself.

It wasn't as if she had no experience with men. After all, Miss Parsons had warned her students that a young lady must always control a suitor's advances. Yet when Jeremy VanderMeer had asked Noelle for a kiss while they strolled through Central Park, she had been too curious not to allow him to touch her gently on the lips.

Noelle dangled her legs over the side of the four-poster bed and frowned. Who was she kidding? Likening Jeremy's chaste attempt at kissing to Luke's kiss was like comparing the pop from a child's toy pistol to the bang from *Old Ironside*'s cannon.

A gambling man wasn't a respectable suitor, either. But despite Luke's faults, he had been honest with her. Marriage and respectability weren't in his future. Her thoughts went back to the flaming red-haired Jubilee, with her carmine lips and powdered face. A strange flutter gripped her again as she thought of the proprietary way the shameless hussy gazed at Luke.

Yes, Luke would appreciate a woman like her. He paid for what she gave him. A fair arrangement with no entanglements. Yes, a woman like Jubilee would suit Luke Savage very well, indeed.

Noelle punched her pillow, then flounced the sheet,

drawing it to her shoulder. Enough of these foolish thoughts. She had a full day's work ahead of her, and she needed sleep. Squeezing her eyelids shut, she willed all thoughts of Luke Savage from her mind.

Men can't change their habits, her mother had often said. Luke was a good man beneath his sporting ways, but despite her feelings, Noelle was a practical woman. Regardless of how well the man kissed, a gambler wasn't the man for her.

Thank heavens she was a sensible woman.

Luke stepped from the Silver Hearts Saloon and breathed deeply of the crisp October air filled with the aroma of sage. Damn, if he didn't feel like whistling as he set out in the direction of Shep's Livery Stable. The morning sun was peeking over the mountain range along the eastern edge of town, splashing gold across the faded storefronts along the west side of Main Street. Beyond, the hills were tinged with autumn's blue mountain asters and golden aspens.

The eye-filling sight surprised him. How often had he gone this way exactly at this time of morning, yet he'd never noticed the pleasing effect before? Even the jingle of his spurs rang with a more resonant sound in the clear morning air.

"Morning, Shep," Luke said as he stepped inside the stable.

Rich smells of animals, leather and hay greeted him. A lanky man stepped from an empty stall and put down a forkful of hay. His leathery sun-burnished face wrinkled with a grin. "Figured you'd be comin' around about now, Luke."

Surprised, Luke asked, "You've taken up mind reading?'' He strode to the last stall where yesterday he had left Noelle's calf.

'''Cause Miss Noelle came in here a while ago, and I figured either you or Mike O'Shea wouldn't be far behind.'' Shep spit out a brown stream of tobacco juice. ''Since O'Shea has already been here—''

''O'Shea?'' A prickle of uneasiness stirred the hair on back of Luke's neck. He glanced at the empty animal pen. The calf was nowhere in sight.

''Yeah. O'Shea rode out early this mornin'. Had business in Lake's Crossing. Be gone a day or two, he told me.''

Luke felt an unexpected surge of satisfaction. ''Aw, that's too bad.'' He couldn't help but smile as he hooked his thumbs in his belt loops.

Shep's gray eyes sparkled with interest. ''Figured you'd make your move on Miss Noelle while he's gone.'' Shep's knowing chuckle irritated Luke more than he cared to admit.

''See here, Shep. The lady can do what she wants. I've no claim on her, nor do I want any.''

''She's a might pretty little thing.'' He squinted one eye at Luke. ''Ah, if I was a few years younger, I'd be throwin' my hat into the ring with you, O'Shea, and all the other—''

''Dammit, Shep. How many times do I have to tell you? I'm not romantically interested in the lady—''

''Nor am I interested in Mr. Savage, if anyone should care to know.''

Luke spun around to see Noelle standing at the back door, the calf beside her. Dressed in a rose floral gown, her golden head bathed in morning sunlight, she was glorious. The sight of her nearly sucked the air from his lungs.

Her cheeks pinked brighter than the color of her skirts. Without a glance at Luke, she stepped inside, urging the calf toward its pen.

Shep leaned on the hay fork; his mouth opened and closed furtively. "I—I didn't mean—"

"Of course you meant no harm," Noelle agreed. "But remember, Mr. Shep. Gossip is the devil's hand-maiden and the passion of idle minds."

Luke grinned, glad to have the chance to see Shep's chagrin, regret and embarrassment rolled into one gaping stare.

Noelle lingered beside the oxen, rubbing their curly heads. Luke brushed his hat and moved beside her. "Sleep well, Miss Noelle?" It amazed him that he could speak.

Noelle slanted a look at Shep, who had put on his hat and was ducking out the back livery door. Then she turned toward Luke. "It's quite impolite to inquire how a lady sleeps, Mr. Savage."

"Sorry, I haven't had much practice with etiquette lately. But you did interrupt my sleep last night, and I figured you didn't get much, either."

"I slept extremely well, Mr. Savage, if it's any of your concern." Her eyes flashed fire before she moved past him.

"Now don't go flying off in a fit, Miss. I came here to offer you a pleasant surprise."

"A pleasant surprise would be for you to disappear."

"Ouch! You've hurt my feelings." He grinned when her eyes narrowed into blue slits.

"I don't mean to be rude," she said finally, "but there's something about you that I find so...so..."

"Devastatingly appealing?"

The cry to battle flashed in her eyes, just as he'd

hoped. He laughed. "Such a touchy female. Have you had breakfast?"

She took in a fortifying breath. "Say what you came here to say and be done with it."

He twirled his hat in the air, catching it with his fingers. "Such a beautiful morning. Thought you'd enjoy a buggy ride out along the south edge of town. I know a lovely woman who lives about three miles from here. I think you'd like her. I know she would enjoy meeting you."

Noelle lifted her chin. "I don't think I care to meet any more of your...lady friends, Mr. Savage. Besides, Curly and Ike are waiting for me. They're moving furniture and preparing to paint the saloon walls."

Luke cleared his throat. "I hate to tell you this, but there's no stores in Crooked Creek that sell paint. Have to order supplies from Lake's Crossing."

Noelle arched her brows. "Mr. O'Shea has kindly offered to fetch paint, along with other hardware supplies that we'll need. I believe he left at dawn."

Good riddance. Luke forced the unsettling thought from his mind that Noelle would be beholden to O'Shea for the favor.

He smiled lazily. "Can we call a truce long enough for a pleasant ride out to meet Emily Brady? Her husband, Daniel, is a prospector. Gone most of the time, and she's starved for female company. I promise you'll be back before Ike or Curly know you're gone. Even your friend, Amelia Bloomer, would approve of Miss Emily."

Noelle grinned, despite herself. "Do you think Amelia would approve of you, Mr. Savage?"

"It's not Amelia I'm asking to go buggy riding." Her smile gave him hope. "What are you afraid of? You just came halfway across Nevada with me, and you *begged* me to bring you.''

''Mr. Savage, the circumstances are completely different.'' She raised a brow and lifted her chin in a resigned way that made him wonder if she was thinking of their kiss. He knew that her pride wouldn't allow herself to show that she had been affected, but he knew by her reaction that she was as moved by the experience as he was.

When he decided that she wasn't going to answer him, she tilted her head and said, ''It is a lovely morning.'' She brushed back a stray flaxen strand from her cheek. ''Very well, Mr. Savage. I'll go with you, but I must be back by noon.''

Luke chuckled as he opened the livery door for her. She brushed past him as she hurried outside a little too fast. She cupped her hand over her eyes when she glanced back at him. ''I'll meet you in front of the Silver Hearts in fifteen minutes.''

Luke put on his hat and nodded. He watched the provocative sway of her hips as she hurried across the dusty street. She was an appealing woman. Maybe it was the clear morning air that surged through his blood, but he felt as charged and happy as if he'd just won the biggest poker stake in all of Nevada.

Whistling, he stepped next door to the barber shop where Shep leaned against the door, watching the morning ritual of the two old regulars, Sid and Amos, playing checkers.

''Shep, will you hitch up a buggy for me?'' Luke felt in his pockets for two quarters. ''And I'd like a few words with you, too.''

Ten minutes later when Shep had finished fastening the team to the buggy, Luke paid him the coins. ''If any strangers ride in while I'm gone, Shep, get their names and tell them to stay put until I get back, will you? I'd like to speak to them. I should be back by noon.''

Shep smiled at the two coins in his hand. "I'll tell 'em, Luke," he said, pocketing the money into his vest pocket.

Shep leaned on the hay fork and watched as Luke climbed into the buggy and picked up the reins. "I knew you was a hell of a lot smarter than O'Shea," he said with a lopsided grin. "There he is, trudging all the way to Lake's Crossin' an' back by himself, while you're here in the spoonin' buggy with the girl."

Chapter Seven

Scattered pines and aspens dotted the grassy slopes along the creek in sharp contrast to the drier terrain of the past few miles. Noelle felt an excitement she hadn't experienced in a long time. She stole a glance at Luke beside her in the buggy. Was her mood caused from the beauty of the sagebrush-covered slopes rising to the distant mountains, or was it this exciting man at her side?

In the past half hour, Luke had behaved as a perfect gentleman. She couldn't help but smile. His charm and rugged attractiveness would touch any woman's heart. Well, not any woman. *She* knew the dangers of such men, thank goodness.

Her light spirits had probably very little to do with the man at her side, she reminded herself. Since she had finally made her decision to remain in Crooked Creek and carry on her father's profession, her future felt challenging and optimistic. No wonder the endless desert and mountain ranges, which only yesterday had appeared life-threatening, were today, breathtakingly beautiful.

"You can see the Brady place from here." Luke pointed to the cluster of green trees to the left. Noelle shaded her eyes. A log cabin and buildings rose in the distance.

"There's a stretch of prairie grass along the river that the Bradys have worked into a good piece of land. I thought you might trade your calf to Emily in exchange for her sewing talent."

"My calf?"

Luke nodded, his gaze ahead on the trail. "Your calf will be a grown heifer before long. Besides, Shep charges a nickel a day to bed the critter, which is money you don't have. Once you meet Emily Brady, I'm sure you'll agree that the Brady place is the best home for her."

A thread of disappointment curled through Noelle. So there was a practical purpose to Luke's offer of a buggy ride. She straightened her bonnet. What had she thought? Chewing her lip, she realized that she'd hoped maybe he had wanted to spend several hours alone with her.

"I'm not romantically interested in the lady." The reminder came back to taunt her, and she felt foolish for her dreamy thoughts.

Silence hung between them as the sprightly team of horses trotted along the hard crusted trail until they arrived at the whitewashed stones outlining Emily and Daniel Brady's property.

Two hounds bayed when Luke turned the buggy into the neatly raked dirt yard. An auburn-haired woman, not much older than Noelle, stepped from the house, a baby in her arms.

Luke and the woman exchanged a friendly embrace. "I brought Naomi something," he said, offering a paper sack to the mother. Emily peeked inside the bag, her smile widening. "Pink hair ribbons!" She let out a squeal of delight. "Oh, thank you, Luke. Just the trimming I was looking for to finish Naomi's new dress."

Noelle took Luke's hand as he helped her from the buggy. She smiled at the pretty young mother when Luke introduced them.

"I can't remember the last time I've talked to another woman from back East," Emily Brady said. Her hazel eyes shone with warmth and good humor. She lifted Naomi and balanced the baby on one hip.

"Come inside out of the sun. Made my grandma's molasses cake last night. There's plenty left."

When Noelle stepped into the single-room dwelling, she felt immediately welcome. Crocheted rag rugs covered the rough-hewn floor. Handmade chairs and a sturdy rectangular table stood beneath one window in the corner. A cluster of family pictures lined the fireplace mantel.

Morning glories peeked from outside the window and in the garden beyond the house, white petunias and orange nasturtiums bloomed. "How can you spare water for flowers?" Noelle asked, surprise in her voice.

Emily chuckled while she poured the coffee from the blue-enameled coffeepot. "This property once belonged to a Mormon family. A while back, these lands belonged to a thriving settlement. The Mormons built a series of cistern wells, which provided plenty of water for grass and crops. When they left to resettle in Utah, most of the lands returned to desert. My husband, Daniel, with Luke's help, restored the well. We collect every bit of rainwater we can and use it for the vegetables and a few flowers."

"What an ingenious idea." Noelle glanced at Luke. "That proves that settlers can bring their families to farm this area and Crooked Creek can become a real town.''

"Crooked Creek *is* a real town," Luke said. "Men here like to raise hell, not petunias."

Noelle took a sharp intake of breath. Angry at herself for the disappointment she felt at Luke's comment, she quickly tried to dismiss it. Of course Luke would discount any thought of women and children coming west with their men. Gone was the sense of closeness she believed had existed between them on the ride out here, this morning.

She smiled self-consciously at Emily, whose hazel eyes missed nothing in the brief exchange between Luke and Noelle.

"May I hold the baby?" Noelle asked, hoping to change the subject. "How old is she?"

"Naomi will be a year old next month." Emily lifted the chubby youngster and placed her in Noelle's lap. The child settled contentedly in the crook of Noelle's arm.

"If you ladies will excuse me," Luke said, picking up his hat, "I think I'll split some firewood I noticed Daniel's got stacked out back."

"He'll be mighty obliged, Luke" Emily said as he ambled out the door. "He's been putting in long days in the foothills."

"I don't know what we'd do if it wasn't for Luke," Emily said after Luke had left the cabin. "Comes 'round to check on me and Naomi when Daniel's gone prospecting."

The idea that Luke would take an interest in the small family seemed out of place for a gambler. Noelle took a sip of coffee, then cuddled the baby in her arms. "I'm glad he suggested that I come visit you and Naomi."

Emily leaned forward and smiled. "Lordy, so am I. I'm half starved to talk to another woman." They laughed, and the time flew as they exchanged stories of their lives before coming West.

Finally Emily got up and refilled their cups. "I'm so very glad you've come to Nevada, Noelle. You'll have to come and see me more often." She brushed imaginary crumbs from the snowy linen tablecloth. "And despite being a bit mule-headed at times, you couldn't ask for a finer man than Luke Savage."

Noelle arched her brows. "But...Luke's my business partner, nothing more."

Emily's hazel eyes darkened. "Life in Nevada isn't like New York, Noelle. For one thing, out here, women need men." Her voice suggested more than romance, Noelle decided.

Noelle blushed. "Mike O'Shea has offered to help me while I get settled. Do you know him?"

"In a mining town, everyone's well acquainted with the lawyer who files our claims." Emily's eyes crinkled against the sun's brightness shining through the window. "Mike's a good man, but there's something very special about Luke." Her face settled into a serious look. "He's never spoken much about his past, but I can sense a certain sadness he doesn't want to talk about. Has to do with his decision to come here, I reckon." She shook her auburn curls thoughtfully. She glanced back at Noelle.

"Now look at me! I forgot to offer you some cake." Emily jumped up and dashed to the small food safe opposite the table and began cutting a slab of molasses cake. "I'm not used to company," she said, placing the wedge of cake on a china plate. "Help yourself to cream. We're thankful for a good milk cow, so there's plenty."

"Thank you, Emily," Noelle said, taking the offered dessert.

"If there's anything I can do to help make your settling in any easier, just ask." Emily cut herself a piece of cake and fed the baby from her plate.

"Well, Emily, there is." Noelle took a sip from her cup when she heard Luke step into the cabin. "Luke, I was just going to ask Emily if she will take the calf."

"A calf?" Emily glanced from Noelle to Luke.

Noelle told the story of how she had found the animal on the trail; when she had finished, she knew Luke had been right to suggest Emily care for the calf.

"Then that's settled," Luke said. "I'll bring the critter over tomorrow."

On the way back to town, Noelle was filled with a mixed sense of emptiness and joy. "Thank you for bringing me to meet Emily." She smiled, thinking of her earlier reluctance to meet another of Luke's women friends. "Emily thinks a great deal of you, Luke."

Luke smiled lazily, and Noelle's use of Luke's first name surprised them both. Noelle said nothing as she settled back into the buggy.

"Emily and Daniel came here two years ago with a large enough grubstake to buy their place. She sits and worries while he's out in those hills with his burros, always hoping the next ledge will bring him that once-in-a-lifetime promise of color.

"You make him sound like a gambler."

"You said it, I didn't."

"Are there any other prospectors with their families in the area?"

"A few. Why?"

"There'll be a need for a school, churches and..."
Noelle turned away to gaze at the rising mountain range
in the distance "...a doctor."

"No need," he answered, his eyes on the trail before
them. "All those prospectors and their families, like
Emily and Daniel, won't be here long. They'll stay for
as long as their money holds out, then they head for the
larger settlements, a little poorer but wiser."

"But Crooked Creek doesn't have to be only a mining town." She felt her patience snap. "With a little
community effort, Crooked Creek could grow as large
as...Kansas City," she said finally. "And if the railroad
comes—"

"The townsfolk find nothing wrong with Crooked
Creek as it is. It's a mining town, period. It doesn't
pretend to be what it's not." Luke turned to study her.
"Can't turn a town into something its folks don't
want." His mouth thinned as his gaze settled on the
team.

Noelle stared at him, her cheeks flaming with frustration. He was the most mule-headed man. No use
wasting her breath talking to him. Besides, they had
spent such a lovely morning, she didn't want to ruin the
little time they had left by arguing.

"I'm planning to offer free dinner plates for the Silver Hearts customers who come to the opening performance of the Great Bellencourt," she said sweetly.

Luke held the reins with one hand. "Speaking of
which...I'm losing money every day the Silver Hearts
is closed. The poker tables can be moved into the center
of the saloon. Shouldn't interfere with your fancying up
the walls."

"Oh, but you can't. I don't want to spoil the surprise."

He frowned. "The only surprise a poker player wants is to see the next draw of his cards." He smiled lazily. "Besides, you receive a healthy percentage of my take. You can buy a lot of thingamabobs with the money."

Her eyes brightened with the thought. "Maybe I could purchase Emily's molasses cakes for the patrons. She might be willing to cook meals for the miners. I could help her, too."

"*Patrons* of the Silver Hearts want to gamble and drink, not eat molasses cake and chatter over tea."

She raised her chin in that certain way that told him he was wasting his time trying to convince her otherwise. "We'll see," she said, folding her arms and glancing out at the stretch of Joshua trees that dotted the land. Luke Savage was a man who had to be shown before he believed.

She'd show him, all right. Noelle sat back in the buggy, watching the stretch of gold sand scattered with wind-beaten sage and brush. She'd enjoy watching him eat crow. Yes, she'd like that very much.

By the end of the week, Luke had made all of the arrangements for the re-opening of his gaming tables. He planned to leave Curly and Ike in charge. If Ike helped Curly pour and serve the first round of free drinks, maybe the gamblers wouldn't miss Jubilee, Iris and Marigold.

Luke opened a fresh deck, cut and fanned the cards with lightning speed. He would never tire of the feel of a stiff, cool and shiny new pack between his fingers.

"Thought I'd find you here." Mike O'Shea moved opposite Luke at the table and put his boot on the chair.

Luke kept his eyes on the cards piled in front of him. "Back from Lake's Crossing, I see." He placed one ace on the stack, then drew another card. "Pile the paint cans anywhere. When Noelle comes down, I'll tell her you're back."

"It's not Noelle I've come to see."

Luke glanced up at him. Mike's sandy-colored hair was slicked down, fresh comb tracks imprinted in the side waves of his head. "Seeing how you're freshly shaved, smelling of bay rum, why, you look slicker than a newborn pup." Luke grinned. "I'm rightly honored that you'd get yourself all gussied up for me, but I'm afraid you're just not my type, Mike."

Mike laughed, knowing better than to take offense. "I wouldn't talk if I were you. I heard Carl say that you've started having an extra shave every afternoon since Miss Noelle arrived." His teasing smile widened. "You can borrow my bay rum if you run out."

"The lady prefers my own manly smell, thank you."

Mike pinched his fingers to his nose in an exaggerated gesture, and both men laughed.

Luke motioned to the empty chair across from him. "Sit down and tell me what's on your mind."

Mike scraped the chair back and took a seat. He absently picked up a card from the discard pile and studied it. "Yesterday, when I was in Lake's Crossing, I asked around about any stranger who answered to Blackjack's description." Mike's eyes met Luke's. "The bartender at Sadie's said that his sister had heard of a man who'd come to town a few days ago. He's lodging with a widow living on the outskirts of town."

"How long has this fellow been in Lake's Crossing?"

"Arrived soon after Blackjack's accident."

Luke leaned back in his chair. "So you believed me when I said that I didn't think Blackjack was dead?"

Mike's gray eyes narrowed. "I'm saying that your suspicions are a possibility."

"What changed your mind?" Luke waited for Mike to continue.

Mike ran a finger along the gold watch chain that crossed his brocade vest. "Before Blackjack's accident, Hilda Mueller had asked me to deed over her boarding-house to Blackjack."

Luke threw the cards on the table in frustration. He admired Hilda; she was a hardworking widow, whose only source of income was the room and board she received from the few old men who preferred home cooking to the more obvious attractions at the dance halls and saloons in Crooked Creek.

Besides, when Blackjack had decided to court Hilda and she accepted, Luke knew Blackjack had probably enjoyed more than just Hilda's wiener schnitzel during those long Saturday afternoons he spent with her. "Why the hell would Hilda do a fool thing like that?"

Mike's fingers toyed with the gold watch chain hanging across his vest. "Apparently Blackjack had promised her marriage." He shrugged. "I never filed the paperwork. Thank God. With Blackjack dead, Hilda's property would have become part of his estate."

"Yeah," Luke said, realizing that if O'Shea had carried out Hilda's wishes, now Noelle would own Hilda's boardinghouse.

Mike raised an eyebrow. "If there's one person in Crooked Creek who thought well of Blackjack, it's Hilda Mueller."

Women! Luke shook his head. He studied the man sitting across the table. O'Shea was practical, ambitious and intelligent. *Exactly what a young lawyer in a new, wild state like Nevada should be. Exactly the kind of*

*man a respectable young woman, like Noelle, would
want for a husband.*

The thought brought a clench to his stomach. Maybe
he was becoming too affected by Noelle. What he
needed was to put some distance between them. She
was not the woman for him, and he definitely had no
choice but to fold and leave the game.

Luke scooped up the cards and reshuffled the deck.
''I'll head out tomorrow for Lake's Crossing and look
into the matter.''

''Want me to go along?''

Surprised, Luke glanced up, then realized O'Shea
was sincere with the offer. Both men knew that if
Blackjack really was alive, he'd do everything in his
power not to be brought back to town. ''Thanks, Mike,
but I might find out more if I go alone.'' Without wanting to worry his friend, Luke added lightly, ''Besides,
Miss Noelle might need you to hang draperies or dec-
orate with flags and banners while I'm gone,'' he said,
chuckling.

Mike laughed, the creases around his gray eyes deep-
ening. ''I'll tell you all about domestic joy when you
get back,'' he said as he was leaving.

Later that afternoon, Luke found Noelle sitting at the
desk in Blackjack's office. She raised her head from the
sketch pad in her lap and smiled when he entered the
room. ''I was just about to go looking for you,'' she
said, a pen in her hand. ''I want to show you something.''

Luke moved beside her chair and glanced at the various rectangular designs sketched by hand across the
page.

''Mike O'Shea just stopped by with your paint buckets,'' he said absently, his mind on the drawings. "Said he'd see you later. He's got a business matter to discuss with you.''

"Yes, I know.'' She placed the pen down beside the bottle of India ink. "Mr. O'Shea is taking me to dinner at the Miner's Café this evening.''

Luke muttered under his breath. *So that's why O'Shea was all gussied up.* "I hope he warned you that everything Hoot knows about cooking he learned as an army cook at Fort Hallek.''

"I'll take my chances.'' She chuckled as Luke came beside her and studied the sketches in her lap.

Luke took a deep breath and let it out slowly. "Is this what you wanted to show me?'' He appraised the various diagrams, and he wondered if she had designed them, too.

"Yes, these are my layouts for the disappearing man act.''

Luke glanced at her. "I know you'd like nothing better than to make me vanish forever, but I won't offer myself as your assistant.''

"The thought has crossed my mind a few times.''

He chuckled, then took the drawing pad and stood by the window, studying the pad in the natural light of the window. A tall cabinet with side panels was carefully drawn alongside a man, who bore a strong resemblance to Ike. Behind the rectangular box, a man-size, framed mirror was placed upon a sturdy shelf, with curtains hanging from rods extending outward from both sides of the mirror.

"If your illusionist skills are as impressive as your drawing skills, I think you'll pull this off.''

A pink blush brightened her cheeks. "Curly and Ike are sworn to secrecy. I told them that if they tell anyone how the trick is performed, I'll make them disappear and never bring them back."

He laughed. "Looks like a lot of equipment. Do you need any help building that frame?"

She looked surprised at his offer of assistance. "Why, thank you, but Curly and Ike offered to build the frames for me."

"So, that's what the sawing and hammering was that I heard earlier."

A glow of satisfaction brightened her face. "Yes, and I've already started sewing the draperies." She took the sketch pad from him. "Emily said she'd come into town tomorrow and help." She moved from behind the desk and went to the window, adjusting the window shutter to shield the sun. "What was it you wanted to see me about, Luke?"

Standing at the window, arranging the wooden slats with the sun streaming upon her, Noelle looked as delicate and fragile as one of his mother's china figurines that she had kept locked away behind glass doors. But Noelle wasn't a china doll, Luke reminded himself. She was a flesh-and-blood woman, with a mind of her own.

His gaze fell to the sketch pad on the desk. She was very talented, extremely intelligent and had a will that matched his own. With Blackjack dead, she had a chance to make a new beginning with her life. But if Luke found Blackjack, Noelle would lose her inheritance. Everything she was working for would be lost. The chances of Blackjack providing honorably for her were nil. Furthermore, Noelle would never forgive Luke for proving that her Uncle Marcel was a crook.

Noelle turned to him. "What did you want to see me about?" she repeated.

For an instant he wanted to say nothing. How he'd

like to turn tail and ride out of town as fast as he could. But he couldn't leave until he settled the matter with Blackjack.

"I wanted you to know that I'll be gone for a few days." He took several steps toward the door. "Thought I'd leave at dawn." He decided not to tell her anything more unless she asked. Besides, what if that man living with the rich widow wasn't Blackjack? No need to alarm her unless he had proof.

Noelle's grin faded and her brows arched in surprise. "Where are you going?"

"Lake's Crossing." His thumbs looped around his belt buckle. "I'll be back as soon as I can."

She glanced away, disappointment clearly etched on her face. She dropped the sketch pad on the desktop, then brushed past him as she hurried toward the door.

"I overheard one of the gamblers tell Ike that a big poker game has been going on all week in Lake's Crossing." She shot the words out. "I'm surprised you're able to wait until dawn to leave." She turned and slammed the door on her way out.

Luke shrugged off the niggling feeling of guilt that her words provoked in him. What would she think if she knew the real reason he was leaving?

He picked up the sketch pad, his fingers slowly turning the pages. The disappearing man, she had scrawled across the first page.

Blackjack. Luke's gaze drifted to the window and the snow peaked mountains beyond. Wherever you've disappeared to, you old sidewinder, I'll find your sorry hide and bring you back, so help me.

Chapter Eight

For the next three days, Noelle forced all thoughts of Luke Savage from her mind. But despite her resolve, she couldn't blot out the painful yearning that crushed down upon her since he'd gone. On Friday, she had just left the office of the bank president, Mr. Carter, when she spied Luke's buckskin tied to the rail of the Red Garter Saloon.

Luke's back! Her heart surged with joy. No, the animal wasn't Deuce, she saw at second glance. She swallowed back the disappointment, her joy trampled like the dust beneath her feet. She steeled her jaw and chided herself for her foolishness. High-stakes card games might go on for weeks, she had overheard Curly say.

Gathering her shopping basket to her side, she hurried across the street before the Friday stagecoach to San Francisco thundered past, swirling thick yellow dust in its wake. Burying her nose into her lace handkerchief, she shook the dust from her skirts and watched the vehicle rumble down Main Street, past the three dance halls and two saloons, before swerving sharply along the north bend in the road. Today's stage marked two weeks since she'd arrived in Crooked Creek, she realized with a start.

How much she'd accomplished in these fourteen days. Curly and Ike had finished helping her paint the saloon's walls only last night. Today, Shep and Ike had hammered the final shingles on the new storage room. She'd sorted through the contents of three upstairs rooms, now vacant, since she'd finally weeded through Uncle Marcel's things, sold what she could, and given away his clothing.

She received a handsome price for the wheelbarrow, filled with pick hammers and mining equipment, she'd found stored upstairs. The stuffed antelope's head and bearskin rug were sold to Carl, the barber, for twice what Mike O'Shea said the trophies were worth. An animal lover, Noelle had been glad to be rid of them.

With Emily's help, Noelle had cleaned and painted the newly emptied upstairs area. She was almost finished sewing new curtains, which would brighten the rooms. The extra space would provide welcome income from lodgers.

She found she was walking with a spring in her step, a sign of her newfound pride in herself. Yet none of it would have been possible without Luke's help. Mike O'Shea had offered his legal assistance to help her buy out Luke's gambling concession. She had refused. Luke had a right to the gambling tables, per his original agreement with Uncle Marcel, regardless of what Uncle Marcel's will had said.

Loud voices coming from up the street drew her thoughts back to the present. Pete Tardiff, owner of the Red Garter Saloon, was scolding two young Indians for loitering in front of his establishment. The pair moved on, but not before Noelle recognized the taller Indian

as the one who had been with Little Henry when they
ransacked her prairie schooner. She watched them scoot
across the street and duck behind Mike O'Shea's office.

A start of outrage riffled through her as she remembered what the Indians had done to her wagon, but she
brushed the feeling aside. Although they had damaged
some of her belongings, Luke turned what could have
been a disaster into a minor incident. The rectangular
mirrors and the devices necessary for the disappearing
man trick weren't harmed, thank God.

What had brought the Indians to Crooked Creek?
Luke said that peace between the townsfolk and the
Paiutes was tenuous at best.

As she neared the Silver Hearts, she recognized
Luke's horse, Deuce, tied to the rail in front of Carl's
barber shop. She pressed a hand to her thumping heart
as a surge of relief rushed through her. She dashed
along the dusty trail, forcing herself not to run toward
the Silver Hearts Saloon. She wanted to wash her face,
brush her hair and change from her dusty clothing into
her fresh, yellow-checked dimity gown before he saw
her.

Noelle entered the saloon and darted past several
miners playing cards at a far table. Ike and Curly were
bending over a large wooden carton, unpacking her father's props.

"I purchased the door hinges and el wrenches from
the hardware store," she said, handing her basket with
the wrapped parcels to Curly. "Mr. Ames said I could
open an account, so I did." She smiled at Curly and
Ike's surprised faces. "If you need any more supplies,
go ahead and order them. I told Mr. Ames that you're
both allowed to charge whatever we need."

The men fairly beamed. She trusted them, and now

this proved her faith in them. She smiled at the blushes rising on Curly and Ike's pleased faces.

"I saw Luke's horse down the street," she called over her shoulder, in what she hoped sounded like a casual remark.

"Luke's already been here," Ike said, unwrapping a man's felt top hat from a round box.

"Dropped off that big package, then took off again." Curly added, pointing to the long, angular bundle near the front door.

"Did he say what was in it?" she asked.

"Said it was a surprise," Ike answered, his attention fixed on a bouquet of yellow silk roses he was unwrapping.

"A surprise? Is that all Luke said?" Curious, Noelle studied the package wrapped in brown paper and tied with string. It could be anything.

"Said he'd be back later. Mumbled somethin' 'bout headin' straight fer a bath and a shave." Ike met Curly's amused look and chuckled loudly.

She wondered if Curly and Ike had teased Luke, too. A thrill rippled along her skin as her excitement mounted at seeing Luke again. Although she loved the way he looked on the trail—black hair windblown, the shadow of beard outlining the hard planes and angles of his face, she was pleased that he wanted to spruce up—as Curly would say—before she saw him.

Racing up the stairs toward her room, she felt almost euphoric. Luke might be on his way here, this very minute. Her hands shook with excitement. She must hurry; it wouldn't do for him to think she was taking time with her appearance just because he finally decided to return. She had no intention of letting him see that she cared what he thought of her.

Through her upstairs bedroom window, Noelle caught a glimpse of Mike O'Shea as he crossed the street and climbed the outside framed stairs to his law office above the bank building.

Mike O'Shea. Since Luke had been gone, Mike had spent almost all his spare time helping her with the saloon's renovations. He'd removed her uncle's unwieldy old furniture from the back rooms of the saloon. He had painted the high ceilings throughout the upstairs rooms that Ike and Curly had feared to tackle. Yet despite the time she had spent working with Mike, he did nothing to make her heart race as the mere thought of seeing Luke again did.

She closed the window curtains. Mike O'Shea had asked to court her, and she had said yes. A tumble of confused thoughts filled her mind. At the time, she couldn't think of a reason to refuse. But now...

Noelle poured water from the ironstone pitcher into the wash bowl, then dipped a linen cloth into the cool water and began to wash her face.

What was she going to tell Mike O'Shea if he asked her to marry him? He knew, as well as she, that a decent woman must marry. Mike was a respectable man, ambitious and intelligent, one her parents would have considered an excellent match for her.

Mike was good-looking enough, with his sandy brown hair and deep-set gray eyes. He was almost as tall as Luke, although Mike's three-piece suits gave him the distinct disadvantage of appearing stuffy compared to Luke's black gambling suits with string ties and snowy white shirts, which contrasted so handsomely against his deep-tanned skin.

Noelle sighed. She respected and admired the young

lawyer, but heaven help her, she didn't feel the same about Michael O'Shea as she did for...

Noelle pressed the wet cloth to her warm cheeks and glared at her reflection in the oval mirror above the walnut chiffonier. Her blue eyes stared back at her—eyes so like her father's. If only she had someone to talk to, someone like her father...

She dipped the cloth back into the water, chastising herself for her pitiful thoughts. Her parents had brought her up to recognize good character in a man. Luke Savage had strong character, she was certain, but he wasn't the marrying kind. She certainly knew what her parents would think about a man like him.

She would talk to Mike, the sooner the better. At all costs, she didn't want to make Mike think she was leading him on, or to hurt him. The truth was that he was a fine man, who deserved a woman who truly loved him—but she wasn't that woman. Perhaps if things were different...

If she hadn't already met Luke Savage...

The unbidden thought surprised and confused her. Just when she thought she had Luke Savage all figured out, her mind and body betrayed her.

Noelle was still puzzling over her wayward emotions when she had finished her ablutions and dressed with infinite care. She'd changed into the yellow-checked dimity gown; the bright color always gave a lift to her spirits.

Too many important things were pressing on her mind. Only one more week remained before the grand opening of the saloon. With costumes to finish, hand-bills to circulate, she wouldn't have time to notice if he was holding those disgusting poker games or not. Besides, she had yet to teach Ike and Curly their parts in the disappearing man performance.

Noelle leaned closer to the mirror and pinched her cheeks. She wanted to look nice for herself, that was all. She brushed back a loose tendril that escaped from her hair comb and studied her reflection critically. A proper young woman, the proprietress of her own establishment, smiled back at her. Pleased with her tidy appearance, she would spend no more time squandering foolish thoughts on Luke Savage. After all, he came and went as freely as Shep's tomcat.

Noelle smoothed the front panel of her dress below her small waist and caught a whiff of her lilac soap. The scent brought the unbidden image of Luke, soaking wet, reeking of lilac water that she had accidentally dumped on him that night he had slept beneath her wagon. Her heart slammed in her throat. Frowning back at her reflection, she felt a new determination. "I'll put that man out of my mind once and for all!"

Luke stepped from the barbershop, his mood suddenly buoyant as he rushed in the direction of the Silver Hearts Saloon. He wondered if Noelle had returned yet. His pulse went crazy when he thought of her, and he realized suddenly that he was behaving like a schoolboy. Damn, what if someone noticed his sudden hurry to see her? He purposefully slowed his gait to a leisurely stroll.

Who was he kidding? Noelle was all he'd thought about, dreamed about since he'd left town. And just now, when he'd returned with the surprise he'd bought for her in Lake's Crossing, and found her running errands instead of smiling at him, like he'd imagined when he'd stepped through those swinging doors, well...

He felt like he did when he was a five-year-old and learned that there was no Santa Claus.

Luke rubbed his freshly shaved chin, the odor of bay rum still tingling his skin. Had Noelle missed him? Would her cheeks flush the color of pink roses when she saw him? Would she smile—that dazzling smile that made him feel like the most important man in the world?

Jeezzo! What was the matter with him? He had no right to feel the things he was feeling about her. No right at all. But what in Sam's hell was he going to do about it?

"Luke!"

Luke turned around and peered at several prospectors, standing in line in front of the bank and assay office.

"Luke!"

His gaze lifted to Mike O'Shea, who waved from the upstairs office window facing the street. "I'd like to see you for a minute, Luke. It's important, and it can't wait."

O'Shea was the last person Luke wanted to see. He swore under his breath, touching his hat brim in reply. Luke started to cross the street, then waited while several cowboys rode past. Moments later, Luke bounded up the steps of the framed building to O'Shea's law office on the second floor.

Luke opened the door and stepped inside the small office. Doffing his hat, he nodded briefly at the man sitting beneath the portrait of President Andrew Johnson. Old Glory hung from a flagpole beside the tall bookcase. Strewn across the desk were official-looking papers piled into neat leather folders.

O'Shea pulled a cigar box from a side drawer and offered one to Luke.

Luke declined with a shake of his head. "Can't stay long, Mike. What do you want?"

O'Shea took a cigar and carefully cut one end, taking his time lighting the smoke. "I'm very interested in what you found in Lake's Crossing," he said finally.

Luke peered at him through a blue wreath of haze. The heavy tobacco aroma filled the small room. "I found the man, but he wasn't Blackjack."

Mike puffed, considering for a long moment. "Sorry, Luke. I didn't mean to send you on a wild-goose chase."

Luke shrugged. "Honest mistake. The man looked enough like Blackjack. Same build. Same thick, dark brown hair mixed with gray." He crossed his right leg over one knee.

"While I was there, I had the print shop make up some circulars," Luke continued. "I'm offering a reward for any information about Blackjack. It will take time, but if that polecat is alive, I'll hear about him, sooner or later."

Mike's dark brows knitted together. "Have you thought what it will do to Noelle if her uncle is alive?"

If Blackjack was alive and Luke was the one to put her uncle in jail, she might never forgive Luke. He'd thought of little else, but he didn't care to share that with O'Shea. "Noelle's stronger than you think," Luke said instead. "If Blackjack is alive, he'll get a fair trial. If he's proven guilty, well…Noelle will have to accept the truth. She's been raised proper, and she'll want to see justice prevail as much as I do." His defense of Noelle surprised him.

Noelle was strong. He grinned. How pleased she would be to have heard him admit it.

He watched Mike lean back and silently study him. He was anxious to leave and see Noelle. Damn, he liked Mike, but when he assessed him in that lawyer's way of his, a small matter might take all day. "What's on your mind, O'Shea?"

O'Shea took a long puff on the cigar. "I want to discuss something with you," he said finally. His gray eyes fixed on Luke.

Luke uncrossed his legs. "Nobody's stopping you."

Mike's hands absently straightened the stack of papers in front of him, his eyes averted. "I've been seeing a lot of Noelle since you've been gone, Luke."

Tell me something I couldn't have guessed. Luke shifted uneasily in the wooden chair, waiting him out.

"Although I've known Noelle a couple of weeks, I'm going to ask her to marry me."

Luke felt as if he had been kicked in the stomach. "When are you going to ask her?" he managed.

O'Shea rolled the cigar in his fingers. "I'm taking her on a picnic later this afternoon. I've asked Hilda Mueller to prepare us a special picnic basket, as only Hilda can prepare." He smiled and rubbed his stomach. "I thought Noelle and I would go for a buggy ride along the west ridge and after our picnic, I'll ask her, then."

A feeling coursed through Luke, a feeling he recognized as jealousy. Although he told himself he had no right to feel a proprietary claim where Noelle was concerned, yet... "Why are you telling me this?" Luke asked finally.

O'Shea stamped out the end of the cigar in an amber glass ashtray. "Because it's in Noelle's best interest."

"Best interest?"

"In other words, I'd like you to put aside any serious thoughts you might have about her."

A warm flush of anger seeped up Luke's neck and warmed his face all the way to his scalp. "I've no claim on her."

Mike settled back in his chair. "That's not what I mean, Luke, and you know it." His gray eyes were serious. "Noelle is the marrying kind of woman. Remember that, Luke. She respects you, and she'll listen to your advice."

"I think the decision is up to the lady."

O'Shea leaned back in his squeaky chair and steepled his fingers in his lap. "Luke, I'm planning to run for governor next election. The mining committee in Carson City feels that I'll be a shoo-in against the incumbent. I can take Noelle out of this town and make her first lady of Nevada. You know she deserves a better life than running a broken-down saloon in a mining town like Crooked Creek."

"I've said all along that Noelle doesn't belong in Crooked Creek," Luke said, his voice giving no sign of his feelings. He couldn't commit to anything more. Not out loud, anyway.

"Fine. We agree." He smiled. "Then you'll do nothing to stop Noelle from marrying me?"

Luke sat up straight and leaned forward in his chair. "Noelle's a smart woman. She doesn't need me to tell her what to do."

O'Shea's smile faded. "Are you're saying that you won't help me?"

"Let's just say that I'll vote for you." Luke grinned

at O'Shea's growing irritation. "But that's probably all the help you'll get from me."

O'Shea's fingers moved back and forth in exasperation. "I don't want there to be any hard feelings between us, Luke, but if—"

"And there's none taken." Luke scraped back the wooden chair and rose to his feet. He put on his hat and brushed the brim with his fingers. "I'll let you know if I hear anything about Blackjack."

Before O'Shea had a chance to say anything more, Luke closed the door and went down the rickety stairs, two at a time.

Despite his feelings, Luke knew that he should be relieved at the idea of Noelle becoming Mrs. Michael O'Shea, the future first lady of Nevada. Mike was a decent, respectable man who could provide her with the life she deserved. But dammit, when he thought of O'Shea with Noelle, it was anything but relief that charged through his blood.

Luke crossed the street, barely missing several wagons that rumbled past. A prospector, pushing an overloaded wheelbarrow filled with mining supplies, called a greeting, but Luke didn't hear. Luke was almost to the horse trough near the Silver Hearts Saloon when he noticed Little Henry's younger brother, Running Beaver, and his cousin, White Cloud, milling about the swinging doors.

A sense of unease swept through Luke. Indians were barely tolerated in Crooked Creek. They knew better than to approach a saloon. Before Luke had a chance to talk to them, the Indians saw him, then moved on.

The rousing piano chorus of "Turkey in the Straw" filled the air as Luke pushed through the saloon doors. Fresh paint and turpentine filled his nostrils. Ike called out a greeting, the cigar clenched between his front teeth never moving. Luke stared at the cigar and wondered how Ike managed that. The stogie was probably a recent bribe from O'Shea.

Luke glanced around, amazed at the sudden change in the place. Beneath the snowy white ceiling, the walls glistened with pale blue paint. The wooden floorboards shone, glassware above the bar sparkled and oil lamps glistened above the green-baize tables.

Ike's tanned fingers never stopped pounding the piano keys. "Hey, Luke. Did ya hear a new tune while you was in Lake's Crossin'?" His broad smile revealed several missing teeth along his top jaw.

Luke chuckled. Ike had the most amazing talent for being able to play any tune after he heard the melody just one time. Whenever Luke left Crooked Creek for another town, he would go out of his way to listen for a new song to bring back for Ike. "Yeah, I heard a new one, Ike. But I'll whistle it for you later. First, I want to see Noelle. Is she back yet?"

Ike grinned. "Miss Noelle is out in the new store-room, hangin' curtains. She said to call her when you came in."

"Never mind. I'll surprise her." Luke picked up the brown-paper-wrapped package he had lugged all the way from Lake's Crossing for Noelle and carried it as he went toward the rear of the saloon.

The smell of fresh wood filled his nostrils. "Hi, Luke," Shep said, looking up from the board he was sawing.

Luke started to answered him, but when he saw Noelle, all thoughts flew from his mind.

She stood by the window, white lace curtains billowing from her outstretched arms. Sunlight bathed her in a wash of gold, her upswept hair caught in a halo of light.

She turned, their eyes met. He wanted to say something, but he could only stare. God, she was beautiful. He was reminded of the marble statue in Blackjack's office—the flawless beauty whose outstretched arms waited to claim her lover.

"Did you have a good trip?" Noelle asked.

He'd forgotten how lyrical her voice sounded. Luke nodded, not trusting himself to speak. She smiled, and he felt a tightening in his loins.

She glanced at the large, clumsy package in his arms. Her thick lashes shaded her eyes. "For me?"

He nodded. "Yes. A surprise. It reminded me of you," he managed to reply. He was rewarded by her shy smile.

"Careful, it's heavy," he said when she moved beside him. "Here, let me carry it over here." He placed the package at the far end of the table where Shep had been measuring lumber.

Noelle untied the string, her eyes widening with excitement. "I feel like it's my birthday."

"It's…practical." He tried to swallow. "It's practical," he repeated, grinning at her.

She ripped the brown paper from the unwieldy form. "Oh!" Her mouth opened as she gazed at the stack of wallpaper rolls. Moments later, she glanced up, her lovely face lit with delight.

"Real wallpaper! I haven't seen anything like this since New York—" She touched his hand in thanks. He felt each of her fingertips sear into his skin.

Removing her hand, Noelle unrolled a segment of one end. "Roses!" Her mouth hung open as she gazed at the delicate nosegays of pink rosebuds tied with tiny blue ribbons repeated across the creamy lace background.

"Oh, Luke, it's the most exquisite pattern. I love it." Her eyes glistened with a sudden rush of tears, and the sight went straight to his heart. He could stand here all day, drinking in the vision of her.

"Thank you, Luke. Thank you, so very much."

Damn, he could use a drink. He cleared his throat as she smiled in that special way that made his heart sing. God, he could go on staring at her for as long as—

"Real pretty paper," Shep said, scratching his head.

Luke frowned, having forgotten that Shep was still there. "I left my horse in your stable, Shep. Whenever you get a minute…" Luke said, glaring at him.

Shep glanced from Luke to Noelle, then back to Luke. "Ah, yeah. I'll go take care of 'im, then I'll be right back, Miss Noelle." He turned and ambled from the room, chuckling loudly as he left.

Luke sighed. "You had mentioned that your bedroom walls needed…" Damn, when she looked at him all soft and pretty like that, he could hardly think straight. All he wanted to do was take her in his arms and—

"I'm so touched, Luke. You're very kind."

You wouldn't think that if you knew what ungentlemanly thoughts I'm having. Luke shrugged. "When you're ready, I'll paper your bedroom walls for you." His imagination soared at the thought of her bedroom.

Her brows lifted. "Do you know how to wallpaper a room?"

Luke thought of Mike O'Shea, painting ceilings and walls while he was away. "Sure. How hard can it be?"

Her lips lifted into a smile. "Have you hung wallpaper before?"

Luke gave her a lazy grin. "I'm a man of many accomplishments, Miss Bellencourt. You just sit and look pretty while I show you a few of my talents.''

Her laughter rang out like music. ''I wouldn't want to miss this.'' She rerolled the paper and placed it neatly beside the others. ''When can you begin?''

Luke remembered that Mike was planning to surprise Noelle with a picnic later today. ''No time like the present.''

She giggled. ''Very well. I'll mix up a batch of paste.''

''Paste?''

''Of course,'' she said, gathering the curtain material in her arms. ''Paste to stick the paper to the wall.''

''Oh, of course.'' Luke grabbed the bundle of wallpaper. ''I'll go ahead and carry these upstairs.''

''We'll have to move the furniture in the middle of the room.'' She smiled back at him. ''Won't take us long. I'll ask Shep to help.'' She turned and started toward Blackjack's office.

''No need. I can do it.''

''Very well.'' She took several steps then paused. ''Oh, Luke. When you go upstairs, you'll find Curly working in the hallway. Will you ask him if he would rent Shep's wagon, then pick up the costumes from Emily's house? She's finished the alterations, and I didn't have time to ride out to her place this morning.''

''You go on and make the wallpaper paste,'' Luke said. ''I'll give Curly the message.''

''Thank you.'' She glanced at him over her shoulder. She furrowed her brow thoughtfully. ''Are you certain you know how to wallpaper, Luke?''

He gave her a lazy smile. ''How can you doubt me, woman?''

She pursed her lips. ''If you say so.''

When Luke reached the top of the stairs, he found Curly on hands and knees, tightening the final bolts of the new handrail.

"Curly," Luke said, hoisting the wallpaper bundle on one hip while he fished in his back pocket. "Noelle wants you to pick up the costumes from Emily's place. And…" Luke counted out five-dollars in coin and handed the money to Curly "…don't take the wagon. Instead, tell Shep you want to use the buggy."

Curly's eyes widened. "The buggy? But I don't need—"

"Take the buggy and don't argue. You don't want to wrinkle those costumes in the back of a wagon, do you, Curly?"

Another thought came to Luke's mind. "On second thought, Curly, I want you to buy the buggy." He grinned, unable to keep a straight face. "Have Shep draw up the bill of sale, and I'll settle up with him later.

Curly beamed, his eyes wide. "I'll go right now."

"And take your time, Curly. It's a beautiful day. Enjoy yourself, take the buggy for the whole day."

Luke chuckled as he watched Curly amble down the stairs. The thought of Mike O'Shea strolling into Shep's Livery Stable, a blanket under one arm, a picnic basket under the other… Damn, he could just imagine O'Shea's face when he discovered the buggy gone and realized who had outfoxed him.

Chapter Nine

"Mornin', Mr. O'Shea," the white-whiskered prospector called out from the wooden seat of his mule-driven, wobbly wagon as the rig bounced along the hard-packed road. His smile revealed several missing teeth.

"Good day, Jedediah," Mike shouted over the noise. He prided himself that he could remember every name of the hundreds of miners who had filed claims with him since he'd opened his law office three years ago. Made a man feel important to have his name remembered.

He pulled the fob chain from his waistcoat pocket, flipped open the gold watch's engraved lid and examined the time. Exactly five minutes had passed since he last checked his timepiece. Damn, he was as nervous as an Illinois hound on the scent of a rabbit.

He put the watch back into his pocket, annoyed with himself. He didn't care much for the feeling. On his graduation day from Harvard, his father had given Mike the watch. "I'll not wish you luck, son, for a man makes his own luck in this world," he'd said.

For most of Mike's thirty-one years, Mike had lived

by that precept. When he'd met his father's famous friend and colleague, Abraham Lincoln, in Washington at the president's inauguration, Mike had decided politics was the life he wanted. Three years ago, when President Lincoln had asked him to help convince the miners to vote for Nevada's statehood, Mike had risen to the challenge. When Nevada was admitted to the Union, he yearned to be part of its dynamic political arena. The memory girded Mike with the resolve he needed to ask Noelle to be his wife. He needed a wife—the right kind of wife—to pursue his political career. Someone with the social graces to woo and win the important men of Washington, but with the adventurous spirit necessary to live here on the frontier.

Yes, with Noelle at his side, anything was possible.

If Noelle will say yes.

Mike patted the gold watch in his pocket. Of course, she'll say yes. Noelle was a lady, and she knew this dusty corner away from civilization held no future for her. She'd agree, and he'd take her home to Springfield, Illinois, where they'd be married in grand style. When they returned to Nevada, home would be Carson City.

His step quickened as he carried the picnic basket that Hilda Mueller had prepared specially for him, and headed toward Shep's Livery Stable.

Women enjoyed romantic buggy rides in the country, and once he had Noelle away from that disgusting saloon she was so fond of, they'd ride out along the northern hills to the crest and gaze upon one of the best views of western Nevada, backdropped by the stunning Sierra Nevada mountains. Ah yes, he'd tell her his dreams for their new home, and their future as the governor and first lady of Nevada. Why, she'd be as eager as he was to tie the knot and begin their new life together.

Then why did he feel so uneasy? Damned unlucky to have Luke Savage return to town, today, of all days. Not unlucky, he reminded himself. A man makes his own luck.

"Shep?" Mike called out. The only answer was the horses' nickering. Mike frowned into the dusty livery window, pausing to let his eyes grow accustomed to the shadows. Where was the buggy?

"Hey, Shep? Where are you?"

"Out here."

Mike peered into the shed. At the opposite end of the building, he noticed the narrow rectangle of sunlight coming from the open rear door. Mike covered the lunch basket with a red gingham cloth to protect the picnic lunch from the barn dust. Then he hurried inside, wondering if Shep was washing the buggy before renting it to him. The idea put a bounce in his step.

Smells of old leather, horse liniment and stabled animals rushed his senses as he strode through the livery. When he reached the backyard, he found Shep hammering a horseshoe over a roaring forge. Mike glanced around. "Where's the buggy?"

Shep gave the red-hot metal another blow. "Ah, well...I'm afraid it ain't here."

"Where is it?"

Shep gave him a one-eyed look. "'Fraid it's gone."

"Gone?"

"That's right."

Mike struggled to hide his impatience. "Where has it gone?"

Shep chewed the wad of tobacco in his cheek. "Curly took it to pick up some curtains from Emily's place."

"Why didn't you rent him the wagon?"

"Didn't want the wagon. Wanted the buggy."

"How long will Curly be gone?"

Shep spit a stream of brown juice on the ground. "Most of the day, I figure." He spit again. "The five bucks he paid me says he don't have to tell me what time o' night he'll be coming back."

"Five dollars!" Where did Curly get money like that? Mike took only a second before the thought of Luke Savage came to mind.

"Luke put you up to this, didn't he?"

"Not me." Shep grinned. "Curly, maybe," he added, his eyes sparkling with mischief.

"That damn son of a..." Mike scratched his jaw. "Well, if Luke wants to play dirty, two can play that little game."

Shep frowned. "Whatcha mean?"

"You'll see. Come on, Shep. I've got an idea how to get back at Luke."

Shep raised both hands and shook his head. "Not me, son. This is between you an' Luke."

"No, it's between me and Luke and your buggy! Hell, Luke could have bought that buggy for five bucks—"

Shep gave Mike a smug look. "Matter o' fact, Luke did."

Mike glared at the older man, and Shep stepped out of Mike's reach. "Hey, I'm only tryin' to make an honest living—"

"Honest, like hell." Mike put the picnic basket down near the doorway. He pulled his money purse from his back pocket, then opened it and handed several crisp bills to Shep. "Here's what I want you to do...."

Noelle balanced the dishpan of wallpaper paste between her arms and carried it toward the staircase. No sooner had she started up the steps when she heard Luke's whistling. She didn't recognize the tune, but she didn't care. The song's happy melody matched her mood. A man's whistling was such a comforting sound, she realized suddenly, and she had missed it while Luke was away.

She had missed a lot of things in that short heartbeat of time since he'd been gone. The slap of cards upon the poker tables, his rich baritone laughter as he joked with the crowd. She didn't have to see him to know he was there, and despite all of her work, the time he'd been gone had left her feeling strangely empty.

At the upstairs landing, she found the hallway almost blocked by the furniture Luke had moved from her bedroom. She sidled past the chiffonier, stepped around the bedside table and over three hatboxes before peering at him through the open doorway.

Luke stood on a chair with his back to her; his size nearly dwarfed the room. The windows were bare; the shades had been pulled down, gold sunlight limning the dark edges, giving the room a sense of intimate secrecy.

Luke's black broadcloth jacket and satin vest lay abandoned over the iron bedstead. His white linen shirt stretched taut across his broad back as he reached for the ceiling. The muscles below his rolled-up white sleeves flexed as he unfurled a roll of wallpaper.

He stretched to the uppermost corner, his fingers easily reaching the ceiling as he measured the sloping angle of the wall. His wide shoulders contrasted sharply with his narrow waist and hips. She held her breath, enjoying the rare opportunity to feast her eyes on him.

He held the yardstick to the ceiling corner, then turned his head, his profile serious as he held the paper to the angle of the wall.

She could hear his even breathing, and she suddenly felt very much alone with him—the only barrier between them was her tightly made bed standing in the center of the room.

This wasn't a good idea.

Her gaze shifted back to the bed, looming large in the middle of her bedroom. How could she have invited him into her private domain, her personal territory, her bedroom?

Mentally, Noelle gave herself a hard shake. She took a deep breath and steadied herself. After all, she and Luke had been alone before. He'd proven over and over that she could trust him. So why…?

Her mouth almost dropped open in shock with the sudden realization—it was herself she didn't trust.

Noelle placed the heavy basin of paste on the floor, afraid she might drop it. Wiping her hands on her apron skirt, she took a deep breath.

Luke noticed her then. He stopped whistling and smiled, fastening his gaze on her intently. She wondered if he knew she'd been lingering in the hall, staring at him. A hot blush rose to her cheeks.

"Is that the wallpaper paste?" He stepped down from the chair and glanced at the washbasin filled with the flour mixture she'd made. He stuck a finger into the pan, then licked it. "Tastes like Hoot's flapjack batter," he teased.

She chuckled. "Better, if you ask me."

His eyes lit with merriment. "Don't worry. If all else fails and the paste doesn't hold the paper to the walls, Shep keeps a jug of furniture glue in the livery."

She placed her hand on her hip and affected a casual air. "Are you doubting my ability, Mr. Savage?"

"I've never doubted your ability to do anything, Noelle."

Something in his voice caused her breath to catch. She answered him with a tight smile, determined not to let her runaway emotions get the better of her.

"Maybe it would be easier if I stood on the chair." She forced herself to concentrate on the work at hand. Craning her neck toward the ceiling, she added, "I've had experience matching patterns."

"Matching what?"

She met his curious look and realized that he was serious.

"The roses along the paper's edge should match one another," she explained, tracing her finger along the edge of one roll. "Here, this rose completes this bud," she said, pointing to the repeat in the pattern.

Noelle watched his intent expression and the realization finally dawned on her. "You've never wallpapered a room before, have you?"

Playfully, he touched the end of her nose with his finger. "How hard can it be?"

The idea that Luke wanted to please her so much that he'd attempt to wallpaper a room without knowing the first thing about it, left her enraptured with joy. But she held herself in with feigned poise.

"Do you doubt *my* ability, Miss Bellencourt?"

She swallowed. "N-no," she whispered. "It's that…" Enjoying the easy banter, she also sensed something else building between them. His brown eyes smouldered, and she had a flash of how he'd looked in her wagon that night, drenched to the skin. Desire had darkened his eyes as it did now.

Quickly, she glanced away to break the spell. "Oh,

I forgot to fetch the stepladder.'' She drew herself up straight. "I'll be right back—"

"I'll go," Luke offered. "Blackjack kept a small ladder in the storeroom." He raked his fingers through his hair. "I'll be right back."

When Luke returned with the ladder, he found that Noelle had already pasted one strip of paper to the wall. She was balancing upon a wooden crate that stood precariously atop the chair seat, her arms holding another paste-laden strip.

"Whoa, be careful." Luke put down the ladder and scrambled to her side, his hands circling her waist. "Let me help you."

"Ooh!" Noelle grabbed his shoulders in an attempt to regain her balance. The wallpaper strip she held in her fingers almost slipped from her hands. "Careful!"

Luke's left hand steadied her back, and his other hand gripped her tiny waist. "You're going to break your lovely neck—"

"I am not!"

"Get down before you hurt yourself." Luke lifted her from the chair and held her in his arms. "Don't ever put a box on a chair and stand on it. I don't want anything to happen to you, Noelle."

Luke's hands gripped her bottom, and she sucked in a ragged breath at his intimate touch. She could feel his rapid heartbeat against his chest as she clung to him. Goose bumps coursed up and along her arms. His dark eyes met hers and sent a shaft of heat down her body.

Without any warning, the paper at the ceiling's edge slowly began to unfurl.

Noelle's eyes rounded in shock. "Oh, no!"

Luke let go of her.

She pointed to the pile of soft cleaning rags in the

hallway. "Hand me one of those cloths on top of the chiffonier," she ordered, "Hurry!"

When Luke dashed from the room, Noelle climbed back on the chair, pressing the wall covering with her hands as best she could, to the wall. At least the paper hadn't completely unrolled into a sticky mess at her feet.

Moments later, Luke handed a large cotton rag to her. She grabbed it with a deft motion.

Luke took a seat on the edge of the bed and watched her brush the surface of the strip with the soft cloth. Immediately, the wrinkles and bubbles vanished from the floral design.

The small corner of the room already brightened with the promise of ribbons and roses, and for the moment, Luke felt a rush of pride in what she'd accomplished in such a short time.

What would she think of him if she knew that he'd offered a reward for any information about Blackjack?

He brushed the thought aside. For now, he'd be content to just enjoy watching the way her shapely body swayed with the steady rhythm of her work.

"There," she said with relief. She stepped down to admire the corner. Her skirts pressed against the bed frame as she leaned back toward him. "How do you like it?"

"What's more important is, how do *you* like it?"

Her eyes glowed with pleasure. "I think it's the most beautiful wallpaper I've ever seen." Her smile lit the room. "And it was very thoughtful of you to offer to help me, Luke. But really, I'm quite able to finish. I'm sure you have other important things to do."

Luke glanced up at the sparkling white ceiling and the image of Mike O'Shea brushing that white paint in

Noelle's bedroom rankled him more than he cared to admit. Damned if he'd allow O'Shea to set foot in here again. "Wallpapering is definitely a two-person deal. You'll need help cutting the paper and somebody to hand it to you," he added for good measure. "Besides, we'll get it done twice as fast."

"Very well. I used the yardstick and razor over there to cut the edges." She glanced in the corner where Luke saw the tape measure, yardstick and *his* straight razor.

"Jeezzo, woman! You didn't cut that paper with my razor, did you?"

"Your razor? What are you talking about? I found that razor in my uncle's desk, along with his shaving mug and soap."

Luke swore under his breath. "Noelle, that's where I keep my personal gear. You've just ruined my only razor!"

"Nonsense. I only used it to cut two lengths of wallpaper. It's probably as good as new."

Luke rolled his eyes. "Here, let me cut the paper while you apply the paste."

She handed the razor to him. "I'll hold the top of the roll for you while you cut the bottom edge," she said, unfurling the wall covering.

"Deal."

During the next few hours, Noelle and Luke worked together, until the last strip of paper had been hung. "There's enough wall covering left over to paper the closet walls," he said, wiping his hands on a rag.

"The closet can wait for some other day," she said, sitting down on the edge of the bed. She glanced over at him, her face beaming in pleasure as she admired the finished room. "It's like the beautiful bedroom I always wanted as a young girl,'' she said. The wistful tone in her voice struck a chord in him.

"What was your bedroom like as a young girl?'' he asked, coming to sit down beside her.

Her smile faded. "I slept on a cot in the living room. My parents had little money after my father had difficulty finding employment as an artist. We rented several rooms over…Harrison's tavern.'' She met his eyes, Luke saw a look of tenderness in their blue depths.

"So you see,'' she said, this isn't the first time I've lived above a tavern. My mother took in washing, and my father did all sorts of odd jobs while he looked for work in the city. They scrimped and saved so I could be educated. It was their dream come true the day I graduated from Miss Parson's School for Young Ladies.''

So you could marry well, he realized. *How thrilled and gratified her parents would have been to know their lovely daughter would one day marry the future governor of Nevada.* "They must have been very proud of you,'' he said, his voice revealing none of his thoughts.

She smiled, her gaze lingering upon the pink nosegays of roses. "My mother always said that someday I would have my own room with flowered wallpaper and…''

Noelle blinked back the memories and Luke's heart sank. God, how he wanted to take her in his arms, to hold and comfort her.

No, you're only thinking of your own comfort, Savage. You want to feel her soft bottom again and run your fingers through her hair until she flushes with the same desire as you feel.

"Glad you like it,'' he said, instead. The words felt like bricks in his throat.

She gave him one of those smiles that stirred his blood. She leaned over him. "Hold still," she said, running her fingertip along his cheek. She sat up straight, higher than he, smiling as she held up the finger to show him the spot of paste she'd removed.

He reached for her hand and licked the paste from her fingertip. Her hand curled back as though he'd burned her.

He took her hand, again. This time, she didn't pull away. This time, neither of them moved as their eyes locked.

Outside, street noises drifted up through the open window, its shade flapping occasionally against the windowsill. But the only sound Luke heard was their rapid breathing. The enticing smell of lilacs drifted from her unbound hair, which spilled over her shoulder. He remembered how she looked, so sweet and innocent, that night in the wagon....

Her lips parted slightly. Her gaze lingered on his mouth as she leaned over him, expectantly waiting.

"Noelle..." He spoke her name more as a plea than a warning.

Her tender lips brushed his mouth in sweet anticipation. Nothing could have prepared him for the overwhelming, sensual feeling her sweet innocence rendered. His arms circled her, pulling her down on top of him. He took her mouth, teasing, possessing as she opened for him. Time stood still as their kiss deepened, her warm breath caressing his face.

Her soft feminine mounds flattened against his hard chest as his fingers caressed her shoulders, back and the gentle curve of her hips.

He traced a line of kisses along her jaw, down to the soft hollow of her throat. He pulled her down beside him, then rolled over, cradling her beneath him, his weight balanced on his arms.

"Luke, I—I—"

"Don't say anything...."

She drew her head back against the feather mattress, exposing the delicate skin at her throat for his kisses. Her breasts heaved as she drew a deep breath. His mouth obeyed, and she moaned with delight, her arms entwining around his neck.

You shouldn't do this! But the words echoing in his brain were drowned out by the urgent desire raging in his blood. *He wanted her, and she desired him.* He ached for her, and he wanted to be the first man to unleash the ecstasy within her.

He cupped her breasts, the nipples taut against her gown. Bending his head lower, he drew the peaks with his tongue. Her fingers entwined into his hair while she cried out in surprise and, he thought, with a jolt of possessiveness, pleasure and desire.

Noelle felt his hardness, and she knew she should stop him, but dear God, she didn't want him to stop. She felt him unbuttoning her dress, then in a few moments, felt his hand on her bare breasts. Her body was hot and desire drove her to meld with him.

He took her mouth again. She kissed him back, exploring the wonders of his mouth. How she loved the taste of him.

She tried to fight the intense feelings she knew she shouldn't be feeling, but God help her, she didn't want him to stop. "Luke, I—I—"

"Don't say anything...."

Through her dazed awareness, she thought she heard a voice calling to him. A man's voice. Deep and familiar.

"Luke?" The man called again.

Luke's head snapped back and he met her gaze. "That sounds like Shep." He pulled away from her and raised the shade, then glanced out the open window.

Noelle got to her feet and tried to straighten her disheveled gown.

"What the hell do you want, Shep?" Luke yelled to the man below.

"Sorry, Luke, but a letter's come for ya. The rider says it's real important. He's waitin' for ya at the livery."

"Tell him to leave it." Luke started to lower the window.

"Wait! He won't. Says it's urgent."

Luke glanced back at Noelle. "Maybe it's a good thing for me to go. If I stay here any longer, with you looking as beautiful as you do right now, I might never be able to tear myself away."

His words brought a glow to her face. She didn't want him to leave, but she knew he should. Besides, she needed time to sort out her confused feelings.

"You'll need to change your shirt," she said, realizing, for the first time, that his clothing was splotched with wallpaper paste, and there was a bulge in his pants she didn't want anyone to see. "Why don't I go for you?" She removed her apron, and pulled a shawl from the closet, wrapping the covering around her shoulders. "I'll tell the rider that I'm your business partner. He'll give the letter to me," she added.

"Okay, you go on ahead," Luke said, unbuttoning his shirt. "But Shep will wonder why I'm not there. I'll change and be right along."

Noelle went to the door, then gave him a little smile

before she left the room. The look almost made his heart turn over.

Luke removed his shirt and raked the lock of hair back from his face while he listened to Noelle's footsteps fade down the hall. "Good thing you left when you did, little one. I don't know how much longer I could have held off—"

Luke shut his eyes and laid back on the bed, painfully aware of his arousal. "Damn, what am I going to do now?"

He opened his eyes and stared at the dazzling white ceiling over his head, and groaned. "I know what I'm *not* going to do. I'll be damned if I'll make love with Noelle beneath the white ceiling that Mike O'Shea painted!"

Chapter Ten

Noelle's knees felt wobbly as she came down the stairs and strode across the saloon toward the door.

Her skin felt warm and radiant from Luke's kisses. She pressed both hands to her cheeks. They were hot enough to burn her. Her heart beat madly beneath her shawl. *Oh, Luke. What am I going to do about you?*

She struggled back the thought. For now, she'd go to the livery and tell the rider that Luke would be along shortly. Hopefully, no one would notice the deep flush on her face.

When Noelle arrived at the livery stable a few minutes later, she found the front door closed. Strange. Everyone knew that Shep never closed the livery stable during the day. She shrugged. Grabbing the knob, she pushed open the door and stepped inside.

"Oh, no! It's Noelle!" a man's voice cried out.

Before she realized what was happening, a sudden gush of sticky liquid flooded down over her.

"Aaa!" She stifled a scream, closing her mouth in reflex. Her arms flailed at her sides as the wet goo ran down her hair, face, inside her neckline and all down the front and back of her.

"Now look what you did!" another man hollered.

"I did? It was your idea!" the first man accused. "Can't you do anything right?"

Noelle spat out a mouthful of goo and wiped her eyes with the hem of her skirts. Her fingers fought through the soaked material of her shawl and yellow gown. "My God!" she cried, shocked as the realization struck that she was covered with blue paint.

She froze, staring at Shep and Mike O'Shea's looks of sheer stunned surprise.

"Have you men lost your minds?" she asked.

"See here, Miss Bellencourt—" Shep began, but Mike interrupted him.

"Why didn't Luke come?" Mike demanded.

Shep dashed for a horse blanket and began to spread it across Noelle's shoulders.

"Stay away from me," she shouted, jerking the blanket from Shep, wiping her face with it. She had walked into a trap set for Luke, she realized, and she was outraged at these two men behaving like mischievous boys.

She eyed the empty paint bucket on the floor. "Who's responsible for this?" she asked, glancing from one to the other of the men.

"O'Shea put me up to it, Miss Bellencourt," Shep said, his Adam's apple bobbing up and down like a yo-yo. "I'm just an honest businessman, miss."

"Noelle, I'm so sorry." Mike stepped toward her, his arms outstretched. Then he stopped, his eyes round with horror. "Oh, Noelle. I'm so sorry."

Behind her, she heard people scampering, voices raised. She turned to see a smiling Pete Tardiff from the Red Garter Saloon, Carl, the barber, and a full-lathered customer gawking beside the two perennial checker players from next door, lining the street in front of the livery stable.

Just then, Luke pushed his way through the growing crowd and rushed toward her. "What in Sam's hell—" The words froze in Luke's throat when he saw Noelle. "Noelle, my God...!"

"Don't touch me!" she demanded.

Luke turned and glared at Mike O'Shea. "What the hell is going on, O'Shea?"

Shep took a step toward Luke. "O'Shea's idea, Luke. He wanted to get back at you for buying the buggy so he couldn't court Noelle anymore, an'—"

"Luke bought the buggy?" Noelle felt humiliated as the paint dripped from her hair, streaming down her face and shoulders. She wanted to cry, but she was much too angry to give in to tears. "Is that true, Luke?"

Luke's mouth tilted up in a crooked smile. "Well..."

"You miserable polecat! You paid enough for it," Mike shouted.

"I'll be happy to rent it out to you, Mike," Luke said, trying to keep his face straight. "That is, whenever I'm not using it."

"You should be ashamed of yourselves." Noelle said, ignoring the blue ooze dripping down her face. "All three of you!"

Mike waved his hands. "Noelle, I had no idea you—"

"What difference would it make if it were Luke?" she stormed at Mike. "It's a childish prank, and I would think you'd have more sense."

"Yes, I agree," Luke added, smiling rakishly at Noelle. "What would the boys in Carson City think if they knew—"

"I wouldn't be too eager to cast the first stone, Savage," Mike warned.

"Stop it this instant!" Noelle stamped her foot. "Enough!" Her face flushed with anger; her fingers balled into blue fists.

Luke pulled a white handkerchief from his pocket and went to her. Gently, he wiped around her eyes with the linen. "I've got just the thing to clean up this mess," Luke said.

"Take your hands off of her." Mike yanked Luke's hand away from Noelle.

"Luke is only trying to help!" Noelle said with irritation.

Luke gave Mike a smug look. "Yes, O'Shea, I was only trying to relieve the lady's distress, which you so unjustly caused. Now, why don't you and Shep clean this mess up?"

Luke put his arm around Noelle's shoulders and led her through the rear of the stable. "If we go the back way, fewer people will see you," he whispered in her ear.

"Just get me away from here," she said, wrapping herself in the scratchy horse blanket. She wished the earth would open up and swallow her.

Luke led Noelle along the back path that stretched behind the buildings along Main street. Unloading wagons and supply carts stood parked along the back steps. Women's laughter billowed from the upper windows of the Red Garter Saloon. Noelle could just imagine Jubilee and the other women gawking and snickering at her.

She didn't care if they did. If she didn't feel so miserable, she'd laugh, herself. She had paint everywhere—

in her ears, on her eyelids, on her nose. She must look a sight.

"I saw a bottle of turpentine in here somewhere," Luke said, opening the back entrance to the Silver Hearts Saloon. Noelle stopped before she put a foot inside the new storeroom that Shep and Curly had finished building only that morning.

"I can't go inside," Noelle said, her gaze on the newly waxed floorboards. "I'll drip paint all over everything." She held her skirts while she glanced up into his dark eyes.

"I've an idea." Luke disappeared inside the back room and came out holding several blankets. "I'll hold up the blanket as a screen, then you can undress and once you're free of your ruined clothing, you can wrap yourself with the other blanket and go inside. I'll remove the paint with the turpentine, then fix you a hot bath."

"Oh, Luke." She felt so miserable, so embarrassed and so grateful to him. "Thank you."

He smiled that special smile that told her everything was going to be all right. She watched him unfold the wool blankets—the same blankets he had slept on the first night when she had found him awake on her uncle's sofa.

"Close your eyes," she said, once he'd held the blanket up for her.

He chuckled. "I'm not promising not to peek," he teased.

"Then raise the blanket higher. Above your head." Despite her misery, she couldn't help chuckle. "I must look worse than I did the night on the trail when I was covered with soot."

"Mmm, just a different color," he said, smiling. "I

think I like you better in the blue. It matches your eyes.''

She grinned. ''Shut your eyes tight.''

Luke obeyed. Noelle watched his lids squeeze shut, then she turned her back toward the closed door of the saloon. At least she had privacy. Her sticky fingers began unfastening each dainty button, beginning at the neck. Sixteen buttons, to be exact.

The simple task was made difficult by her fingers sticking together. She flushed, remembering how Luke had unbuttoned the same buttons in seconds, only a short while ago.

Removing her shawl and dress, she let them fall in a ruined heap at her feet. Then she stepped out of her underskirts, shoes and stockings. She wiped her fingers until most of the blue stain had been removed from her hands. Thankfully, her thin chemise and drawers were free of paint.

A breeze ruffled her chemise and Noelle shivered, then she pressed against the blanket that Luke held up for her. ''I can manage now,'' she said softly, wrapping herself in its soft folds.

''I'm really sorry about all this,'' he whispered.

''I know you are.'' She glanced at him over her shoulder. The wind ruffled his hair, the black shadow of beard highlighting his cheeks and jaw. She knew now what his touch felt like against her sensitive skin. Now that she knew, the memory created a sensation of incredible desire she couldn't ignore. She wanted him to touch her. She yearned for him to touch her.

His smile faded, and she knew that he guessed what she was thinking. When did he learn to read her so well?

''Sit down on the step, and I'll begin with your hair.''

Noelle obeyed without question. He sat down beside her, and she watched him dampen a cotton cloth with turpentine. The aroma reminded her of the first time she'd crossed the Eastern slopes of Nevada and smelled the pine groves that dotted the mountains.

He leaned her against his chest, while his tanned fingers began to wipe blue paint from the long strands of her flaxen hair. He took his time, parting and brushing the strand of curls that hung from her shoulders.

The warm air tickled her sensitive skin, and she closed her eyes and leaned back against Luke, allowing his gentle touch to caress her. When he had finished her hair, she felt the soft cloth glide over her forehead and across her brows.

When he'd finished with the turpentine, he reached into the bucket he'd brought with him and wrung out another cloth. Warm, soap-scented moisture touched her forehead, wiping away the turpentine.

Tenderly, he wiped around her eyes and lids. She sighed as his fingers worked their magic. When he rinsed her face, each touch was so incredibly gentle, so exquisitely soft, that she could only imagine that his large, wide hand claimed the cloth.

The sun kissed her skin with its fire, or was it the memory of Luke's kisses and his nearness that warmed her blood with such intensity? She felt as light and free as a wisp of cloud floating across the heavens. She wanted to remain like this, forever.

His touch drifted down along her jawline and the delicate column of her throat. She shifted slightly, remembering the fiery trail of kisses he had planted there, less than an hour ago.

How she longed to be with Luke upstairs, as they had been in her bedroom. A blush of sensation followed that image. Yet here, outside, she felt safe, allowing herself to be disarmingly lulled with wondrous thoughts of him.

What must it be like to be loved by a man? No, not any man. What would it be like to be loved by Luke?

She opened her eyes. That was impossible. Even if Luke wanted to love her, she mustn't allow that to happen. What if she were to become pregnant?

Pregnant, with Luke's child. The thought brought an incredible yearning to her most inner heart. A child with the man she loves. But a child born to an unwed mother would be cast aside by society, an innocent victim. Her child didn't deserve to be a bastard!

She sat up, suddenly aware that her growing sense of safety was nothing but an illusion. The truth was that women who fall claim to their vulnerabilities are destroyed by society, and their children with them. She was in danger of becoming a woman like Jubilee. But Jubilee knew how to take care of herself, and Noelle knew nothing about how to prevent pregnancy.

Why was it that one look at Luke Savage and her common sense disappeared like water down a desert sinkhole? Someone had to be responsible. Noelle had felt herself giving in, and she mustn't. She must remain strong and in control.

"P-please..." She caught the end of the cloth in her fingers. "Thank you, Luke, b-but I can finish. I'll go and prepare my bath."

He said nothing, his grip firmly on the cloth.

She turned and raised her face to his. "Please, Luke."

He didn't speak, but those deep passionate brown eyes said everything. *A gambler isn't expected to be the responsible one.* As though he read her thoughts, his fingers relaxed and the cloth fell into her waiting palm.

With as much dignity as she could muster, Noelle wrapped the quilt tightly about herself and got to her feet. Rolling her discarded clothing into a ball, she grabbed her shoes and stockings, then scampered through the door to the safety within.

Luke stared at the doorknob long after she'd left, knowing full well that Noelle Bellencourt wasn't the kind of woman to take a man's attention lightly. No, she expected responsibility, commitment and marriage. She was the wrong kind of woman for a gambler like him, and they both knew it. So why didn't he feel a sense of relief when she ran away?

Relief, hell. He hadn't felt relief since he'd first met her, if he was honest. So, why didn't he just take off for a few days, wander down toward Virginia City, like he used to do when he felt the wanderlust call to him?

You're a damned fool, Savage. It's not wanderlust that's got you coiled up and striking back like a snake trapped in a barrel.

Noelle made him wonder about things he had no right to wonder about—like what it would be like to have a little girl with morning glory blue eyes and flaxen curls call him daddy? Or what it would be like to grow wrinkled and silver-haired together with Noelle—as his grandparents had—exchanging those secret, loving glances when they thought no one noticed?

Luke put the cloth back into the bucket of soapy water and leaned against the door. Overhead, an eagle soared silently, its white tail spread wide and golden in the sun.

He could still feel her soft weight against his chest and her slight tremble when he'd first touched her skin. She should have run like hell.

One thing was clear, he couldn't trust himself to be

alone with her again, and he could do something about that. He'd take a room at Hilda's boardinghouse and only go to the Silver Hearts saloon during the poker games when he wouldn't be alone with her. But quenching the fire that she stirred in his blood was another matter.

A few minutes later, Luke strode past the stage depot, then crossed the road, turned left toward the dead end until he came to Hilda Mueller's boardinghouse. The hinges of the wind-weathered sign—Rooms for Rent: Clean Gentlemen Only—creaked in the breeze as he stepped up to the porch of the two-story, white frame house and knocked on the screen door.

George and Rufus, two retired prospectors, peered back at him from their straight-backed rockers. "Howdy," they said in unison. "Stayin' t' supper?" George asked, cupping his ear as he waited for Luke's answer.

Luke shook his head. "No, George." He hoped George and Rufus wouldn't engage him in conversation. He'd have enough trouble with Hilda's curiosity when he made his request for a room.

He rapped on the door again. This time, the light clatter of footsteps upon wooden floors made him glance through the screen door.

"Why, Luke Savage. What a surprise!" Hilda's gray eyes crinkled with her smile. She stepped back, allowing him room to step inside the narrow hallway. Then she ducked her head out the door and peeked around, as though looking for someone. "I hoped that Blackjack's niece might be with you." Hilda stepped back, then wiped her hands on her faded apron. "Noelle is such a lovely young woman." Her grey eyes sparkled with an inner glow that raised Luke's hackles. Everyone knew Hilda was a frustrated matchmaker.

"I'd like a room, Hilda."

Her eyes lit with curiosity. *"Ja,"* she drawled, assessing him for a moment. Then she tossed her head toward the hallway. "Come inside," she ordered, obviously deciding not to ask the questions that built behind her bright eyes. "I have the last room on the left available. I show you."

"I don't need to see it, Hilda. I'll pay you a week's room and board. If I can have the key, then I'll be going. Miss Noelle is performing her magic act tomorrow, and I promised I'd help Curly and Ike assemble the props."

"Sit down while I get the key," she insisted, motioning to the several chairs in the kitchen. "And help yourself to my bread pudding, warm from the oven."

"Thanks, Hilda," Luke said, knowing better than to refuse. He knew, as well as her boarders, that Hilda believed all of man's ills could be cured by either a quotation from the Good Book or an ample serving of dessert topped with whipped cream.

Luke seated himself by the window. On the wall next to the cookstove, a framed Home Sweet Home called out to him in cross-stitch.

He glanced outside. Dazzling white sheets and pillowcases flapped from the clothesline stretched across the yard from the porch to the shed. He drummed his fingers on the table, then forced himself to stop, irritated that he felt so boxed in by the stifling hominess.

When Hilda returned, she handed Luke a key. She glanced at the pan of untouched bread pudding sitting upon the warming tray of the woodstove and frowned back at him.

Luke got to his feet. "Save me some pudding for later," he said, hoping to appease her. Hilda's thin face broke into a warm smile.

"*Ja,* I will. Now, you go help Miss Noelle. She's invited me to her performance this Saturday night." She picked up a knife and resumed peeling the potatoes in a blue crock on the table. "I can hardly wait to see the changes she's made to her uncle's building." Her hand quieted and her gaze drifted out the window. "I still can't believe that my Blackjack is gone."

Luke rolled his hat brim with his fingers. "I'm sorry for your loss, Hilda. Mike O'Shea told me that you and Blackjack were…"

"*Ja,* Blackjack had asked me to marry him, and I told him *ja.*" She lifted her chin and sniffed. "We were to be married this spring."

Luke set his jaw. No need to try to explain that Hilda was better off alone than with a man like Blackjack.

Hilda's gaze remained fixed on the mountains beyond. "How sad that Blackjack didn't live to see his grown-up niece." Her eyes brightened, and she blinked. "But I tell Noelle what a fine gentleman her uncle was."

Luke bit his tongue to keep from saying something that he'd regret later. He tucked the key into his pocket and strode toward the door. "Thanks, Hilda. Don't forget to save me a piece of that pudding."

When Luke returned to the Silver Hearts Saloon a short while later, he was relieved to find the place almost empty except for Ike, who was seated at the piano, plunking out a tune.

"Miss Noelle is in the storeroom, practicin' her act."

Ike spoke with an unlit cigar clamped between his teeth. "She asked not to be disturbed."

Luke frowned. "I didn't ask where Noelle was, did I?"

Ike glanced up, startled. "Humph! You're sure in a good mood." His hands glided across the keyboard, a slow, haunting melody filling the room. "This'll pick up your spirits." He smiled broadly as he waited for Luke's reaction. "What do you think of this tune?"

Luke hesitated a moment, then moved beside the upright piano. "Is that the melody I brought back for you from Maude's Place at Lake's Crossing?"

"It's yer ditty, all right. Only I'm playin' it like a waltz." His fingers slid over the yellowed keys, his left hand weaving back and forth in three-quarter time.

Luke tapped his foot to the music. "That's an amazing change, Ike. It's downright beautiful."

"Can't take the credit," Ike said. "When I played this for Miss Noelle, she suggested I slow the tune some." His grin stretched wide as a mile. "She was right. It's mighty purty played slow."

A bittersweet feeling claimed Luke at the mention of Noelle's name, but he pushed it aside. "If anyone should ask, I'll be at the gambling tables."

By midafternoon, Luke's luck had gone from bad to worse. Usually poker took his mind off of things, but nothing seemed to dent his bad mood.

Hoot, the owner of the Miner's Café, glanced at the players sitting at the poker table, then he looked at Luke. His muscular arms crossed in front of his burly chest. "Luke, are ya goin' t' play or not?"

Luke glanced at his cards—one of the worst dealt hands he'd ever seen. "I'll have to fold, gentlemen," he said to the other men at the table. He folded the cards on the table, facedown, then pushed his chair back as he stood.

Hoot turned to the man waiting at the bar. "What about you, Jed?"

The white-whiskered prospector cocked one eye. "Count me in, Hoot. Whose deal?"

Luke strode to the bar where Sheriff Wade stood talking to Curly. He moved beside Luke, his face serious. "Can I see you a minute?"

"Of course," Luke said, following the sheriff around the gambling tables toward the door. No one spoke until they were outside.

Sheriff Wade struck a wooden match against the hitching post and lit a hand-rolled cigarette. A puff of blue smoke haloed around him as he shook out the burning match. "A cowboy came to town this afternoon, lookin' for you, Luke. He wouldn't say what it was about, but I think it might have to do with Blackjack."

"Where is the cowboy now?"

"Clearin' the dust from his throat at the Red Garter, I imagine. Anyway, if he gives you any information about Blackjack, I want you to tell me." The sheriff took another drag on his cigarette.

Luke sensed that the sheriff was beginning to realize that the wily Blackjack might be alive after faking his own death.

"I told him where to find you, Luke. If you set out after Blackjack, I want to go, too. If he's alive, then he played a-low-down trick on the townsfolk of Crooked Creek, and I feel responsible to bring him in."

"Thanks, Sheriff, but if Blackjack is alive, I'll bring him back to face charges."

The sheriff steeled his jaw and frowned. "Then stop by the jail and let me deputize you."

"I don't need to hide behind a badge, Wade."

"I know that, son. But it will make it legal."

Luke hesitated. "All right. I'll stop by the jail on my way."

"Then if you find Blackjack—" Wade said.

"*When* I find him."

Sheriff Wade shook his head. "When you find him, he'll get a fair trial."

From up the street, Emily, holding her infant daughter asleep in a basket, called out to them. "Sheriff, don't leave without taking one of my posters!" She hurried toward them, several handbills tucked under her elbow.

Luke and Sheriff Wade tipped their hats as Emily gave the lawman several rolled-up parchments. "I've just finished lettering the handbills for Noelle's grand opening. Tack this poster in front of the jail, Sheriff. And here's another one for Ben at the stage depot."

"I heard them talkin' about the Silver Hearts grand opening at Carl's barber shop this morning," Wade said, glancing at the paper in his hand.

"Tomorrow night, Sheriff. Be sure to tell everyone to come."

Wade raised his head and tilted his eyeglasses to read the neatly lettered script. "Miss Noelle Bellencourt..." He squinted. "What's a presti...digit...ator?" he asked, sounding out the syllables.

Emily exchanged a look with Luke. "A prestidigitator is an illusionist. A magician. It means that Noelle will be performing her sleight-of-hand tricks tomorrow night."

Wade wrinkled his brow. "By gum, Miss Emily. Then why don't you just say so?"

Emily chuckled. "And on your way back to the jail, Sheriff, will you please run this poster over to Mike O'Shea's office for me? I want to go inside and see if I can help Noelle."

"No need to ask for O'Shea's permission, I'll go ahead and tack the poster to his door." Sheriff Wade hesitated, enjoying the growing expression of curiosity on Emily's face.

"Where is O'Shea?" Emily shifted the basket containing her sleeping daughter from one arm to the other.

"He's left for Carson City to meet with the governor's committee," Wade answered. "Won't be back till Saturday." He tipped his hat to Emily, then strode off.

Emily glanced at Luke, a determined look in her eye. "Let's go inside and get out of the sun. Besides, I've got a matter to discuss with you."

Chapter Eleven

Luke pushed open the saloon doors, and Emily strolled inside, taking a seat at one of the empty poker tables in a quiet corner of the room. Glasses sparkled from racks above the highly polished bar. The smell of lye soap and furniture polish permeated the room. Shep, standing on the stepladder near the bar, grunted a hello as he adjusted a lamp on the overhead chandelier.

"Hasn't Noelle done wonders for this place?" Emily said, lifting her child from the basket and putting Naomi on her lap. "Make a fine wife someday…that is, if she can find a man good enough for her." She shot Luke a teasing grin.

Luke took a deep breath as he straddled the chair across from Emily. "Noelle's a mighty fine woman, no one will disagree with you on that score." He could sense Emily was wound up in a fit of matchmaking. He knew she meant well, but, damn, he wasn't in the mood for her interference.

"I heard the men wagered among themselves who would be Noelle's partner in the illusionist act. Ike won." Emily's hazel eyes lit with amusement. "Funny how some sensible men can behave like boys at the sight of a pretty woman.''

Luke shrugged. He was fond of Emily, but she was married to a hardworking prospector—a man who was content to come home at night to a wife and child, after digging in the black earth all day, waiting for the one lucky chance to hit silver. How could Emily understand a gambler like Luke? Hell, he didn't understand himself.

''I hear you bought yourself a buggy.'' Emily's eyes glittered with amusement as she fiddled with Naomi's dress sash. ''It'll take more than buying that old buggy from Shep to stop O'Shea from courting Noelle.'' Her expression grew serious. ''Did you know that O'Shea is planning to ask Noelle to marry him?''

Luke sighed. ''Yes, but it's none of *my* business, Emily.''

Her thin lips drew into a determined line. ''Didn't say it was, Luke. But how can you stand back and let this happen?''

''Because I have no right to say anything. Noelle is a grown woman. She should marry a man like O'Shea. Did you know he's planning to run for governor?''

She wrinkled her nose and made a dismissive gesture. ''Luke Savage, I never knew you to be a quitter.''

He shifted uneasily in his chair. ''Let me hold Naomi,'' he said, hoping to change the subject. ''She must be getting heavy for you.''

Emily's mouth relaxed in resignation as she lifted the child into his arms.

''Look how our little dumplin' has grown,'' Luke whispered to the sleepy child. Naomi yawned, then closed her eyes contentedly as she nestled against his chest.

"I'm sorry if I spoke out of turn, Luke. But I've come to know and care about Noelle in these past weeks. I think she might refuse O'Shea if she thought you'd settle down."

Luke sighed as he brushed his hand over the top of Naomi's russet curls. "Did Noelle say that?"

Emily hesitated, her gaze upon her daughter in Luke's arms. "No, not in so many words. But sometimes it's not what a woman says, but what she doesn't say that counts."

"Noelle's old enough to play her own hand, Emily. Besides, she knows that a man like me would give her nothing but grief."

"Sometimes I think you're the most stubborn, cussed man, second to my own Daniel, that I've ever met!"

He shrugged. "Some of us just aren't the marrying kind, Emily." He glanced down at the child, asleep against his chest, and he felt Emily's gaze studying him.

"For a man who's not the marrying kind, fatherhood looks pretty good on you, Luke." The smile was gone from her face, and her hazel eyes showed concern.

"You've got a good man, Emily. But we're not all like Daniel."

"I'm convinced you want to believe that. But for the life of me, I can't figure out why."

He grinned. "I'll leave you to your little puzzle, Emily. I told Curly and Ike that I'd clear away the poker tables from the front of the saloon so they can set up the chairs for Noelle's performance."

He got to his feet, then placed Naomi into Emily's arms. As he strode toward the back of the saloon, he could still feel Emily's gaze upon him.

The afternoon wore on, and Luke was grateful for the time alone. He had almost finished stacking the last of the tables in the new storage room when he heard Emily call to him.

"Hurry, Luke. You don't want to miss this."

Luke parted the flour-sack curtains and poked his head through the blue floral print that served as a door to the new addition. "What is it, Emily?"

"Noelle is beginning the dress rehearsal for the disappearing man trick. Come on, the show is about to begin."

"I can't, Emily. I'm not finished—"

"Nonsense. You've been working all afternoon. Take a load off of your feet."

With a sigh of resignation, Luke escorted Emily to the front row of chairs. Ike and Curly stood a few feet away, their heads together in serious discussion. Shep put a finishing spit polish on the glass lamp, then stepped down from the ladder. He waited for Emily to be seated in one of the rockers that usually inhabited Carl's barbershop before Shep folded his long-legged frame into a large, overstuffed chair.

Luke leaned back and wondered what Blackjack might say if he could see the changes that Noelle had made to the place. Lamps flickered overhead, casting expectant shadows across the carmine velvet drapes drawn tightly across the stage. A gold fringe valance hung across the width of the stage—a valance Luke remembered seeing flounced across Jubilee's bedroom, when she had lived upstairs. The card tables had been stacked out of sight, replaced by three rows of an odd assortment of seating. Besides the gamblers' chairs, he recognized the lumpy velvet sofa from Blackjack's office and the deacon's bench from Carl's barber shop.

Little Naomi, bouncing excitedly in her mother's lap, stuck her chubby fist in her mouth. Luke brushed the child's rosy cheek with his index finger, and was rewarded with Naomi's glowing smile.

"Naomi's cut another tooth. That makes five," Emily added.

"Five!" Shep chuckled. "That's one more than Ike's got." He slapped his knee and chortled.

Ike glared back, straightening his shoulders. "That's five more teeth 'n you'll have if you don't pipe down." His wide mouth split into an easy grin.

"I'm as nervous as if it were me performing up there," Emily said. "When will the show begin?"

"Should be startin' any minute now," Shep replied. "Curly, quit pacin' back and forth an' take your place over there." Shep pointed to the center of the stage.

"Quit bein' so bossy." Curly placed his fists on his hips. "I know where I'm supposed to stand."

Ike took a seat at the piano and pounded out a rousing chorus of a Stephen Collins Foster tune, his cigar clenched firmly in his teeth while he grinned at the audience.

Curly stepped to the center of the room. "It is my pleasure," he began, "to introduce to you folks of Crooked Creek, Nevada, the Great Bellencourt...."

After Curly's introduction, Noelle, dressed in a fitted black suit, stepped from behind the red velvet curtains. Her blond hair was swept away from her face, cascading down her back. A black top hat angled on her head at a saucy angle. The perfectly fitted black wool jacket and skirt hugged her feminine curves to extreme advantage.

Luke's mouth felt dry, and he shifted uncomfortably in the chair while the small audience of friends applauded her entrance. Noelle smiled, removed her hat and bowed with a flourish. The motion of her head sent her long, curtain of flaxen hair shimmering around her shoulders.

She appeared so tiny as she strutted across the platform, bearing the style and presence of a natural performer. In the black fitted costume, she appeared more desirable than the scores of flimsily clad dance hall girls who had filled that stage before her.

Luke watched as she pranced back and forth, her delicate hands pulling brightly colored silk scarves from her black top hat, to the appreciative oohs and aahs of the small crowd. He recalled her small yet capable hands brushing across the rosebud wallpaper, and the slight tremble of her fingers against his when she met his kiss.

He fought back the unbidden thought of Noelle and Mike O'Shea together, his hands moving over her, inhaling the sweet scent of lilacs from her hair. Luke's fists clenched at his sides as he shook himself from the tortuous thoughts.

He joined the applause as Noelle made an egg disappear from Shep's handkerchief, only to find it again inside a bouquet of silk roses that bloomed from inside her black top hat.

''Thank you,'' Noelle said, bowing briefly. Then she asked Curly for a silver dollar. Dropping the coin into a glass of water, she covered the glass with Shep's handkerchief, and with a tap of her wand, she removed the cloth. To everyone's amazement, the coin had dissolved.

Curly's jaw dropped. Noelle apologized for losing his coin, then she brushed her hand behind his left ear, revealing the shiny coin in her hand, much to his delight.

Luke sat, entranced.

With the small stick she removed from under her arm,

Noelle pointed to the man-size, wooden cabinet, which stood in the center of the platform. Wings of thick draperies hung from each side of the box. A wide panel extended across the top of the frame, which Luke remembered, hid the full-length mirror, essential to create the illusion.

Curly, dressed in a blue suit, fidgeted nervously with his bow tie. His usual jolly expression was full of misgiving.

Ike finished the tune, then began a loud drumroll on the piano. At the cue, Curly stepped forward, taking his position.

"And now, ladies and gentlemen," he began, "the Great Bellencourt..." his deep baritone voice boomed even louder "...will make a man disappear into the great unknown, then try to bring him back again...." Curly gestured toward Noelle while Ike pounded out another spectacular drumroll on the ivories. "The Great Bellencourt."

Loud clapping followed, and Curly bowed, his face beaming. Ike stood up and took his place beside Noelle while Curly pulled the piano bench near Luke and took a seat.

"Noelle altered her father's suit to fit her—all by herself," Emily whispered to Luke. "Mighty talented woman," she added. Her accolades reminded Luke of the mothers who had brought their eligible daughters to the dancing socials he was forced to attend as a boy in Philadelphia.

Luke smiled pleasantly at Emily, then returned his attention to Noelle.

"Do I have a volunteer from the audience to act as my assistant?" Noelle asked, unable to hide her smile. Ike, cigar clenched in his teeth, lumbered toward her.

"Ah, this brave gentleman dares to offer himself as a traveler into the unknown." She turned and gestured to Ike, who hooked his thumbs under his suspenders and took a deep bow.

Luke clapped, unable to keep a straight face. Noelle bowed to Ike, then led him to his place at the tall, wooden cabinet. As practiced, Ike stepped inside and turned to face the audience.

Curly hooted, and Shep threw a wadded spitball at him.

Ike's face paled, and he glanced uneasily at Noelle.

"You're doing great," Noelle whispered to him. "Remember what we practiced, and everything will be fine."

Luke couldn't help but grin. Neither Curly nor Ike would ever be caught dead performing in front of a crowd unless they had been totally charmed by Noelle. He thought of his own fascination with her. She hadn't been out of his thoughts since he'd first met her. Damn, she was an itch he couldn't quite scratch, and if he was smart, he'd stop trying. He'd take his savings and open a gambling house in Lake's Crossing, or try his luck in California.

If he was smart, he'd head back to Hilda's, right now, and see if he could find that cowboy who'd come to town looking for him. Once Luke settled with Blackjack, he'd be free with Crooked Creek, and he could start over in another place.

Luke watched Noelle as she tapped the wooden cabinet with her wand. He couldn't help but recall that before he'd met Noelle, he would have raced after any information about Blackjack faster than a spring flash flood rushes through a canyon. But for some strange reason, Luke didn't want to leave just yet. If the cowboy had come for the reward, then he wouldn't leave town until he saw Luke.

With Ike standing inside the wooden box, Noelle circled her magic wand in the air, then closed the door.

"Ladies and gentlemen," she announced. "You noticed that my volunteer has been positioned inside the cabinet." She smiled confidently, then raised her wand. "I will close my eyes and concentrate as I will the spirit and body of this man to disappear into thin air!"

The room held an expectant hush while Noelle lowered her head, wand poised in the air. After a few moments, she stepped back and moved toward the cabinet. With a deft motion, she tapped on the door, then opened it.

The cabinet was empty. A gasp rose from the small audience, and although Luke knew how the trick was performed, for one startling moment, Luke actually believed Ike had disappeared.

"Amazing!" shouted Emily, clapping.

"Hmm," said Curly, scratching his head and rising to his feet. "Where's Ike?"

Noelle laughed. "Quiet, ladies and gentlemen." She glanced at Luke, who was surprised to find himself on his feet, clapping. His gaze met hers, and his chest felt tight with an emotion he didn't want to feel.

Noelle bowed, then stuck her wand inside the box. She pushed back the draperies, proving that Ike wasn't anywhere to be found.

"Now if my audience will kindly try to imagine another drumroll," she suggested, closing the door to the cabinet again. Noelle lowered her head. "Again, I will close my eyes and concentrate as I will the spirit and body of this man to reappear from the other side!"

Noelle lifted her head, then waved the wand in several circles before tapping the door. She held the pose for a moment, then faced the crowd.

"Ladies and gentlemen. Let us see if my magic has brought back our friend's spirit and body from the beyond."

This time, Ike pushed the door open. With his cigar still clamped in his teeth, Ike stood grinning at Noelle.

"Keep your eyes on the audience, Ike," she coached.

Ike stepped from the box to applause and hoots from his friends. "Spectacular!" Luke yelled, as he came forward and slapped Ike on the back. He turned to Noelle as the others crowded around Ike.

"You were wonderful, Noelle," Luke said. "I'm really impressed. I know how much this means to you." He took her small hand in his.

Never had Luke seen such heartfelt happiness shine from a pair of eyes. "Thank you, Luke." Her hand felt like ice. "I didn't think I'd be so nervous."

"It didn't show," he said, realizing that her hands were cold because of fear. He wanted to take her in his arms and protect her. He didn't ever want to see her frightened again.

He released her hand and stepped back.

"I appreciate that you canceled today's poker games so I could have the room for the rehearsal."

"Think nothing of it. Everyone's excited about the grand opening, and from what I hear, you'll have a packed house for this Saturday's performance."

She smiled. "I hope you'll be here."

Emily pressed forward, giving Noelle a hug. "I'll be heading back to the ranch. Daniel will be beside himself if I'm not home before dark."

"I'll ride back with you beside your wagon, Emily.

I know you're perfectly capable to go back alone, but I'll feel better if I ride along.''

"Thanks, Luke. I noticed some Indians in town when I first arrived today. They're probably harmless, but I'd be obliged if you'd travel along with me." Emily turned to Noelle. "A little fresh air might do you good, too, dear. Why don't you come along with us? That little calf of yours would enjoy seeing you again."

Noelle glanced from Emily to Luke. "I-I don't think—"

"No thinking about it, Noelle. It'll be beautiful riding back to town. Why, the willows along the river are turning gold already, and the hills have such a heady scent of rich, fallen leaves that is almost painful in its sweetness."

Noelle laughed. "Very well, you've convinced me." She was smiling when she glanced at Luke. "Are you sure you won't mind, Luke—?"

"Of course he won't mind," Emily said with a snap. She picked up Naomi. "Luke, don't just stand there. Get your horse and one for Noelle saddled. I'll wait for you in the wagon."

"It'll take me only a minute to change." Noelle collected her top hat and wand, averting her gaze from Luke as she headed for the stairs.

Damn, this was the last thing he needed. No doubt, Emily had planned this all along. But one look at Noelle's face when Emily had invited her, and Luke was certain that Noelle wasn't any happier about being alone with him on that ride back to town than he was.

If Noelle had any doubts about being alone with Luke on the trail back from Emily's place, she gave no hint. In fact, he had enjoyed Noelle's easy banter about the humorous antics that Curly, Ike and Shep had been up to these past few days. His time with Noelle had reminded him of two good friends who simply enjoyed each other's company.

He leaned back in the saddle, letting Deuce follow the hard-packed trail as he listened to the horses' easy gait. Noelle, who rode beside him, was suddenly quiet.

"Your parents would be very proud of you, Noelle. I couldn't help thinking of your determination when you insisted I bring your father's boxes of props when your wagon wheel broke in the desert."

"It took the threat of my Hawken rifle, if I remember," she said, laughing. Her smile faded. "Seriously, I owe my success to you, Luke. You didn't have to accept my decision to close the saloon. It was only later, when Mike O'Shea explained the terms of my inheritance that I understood that I may have inherited the building, but you owned half of my uncle's business. I didn't own the controlling share, and therefore, I had no right to close the saloon. Yet the time allowed me to prepare for what I wanted to do, and you allowed me that. I'll always be grateful to you, Luke."

Luke felt an uneasy catch at the mention of O'Shea's name. Damn, he didn't want her gratitude. He didn't want her to start looking at him as some kind of hero.

"I didn't mind. I still had the gambling tables. Besides, you didn't ask to get saddled with a saloon after your uncle left," he added.

She raised a brow. "My uncle died, Luke." Her chin raised a notch. "You're still persistent in your belief that my uncle staged his death, aren't you?"

Sweet Jeezzo, why couldn't he keep his big mouth shut! He glanced across the desert, the purple ridge of mountains ahead of them. "It'll be dark soon, we better hurry." He urged Deuce into a trot.

"Answer me, Luke!"

He turned toward her, expecting her to look offended. Instead, she looked innocent and questioning. His heart melted.

"All right, I owe you the truth, Noelle. Yes, I still believe your uncle is out there, somewhere."

Her horse nickered at a jackrabbit. She held the reins evenly. "And you'll spend the rest of your days trying to prove it?"

He glanced away. "I honestly don't know."

She rode quietly for the next few minutes. "For what it's worth, Luke...if my uncle is alive, I hope you find him. Regardless of what you might think of him, he's my uncle, and if he's alive, I want to know it."

Chapter Twelve

The moon peeked above the purple horizon that cloaked the western mountains when Luke and Noelle arrived back in town. Luke helped Noelle dismount from her horse, then returned the animals to the livery stable. He found her waiting for him as he came out the back door. Silently, they walked the short distance along Main Street, until they reached the path leading to the rear of the Silver Hearts Saloon.

A soft light permeated the back room's window. Although she had told Ike to close early, the sound of a tinny piano told them that Ike hadn't left yet.

"Thanks for the ride, Luke. The fresh air helped clear my head."

"I enjoyed the company," he said, meaning every word. He should see her inside, check the locks, then leave. But he didn't want to let her go...not yet.

"Let me see you inside," he offered, opening the door.

"There's no need. Ike is inside. He'll check the doors and windows."

He stood looking at her in the moonlight. She was beautiful. Her hair, almost silver in the moonlight, haloed her face like lace filigree. A whiff of lilacs touched his senses as she tossed her head.

"Listen, isn't Ike playing the song you brought back from Lake's Crossing?" she asked.

He smiled. "Yes, but Ike told me that it was your idea to change the melody to a waltz."

"The tune reminded me of an old waltz my mother and father used to dance to, and when I hummed the melody for Ike, he immediately improvised the rest."

Luke grinned, the moonlight striking his face with a soft glow. The dimplelike scar beneath his cheek was barely visible. He was looking at her now, as he had when she first noticed him in the audience this evening.

How happy she'd been to see him watching her perform. She had so wanted to please him, to make him proud of her. Yet why should she care? What was this thing between them? All she knew was that he was the most important man in the world to her.

"I should be going inside." The music floated over and around them as they remained transfixed, their eyes holding each other captive.

"I don't remember the last time I waltzed," Luke said, leaning against the doorway.

Moonlight etched his strong, chiseled features with lunar magic. She watched Luke's mouth quirk as he waited for her answer. That sensuous, beautifully carved mouth. She remembered his kisses, the molten feeling of desire as his lips trailed their fiery path to her heart.

"Do you remember the last time you waltzed?" he asked.

She blinked, tapping her foot to the music, hoping he hadn't noticed that she was staring at him. "Yes, I'll never forget my last dance. It was a year ago, and I had just graduated from Miss Parson's School for Young

Ladies. She gave a cotillion for the graduating class at one of the hotels in New York. The gentlemen she invited were barely old enough to leave their mothers.'' The memory brought a lightness to her voice. ''We had to teach most of the boys how to waltz—that is—the boys who would dare leave the sidelines and venture onto the dance floor.''

''That's the difference between a man and a boy. No man would miss a chance to dance with you.'' His voice was like a low whisper in the night. He closed the distance between them as his right hand slid around her waist. His left palm caught her right hand. He paused long enough for her to walk into his arms, then he swept her back into the first step of the haunting melody. Her hand slid up his arm, instinctively circling his shoulder, while he whirled her into the incredible enchantment of three-quarter time.

She felt as if they were floating. Round and round. She followed his lead as effortlessly as if they were one. His arms held her with strength, yet gentleness. Control, yet surrender. She felt exhilarated with the sense of freedom, yet she felt caught within his spell, as well.

Round and round they twirled, the storeroom transformed into a symphony of shadows by the spell of moonlight.

She was mesmerized by the nearness of Luke. Beneath her fingertips, she felt the hard play of his muscles as they waltzed, caught up with the lilting rhythm. His male scent—mixed with the spicy aroma of leather and sage—brought a headiness that drugged her senses.

She held him, no, clung to him, hoping this moment would never end. Luke was like quicksilver, summer lightning, brilliant yet fleeting. She had to hold on, lest he disappear.

She opened her eyes and leaned back, needing to see him, to know he was real. *A gambler never stays long in one place.* For now she didn't care. He was here, now, and that was all she wanted.

His soft breath caught in her ear as they swayed to the music. Her heart pounded an urgency that began deep inside her, its quickened tempo so loud she wondered if he could hear it, too.

His lips nibbled at the shell of her ear, causing incredible sensations of yearning within her. Her breath caught, as she lifted her face to his. She sought his mouth with a hungry longing that almost frightened her.

His lips found hers the way the sun's first rays kissed the morning's dew. Burning, intense and primal. Unbidden desire rose from a secret place deep inside her. She felt herself being lifted in his arms.

"Noelle, tell me to go," he pleaded, his voice a hoarse whisper.

"No, I don't want you to leave." She tightened her arms around his neck. *I want to stay like this, forever.* But she knew if she said those words, it would frighten him away.

He took her mouth again, this time, urgent, demanding. For an instant, a warning sounded in her brain, but she pushed it back. She knew he would leave her, he had always been honest with her about that. She would accept it when the time came. Now, she needed to know what it was like to be loved by him.

In her dreams, she had thought that their first loving would fill her with uncertainty and trepidation. But not now, when he was so very real, so very close to her; reality of him gave her a boldness she had never believed possible.

"We're alone. Ike left some time ago," he whispered into her hair.

In her mind, she still heard the lilting melody of their waltz. She looked into his smouldering gaze. *How long had they been dancing to their own rhythm?* she wanted to ask, but one look into his dark, passionate eyes, and another question formed.

Will you make love with me?

As if Luke read her mind, he lifted her into his arms. Her hair fell forward, brushing his face with silken delight. How he wanted her. His body ached for her. And there was no mistaking the answering need and desire in her eyes. "Are you sure, my darling?"

Her answer was a pleading sigh. "Carry me upstairs," she whispered hoarsely.

He carried her through the darkened shadows, past the locked front door. Instead, he laid her gently upon the blue velvet overstuffed sofa that was his bed when he stayed overnight in the saloon. He took the folded quilt from the corner of the sofa. "Here, let me spread this out for you," Luke whispered.

She smiled at his thoughtfulness. His lips sought hers, their tongues tangled as their kiss deepened. His tongue plunged and withdrew, plunged and withdrew, the repeated motion driving her into a whirlwind of desire.

Only when she felt the soft whisper of fabric brush along her skin, was she aware that he had removed the top of her gown, baring her to the waist. His unbuttoned white shirt split open, revealing the large expanse of his black-furred chest. Her hands spread across his muscled torso, her fingertips delighting in the springy dark mat.

His mouth trailed a line of kisses downward, stirring a fire so intense, it took her breath away. When he took her nipple, she was filled with a sudden urgency; she thought she might cry out in pure pleasure.

Her fingers explored the corded muscles of his arms and back. She delighted in his reflexive shudder.

He raised her against the cushions, and lifted her skirts while he lowered his head. She writhed with an incredible longing, as she felt the delicate fabric give way. His touch brought a sudden wave of surprise when she realized the soft moans of need that echoed the darkness came from her own torment.

"Lean back, I want to pleasure you" she heard Luke say.

"You do pleasure me, my love."

"No, this is only the beginning, Noelle. There is so much more I want to show you." He took her breast, his mouth bringing the bud to a throbbing crescendo. While his thumb and forefinger kept the rhythm, she felt his tongue move downward again, laying the tenuous threads of immediate urgency.

Beneath her skirts, she felt his hands stroking her, moving her forward to something she didn't know, didn't understand. His touch was so gentle, so incredibly gentle that she thought she might die of it. When she thought she could bear it no more, he moved again, hovering at the core of her femininity.

Never could she have imagined such a building of desire that consumed her very being. Before she knew what to do, what to say, desire exploded all around her as his tongue blossomed her need into splintered ecstasy. Her thighs clamped around him, as she writhed wildly. She clutched his shoulders, arching with delirious pleasure. On and on, rapture shattering around her.

Luke held her, kissing her with an urgency that kept her from spinning back to earth. How long he held her, she didn't know. Eventually, she raised her head, her skin flushed with his kisses.

"I had no idea…" The sound of her joy mingled with his.

"I trust that means you liked it," he said, that lazy smile melting her all over again. She answered him with a kiss on the top of his head; he cupped her tender breasts in his palms, brushing the sensitive tips with his tongue and fingers.

She yanked his hair playfully. He kissed her again, fully on the mouth, this time. She wrapped her arms around his neck and moved against him. She felt his hard shaft press against her thighs.

Suddenly, she realized that he had pleasured her, kept her from being pregnant by denying his own pleasure.

"It's all right, my darling." He kissed away her further plea. "My pleasure is knowing that we have this between us. No one can ever take that away from us."

Her eyes stung with tears. "Oh, Luke, I love you."

She felt his back stiffen at her sudden outburst. Oh, how she wished she could take back her words. "It's all right. I know you're not the marrying kind, Luke." She forced a smile and willed back the threat of tears. "I knew what I was doing."

But she didn't know. If it wasn't for Luke's sacrifice, she might be pregnant. The thought gave her pause. When did the tables turn, and he become the responsible one?

"Noelle, I know you didn't plan this. I—I know you're innocent…and you still…I mean…"

She wrapped the quilt around her and hurried to her feet.

He picked up his tie and shirt from the floor. "Do you want me to help you—?"

She pulled away from him. "No," she said, drawing the quilt around her. With one hand, she straightened her skirts around her. "I'll lock the door after you," she said, afraid she might cry before he was safely gone.

"Noelle, I—"

"Please, Luke. It's late. You better leave now."

She followed him through the storeroom, where a short while ago they had waltzed to the music of their souls. Now, the moon had drifted behind a low bank of clouds, and the magic had vanished as swiftly as their parting.

At the door Luke turned, his rough fingers cupped her chin in a tender caress. Then, without another word, he turned and was gone.

Noelle bolted the door, then sank against the wood, the feeling of loss more powerful than she could imagine.

So this is my punishment, she realized, now fully aware that once she had known Luke's touch, no man could ever satisfy her again.

Before Curly and Ike had opened the saloon the next morning, Noelle had saddled a horse from Shep's livery stable and ridden out to Emily's place. The early morning air held the threat of snow. Noelle snuggled deeper into her coat as she dismounted, then strode toward Emily, hanging clothes in the yard. Noelle needed to talk, and Emily was the only person who might understand.

Behind the cabin, a moo sound broke the morning's silence, and Noelle glanced over to see the brown-and-white calf grazing beneath a tree. "How she's grown!" Noelle said, striding toward the animal. She scratched the wiry curls atop the calf's head while it nuzzled Noelle under her arm.

"By Golly, I think that critter is genuinely glad to see you." Emily laughed as she finished pinning a diaper to the clothesline. "I know I am." Her laughter was infectious.

Emily moved the laundry basket, then took another diaper. "Did you and Luke have a nice ride back to town last night?"

Emily's blunt question took Noelle by surprise. She blushed. "Er…yes. I came to ask you some advice, Emily." Noelle picked several diapers from the basket and pinned them to the clothesline. "I hope you don't mind."

"Mind?" Emily's brow raised. "Land's sake, I can't tell you how grand it is to have another woman to talk to." From the moment Noelle arrived this morning, Emily knew that Noelle needed to talk to someone. "Hmm, wouldn't have something to do with Luke, would it?"

Noelle hesitated. "How did you know?"

Emily took a clothespin from her mouth. "My dear, whenever you mention Luke, your face shines brighter than a gold nugget in the sunshine." She snatched the last diaper from the basket and hung it beside the others. She watched Noelle's face darken with a pink blush.

"Come on, let's go inside out of the wind. I'm steeping a pot of tea, and we can have a nice chat while the baby sleeps."

Emily balanced the empty basket on her hip and shooed the chickens away from the front porch while she led Noelle into the cabin.

Inside, Noelle took a seat beside the window while Emily busied herself pouring tea and cutting two slices of freshly baked bread.

"Mike O'Shea will be returning from Carson City

today, and I know he'll propose the first chance he'll have.''

Emily placed the tray upon the table. "Mike is a respectable man who will make some woman a wonderful husband." She studied Noelle's troubled face. "But do you think it's Mike who would make you happy?"

Noelle frowned. "I think the question should be, will I make him happy?" Her brows lifted. "Oh, Emily, I just don't care about him...in that way."

Emily gave a sympathetic nod. She knew what she had guessed was correct. Noelle and Luke had fallen in love, and regardless of what either of them said, they were both too stubborn to admit it.

Noelle bowed her head. "If my parents were alive, they'd encourage me to marry a man like Mike." Her frown deepened. "He's a good man. He's ambitious." She glanced up. "Did you know that he's planning to run for governor?"

Emily sipped her tea. "He'll probably win. He usually gets what he sets his cap for."

"But when Mike looks at me, I feel...nothing."

"What do you feel when Luke looks at you?"

Noelle plunked the cup down in the saucer with a clink. Silently, she gazed out the window, her chin quivering.

Emily watched her, remembering her own snap decision to marry her prospector husband, Daniel. Despite her parents' warnings, she traveled the road West and never regretted a day of it. "When it's right between a man and a woman, Noelle, you'll know what to do."

Noelle sighed. "I wish it were that easy. My parents worked so hard and sacrificed so much to educate me. They wanted me to marry a respectable man, one who

would be a strong father for our children.'' She turned
toward Emily, her blue eyes bright with unshed tears.
''I love Luke. I've tried not to, but the truth is, I'm
hopelessly in love with him. But he doesn't want marriage.''

Emily put down her cup. ''Noelle, I've watched the
two of you when you're together.'' She smiled again.
''Luke cares for you, my dear.''

Noelle's sad gaze lingered along the snow-dusted
ridge of mountains. ''Oh, Emily! I know he does. But
that's not enough. I'm not foolish enough to believe a
man can change. Luke has always been honest with me.
He never claimed to be a family man.''

Emily put down the corner of bread and honey she
was eating. Wiping her fingers on a napkin, she met
Noelle's forlorn look. ''Let me tell you something about
Luke. We've known him for nearly three years now. He
rarely talks about his past, but I know there's pain there.
I don't know if it's a woman, or the war, or both. Whatever it is, I think it's his pain that holds him back from
being who he is. I hope someday he'll dare to reach for
the happiness he deserves.'' Emily leaned back and
studied her. ''Maybe your love will give him that courage, Noelle.'' She sighed. ''I can only hope so.''

''Oh, do you think it's possible, Emily?''

''Of course.'' She smiled tenderly. ''Daniel and I
owe Luke more than we can ever repay him. About a
year ago, Luke came to help Daniel with our well. I
was pregnant with Naomi, my time near. My water had
already broken, and I knew what I had to do. I'd helped
my sisters give birth plenty of times. I didn't want to
tell Daniel, he had enough on his mind. Besides, he's
always fussing about me so.''

Emily gave a weak smile. ''That afternoon when

Daniel came in to see how I was..." She shook her head and sighed. "Noelle, I'd seen birth before, but it wasn't the same as giving birth. I knew it was painful, but I never expected such unrelenting pain. I tried to shield my husband, but looking back, I knew I hadn't fooled Daniel for a minute. The next thing I knew, Luke had arrived and told us he was a doctor.

"Well, at that time, all I thought about was the baby. I knew something was wrong and...I was afraid I was going to lose my baby."

"Emily! What did Luke do?" Noelle leaned forward, her hand gripping Emily's clenched fist.

"I must have drifted in and out of consciousness after that. But I remember Luke's soothing words as he positioned me. He told me what to do, how to breath, when to push.

"Then finally, through the waves of agony, I remember hearing this faint little mewing sound. A baby's cry. Dear God, but it was a miracle, and if it hadn't been for Luke, we wouldn't have our little Naomi. Daniel might have lost me, too."

Emily wiped the tears from her eyes. "Luke explained that Naomi's birth was what they call a breech birth."

Noelle nodded, familiar with the term used when the baby is born feet first. She had heard of the painful process where the doctor must turn the infant around before the birth can be successful. "I'm so glad that Luke was there for you."

Emily smiled. "Luke's gambling ways are only skin-deep, to my way of thinking. You said that a man can't change. But if the man is generous, kindhearted, and reliable, then he can surely return to what he once was."

"Emily, are you saying that you think Luke will someday want to settle down?"

"I'm saying that I think if Luke finds the right woman, who's to say he won't marry and want to settle down?"

Noelle hesitated. "The right woman." She shook her head. "I'd like to believe what you say, but I don't think marriage is for all men. Look at my Uncle Marcel."

Emily sniffed. Lifting her grandmother's blue-glazed teapot, she refilled Noelle's cup. "Luke is nothing like your uncle."

Noelle leaned back and stared quizzically at her. "Luke insists that my uncle was dishonest. What did you think of Marcel?"

"I didn't know him very well." She took a deep breath. "Daniel might be able to tell you more." She leaned back as she thought. "An attractive man. Always well dressed. Wore a black suit and high-top hat wherever he went."

Noelle traced the gold rim of the china cup with her fingertips. "I must be getting back. I want to rehearse again before tonight's grand opening." She took a sip of tea. "What time will you and Daniel be coming?"

"We want to be early enough to get good seats. Daniel went into town for supplies, he should be home in a little while. We wouldn't miss it." She smiled and rose from the table.

Noelle gently squeezed Emily's wrist. "Thank you for listening to me, Emily. It's such a comfort to have you as a friend."

Emily smiled warmly. "Come whenever you can, Noelle."

The women ambled to the hitching post where

Noelle's horse was tied. "Next time, I hope Naomi is awake so I might hold her," Noelle said, gathering the reins in her hands. She mounted the horse as Emily glanced up to see her husband driving their wagon from town.

"Here comes Daniel now." Emily watched as Daniel stopped the team near the watering trough. He tipped his hat to Noelle as she rode by, then he stepped from the wagon to kiss his wife.

Emily leaned into Daniel's embrace as they watched Noelle ride off, the tan billows of dust trailing behind her. When horse and rider were out of sight, Emily turned to help unload the rolls of chicken wire from the wagon bed.

"Just heard at the livery stable that there's a cowboy in town who claims to have seen Blackjack in Virginia City. Did Noelle say anything to you?"

"No. I think if she'd known, she'd have mentioned it."

Daniel's bushy eyebrows lifted. "Seems that Luke put up a reward for information about Blackjack. An' this cowboy spoke to Luke and staked a claim to the reward money."

A thread of worry crept up Emily's spine. "I hope she hears the news first from Luke. She might take it easier."

Daniel shook his head and squinted against the sunlight. "Don't seem likely. Luke's already left for Virginia City. Saw him leaving when I arrived in town this mornin'."

"Oh, Daniel. Sometimes I wish I would mind my own business and not talk so much!"

Daniel stared at his wife. "What brought this on?"

She glanced in the direction of town. "Because I

think I've just encouraged Noelle to hope for something that may never come true.''

He laughed. ''I think all of Nevada is built on hope, Emily. Besides, I like you just the way you are.''

He put his arm around her as they strolled back toward the cabin. ''Oh, Dan. I hope Luke Savage doesn't break that poor girl's heart.''

When Noelle returned to the livery stable, she noticed Luke's horse was missing from its stall. Strange. This time of day, he would be preparing for the poker games, greeting the men who rode into town from all parts just to sit in with the great Luke Savage.

She felt a frisson of disappointment, then immediately chided herself for it. Luke owed her no explanation for his comings and goings. She was becoming as possessive as a long-married wife.

She gathered her skirts and hurried along the boardwalk. A small cattle drove thundered along Main Street. Dust covered her as the thundering hooves lumbered along the road, cowboys yelling commands as they flanked the moving herd.

She shook out her skirts before going inside the Silver Hearts. Although she knew he wasn't there, Noelle glanced in the corner where Luke would often sit alone, shuffling cards, or engage Curly or Ike in those colorful, boastful stories the men loved to tell about each other.

But the corner table was dark, the lamps left unlit. Nowhere was the sound of his rich laughter or the happy whistling that had become so much a part of her life.

Curly glanced up from polishing the bar as she strode inside.

''Mornin', Miss Noelle,'' he said, giving her a beaming smile. He wiped a circle upon the bar's surface with the snowy polishing cloth in his hand. "Luke said to tell you that he left a note in the office for you."

She felt a sense of foreboding. "Thank you, Curly. Did Luke say when he'd be back?"

"I heard Luke tell Ike that he was sorry he was going to miss the saloon's grand opening."

A deep wave of disappointment crushed through her. Without another word, she dashed into her uncle's office.

Sunshine slanted through the window above the desk, splashing gold patterns of light along the dark green walls, but the sun did nothing to warm the chill she felt. On the desk, propped against the statue of the lovers, was the envelope with her name scrawled across the front. She studied the bold, black script. Although she had never seen Luke's handwriting, she knew that the fine, strong hand was his.

She leaned against the top of the desk and held the letter, suddenly afraid to read what was inside. But she forced herself to open it and read the paper.

My dear Noelle,

Word has reached me that a man, bearing your uncle's description, is conducting business in Virginia City. I hope you understand that I must pursue this lead. Good luck on your performance this evening. My thoughts will be with you.

Luke

The words were blurry with tears when she reread the note. How she'd like to believe that Luke had her interest at heart and was pursuing Uncle Marcel to bring him back for her. But she knew the truth. Yes, Luke had always told the truth. He was obsessed with finding her uncle so he could prove to her that Uncle Marcel was a swindler.

Why can't Luke accept that Uncle Marcel is dead, and let the poor man rest in peace? *Because Luke will never rest until he exacts his justice.*

"You don't want justice, Luke Savage! You want revenge!"

She crumpled the letter, then threw it into the unlit fireplace. She daubed at her eyes and headed upstairs to her room.

Damn Luke Savage! She had an act to perform tonight, and she would force all thoughts of him from her mind.

Chapter Thirteen

From the shadow of Sun Mountain, Luke watched the sunset above Virginia City turn from rosy pink to dark crimson and purple ribbons of color. Luke wondered if Noelle was noticing the spectacular sunset, too.

Of course she wasn't. By now, Noelle would have found the note he'd left her, and she'd be much too angry and disappointed with him to think about sunsets.

Luke wiped the trail dust from his face with his bandanna, then tied the cloth around his neck. Damn, how he wished he were back in Crooked Creek, to comfort her, to still the nervousness she would face trying to resurrect her father's act in front of the townspeople. But Noelle's anxiety entailed more than that.

She was facing the path she'd cut out for herself once she'd decided to make a new life with her uncle. Now, she believed that Luke was destroying what chance she had to fulfill her dream. If Luke found Blackjack, she'd lose the inheritance and all she'd worked for. Noelle had every right to hate Luke.

Then why didn't he turn around and forget all about Blackjack? Let the bastard promise other good women like Hilda Mueller that he'd marry them. Let Blackjack

sell other gambling concessions that he didn't own to
trusting, new business partners? It wouldn't cost Luke
anything. Why did he care?

Luke pulled the tobacco pouch from his pocket, and
began to roll a cigarette. He really didn't know why he
cared. Maybe it was because he couldn't bring his
brother, Chad, back from the dead. He couldn't undo
the war and its mistakes. But he could bring Blackjack
back if he was alive, and Luke felt it in his bones that
he was.

Urging his horse forward, Luke followed the trail
through the sage-covered mountains toward the outskirts of Virginia City. Luke knew he had no choice but
to follow his plan. Regardless of the personal cost to
himself, Luke had a job to do.

Several hours later, the adobe jailhouse at the edge
of Virginia City appeared on the horizon. Luke pulled
his hat brim down over his face as he guided Deuce in
the direction of the small building with the barred windows. Once he contacted the marshall, the lawman
would lead Luke to the man who might be Blackjack.
It was only a matter of time until Luke found out if
he'd been sent on another wild-goose chase.

Luke pulled up his collar against the changing wind
and listened to the lonely howl of a coyote. His gaze
drifted over the sprawling city, so fertile and deep with
the heavy black soil that had proven incredibly rich in
silver for those lucky enough to find it.

Luck. Luck was all that separated the poor bastards
who pushed their worldly goods in wheelbarrows down
the paths of Tent City from the silver barons who lived
along Mansion Row.

*If you're down there, Blackjack, so help me I'll find
you.*

* * *

Outside the Silver Hearts Saloon, two young Indians peered through the window and watched in awe as cheers and clapping filled the air. Never had White Cloud and Running Beaver seen such powerful magic as that possessed by the small woman with hair like silvery gold. To pull colorful ribbons from an empty hat, to make a silver dollar disappear, only to reappear from a man's ear was strong medicine. But when the woman locked the big man inside a box, then made him disappear—the sight was truly frightening.

Running Beaver's skin had grown cold with dread. Then when she had waved the magic stick again, and she threw back the lid of the box—to everyone's amazement—the man reappeared.

White Cloud turned to stare at his cousin, and Running Beaver realized that he was thinking the same thoughts. The woman possessed magic that would bring a man back from the darkness.

Running Beaver's teeth chattered with more fright than he'd ever known in his sixteen years.

"Little Henry needs the woman's magic," White Cloud whispered in their native language. "And your father will reward you with a white feather as he did Little Henry."

Running Beaver's jaw tightened as he remembered the shame he felt when at the tribal ceremony, his older brother, Little Henry—only one winter older than himself—had received his second white feather. It had been awarded as a special honor for bringing their father, the chief, the chestnut brown gelding which had belonged to the woman's driver. Besides, Little Henry had been younger than Running Beaver when he had received his first feather—for killing a noble deer. Running Beaver wondered if he'd ever bring honor to his father by receiving a sacred white feather—yet his older brother had been rewarded two.

Running Beaver turned to his cousin. "You, too, White Cloud, will earn your first feather from my father. For I'll need your help."

White Cloud's dark eyes widened. "Your father will give me one, too?"

Running Beaver nodded. "What we do will be a great coup. But dangerous."

White Cloud frowned. "But how? She roosts upstairs like a hen in a tall bush. Too many people watching for us to steal her. We will be caught."

Running Beaver smiled. "I have an idea that will bring the woman and her magic to us." His smile widened when his cousin stared at him in growing confusion. "Do not trouble yourself, cousin. I may be a year younger than Little Henry, but my plan will prove to our father that I am as wise. But first, we must keep out of sight until all of the people leave."

"Congratulations," Emily said, as Noelle took her final bow to the wild applause and whistles of the crowd. At least one hundred prospectors, cowboys, miners and people from all walks of life had packed into the Silver Hearts Saloon for the experience of their lifetimes. Curly and Ike were shaking hands, accepting compliments and well wishes. Both men's faces beamed with pleasure.

Emily hugged Noelle for the second time in five minutes. "I wish Luke could have been here to see your entire act. Oh, Noelle, you were magnificent!"

Noelle held her tongue in check. "Well, Luke's not here, is he?" She strode with Emily as they moved toward the crowd of well-wishers near the door. Michael

O'Shea caught her eye as he stood, waiting for her. He'd tip his head, shake hands with the customers, but his glance remained fixed on Noelle.

Emily's eyes widened when she saw him, then she turned to Noelle, the unspoken question shining from her hazel eyes. *Was Noelle going to accept Mike O'Shea's marriage proposal?*

"Yes, I'm giving Mike my answer tonight," Noelle said to Emily, her expression open and expectant.

"You're a smart woman, Noelle, and I trust your judgment." Emily's face suddenly remained passive behind a stoic mask. "I know you'll do what's best, Noelle." Emily paused as Mike O'Shea came up beside them. Turning to Emily, he said, "Excuse me for interrupting, Miss Emily, but I'm planning to take Noelle to Hilda's boardinghouse for a private meal." He extended his arm to Emily. "May we see you to your wagon?"

"My Daniel is fetching our wagon, thank you," Emily said, refusing to take his arm. She turned toward Noelle.

"Why don't you spend a few days with Daniel and me until Luke returns? The change of pace will do you good. You've been working so hard—"

"Thanks, Emily, but I'll be fine." Noelle didn't want to be rude, but she could only think to get away from everyone. She should be happy—the act was a success, people had been buying tickets all week long, and thanks to Luke's encouragement, she had charged more for the performance than her father had received in New York City.

Despite all of Noelle's success, she felt none of the jubilation and exhilaration she had expected. All she wanted was to be alone.

Hilda Mueller came beside her and shook her hand. "Miss Noelle, you took my breath away when you made Ike go poof!" Hilda waved her hands, then clasped a hand to her throat. "Truly magic! If only Blackjack could have lived to see you perform the acts he did as a young man with your father!"

Noelle took the older woman's pudgy hand in her own. "I was thinking about that myself," she said softly. "Thank you, Hilda, for coming." She glanced at the line of people waiting to shake her hand. "And thank you all for coming."

Tears welled in her eyes, and Noelle broke away and hurried toward the office. She didn't notice Mike follow her until he came up behind her when she stepped into the office.

"Oh, Mike," she said with a start. "Come in," she whispered, wishing she didn't have to face him right now. But she had given her promise that she'd speak to him this evening; this was one matter that couldn't wait.

"Congratulations, Noelle," Mike said, shutting the door after him. "I thought we might have dinner and—"

"I'm sorry, Mike, but I couldn't eat a bite." She pressed her hands to her throbbing temples. "I—I'm very tired, but I did want to talk to you."

Mike took her hand, but she delicately pulled away. "Please, Mike. I've thought over your proposal very carefully, and although I'm very flattered—"

"Noelle, you look pale. You're obviously tired. Why don't we wait until—"

"No, Mike." Her voice was firm. "My decision will be the same in the morning as it is now." She didn't want to hurt him. She knew the pain and misery of loving someone who didn't love you enough to want to share your life. But in her heart, she knew that Mike didn't really love her. "Please try to understand, Mike. You're a wonderful man, someday you'll find a wonderful woman who'll make you truly happy. But I'm not that woman."

Mike gave her hand a conciliatory pat. "We'll talk about this tomorrow, my dear, after you've had a good rest."

"No, Mike. We'll not speak of this again." She brushed past him and opened the office door.

"Noelle!"

She ignored him as she crossed the room on the way to the stairway. Emily and Hilda glanced up, surprise and concern on their faces as they watched Noelle dash up the stairs.

Hilda moved beside Mike O'Shea, who stood at the bottom of the staircase and stared up at Noelle. She hesitated halfway up the steps, then turned around to face Mike and Hilda.

"Mr. O'Shea, aren't you and Miss Noelle coming to the boardinghouse for dinner?" Hilda asked.

"I'm sorry, but—" Noelle glanced from Hilda to Mike, then Emily and Hilda. She felt her throat tighten. "Please, if you'll excuse me, I have a headache, and I'm so exhausted." Despite her excuse, Noelle knew that Emily was the only person who would be aware of the real reason for Noelle's abrupt exit.

She turned around and dashed up the remainder of the stairs, hoping she could make it to her room before the tears flowed.

Any joy Noelle felt for the opening success of the new Silver Hearts Saloon was a hollow victory. All she wanted was to be alone with her misery.

* * *

Later that evening, when she thought everyone had left, Noelle came downstairs to find Ike locking the doors and windows.

"I'm turning in early, Ike." she said. "Thanks for locking up for me."

Ike gave her a comforting smile. "Certainly, Miss Noelle. An' th-thank you, again, Miss Noelle." His long face blushed with pride. "Don't think I'll ever forget that hush in the room when you opened the cabinet door, and they saw I'd vanished." His jaw dropped open again.

"You, Shep and Curly were wonderful. I couldn't have done it without you." She kissed his leathery cheek. "Thank *you,* Ike."

Ike's face turned as scarlet as the new velvet drapes. "'Night, Miss Noelle."

She went up the stairs to her room. An empty longing pervaded her feelings. *She missed Luke. Despite all of her words to the contrary, she loved him.* It hurt to know that he couldn't have waited one more day before charging off for Virginia City in search of her uncle.

Noelle pushed open her bedroom door and lit the lamp. The lovely room, with the pink rosebud wallpaper stood waiting for her. She sat on the bed, the creak of the ropes beneath the mattress reminded her of being here with Luke and the memory of his kisses. The lamp's flickering glow against the rose pattern he had picked out for her brought a feeling of tenderness she couldn't force away, even if she had wanted.

Noelle went to the window and looked out over the street. In the short time that she had lived in Crooked Creek, she had changed a great deal.

In the night's breeze, the colorful banner proclaiming the Silver Heart's Grand Opening billowed from the corner of Mike O'Shea's law office and stretched across the street where it fastened to the saloon's roof's edge. Music and laughter floated up from the dance halls along the street, but unlike her first night—when she had learned of her uncle's fatal accident—Noelle's sadness was fraught with longing.

The waxing November moon rose in the distance. Although the mountains loomed along the northern horizon, she couldn't see them in the pale moonlight, yet she knew they were there.

It had been that way this evening. Although Luke hadn't been in the audience tonight, she had sensed his presence. It was as if she were branded by him.

Luke haunted her soul. His touch lingered along her skin, his scent invaded her senses, his warmth lifted her spirits, his rich laughter echoed through the corridors of her mind.

She glanced up at the moon, surrounded by a thousand stars across the heavens. She had been alone before, but this time, there was an aching loneliness that nothing could dispel.

She shut her eyes against the memory of Luke's kisses and the exquisite torture he had shown her.

"Oh, Luke," she called out, against a new onslaught of pain. "If only…"

Noelle wrenched free of such disturbing thoughts. She had proven to herself that she was a strong woman, and she could do this final thing, too. If Luke didn't want her enough to change his ways, then she would change hers. She would turn Luke Savage into a faint memory and forget that he'd ever touched her heart.

She wouldn't think of Luke's loving or her body's yearnings that betrayed her resolve, even now. She wouldn't dream of Luke. She'd turn the thought of Luke

Savage from her mind until she could see him for the illusion that he'd become to her.

Fragments of images slipped in and out of Noelle's troubled dreams. Finally, she sat up, her mind groggy. Again, a plaintive cry broke the night's silence. An animal? A baby crying? Had she dreamed the noise?

Fully awake now, Noelle realized that the sound that had awakened her was coming from outside. She heard it again.

Noelle slipped on her wrapper and peeked out the open window. A faint purple cast lit the eastern horizon. It would be dawn soon. Perhaps she had been mistaken about the sound, after all.

The lights from Red Garter Saloon down the street were dimmed, and a single lamp twinkled from the jail at the far end of the street. The dusty street below was empty, except for a horse tied to the rail in the shadows. Strange. A man wouldn't leave a horse alone on the street if he expected to find it in the morning.

Just as she was about to close the window, a tiny voice echoed in the darkness. A baby's cry?

"Who's there?" she called out into the night. But now, the sound appeared to be coming from the alley behind the saloon. Noelle recalled her mother's stories of poor women, who, unable to care for their infants, would leave their babies on the doorsteps of charitable families.

In the dark, Noelle dressed quickly, hoping if such were the case, she might still find the mother. Maybe the mother was one of the women who worked at the Red Garter or other such establishments in town.

Noelle dressed hurriedly. She was buttoning her dress as she rushed to the stairway. It took a few moments for her eyes to adjust to the darkness. Feeling her way along the banister, the floor creaked as she found her way down the steps.

Moonlight guided her as she moved toward the sound coming from the back door. She had almost reached the storeroom when the crying stopped.

Noelle hesitated, listening. Out of nowhere, a feeling of alarm clutched at her heart. She rushed to the back entrance and pushed back the curtain, peering out the door's window, but she saw no basket with a baby on the steps. Nothing.

Opening the door slightly, Noelle held her breath as she stared into the shadows. Although the crying had stopped, she sensed someone was there.

Chapter Fourteen

Noelle's imagination leaped with the frightening images whirling in her mind as she gazed at the murky shapes along the alley. No, she *was* letting her imagination run away with her good sense.

She heard a noise beside her, and she jumped. Before she could dart back inside and slam the door, a man lunged at her. A scream rose in her throat, but a strong hand clamped over her mouth as he pushed her against the door. Her heart hammered in her chest as she struggled against him, but his other hand grabbed her wrists, then he dragged her inside the storeroom.

Did he want to steal whiskey? To open the safe? To do her harm? She tried to pull free, cursing herself for not bringing the Hawken rifle, which she kept upstairs in her bedroom closet. How could she have been so foolish?

"Do not be afraid, magic woman." The young man, not much taller than she, stared at her. In the moonlight, she recognized him as one of the Indians who'd pilfered through her prairie schooner wagon when she had first met Luke in the desert.

Which of these men had made the sound of the crying

baby to lure her downstairs? Outrage replaced her fear as she realized their cunning. What could she do? She pushed at his face, but his grip was as strong as steel.

The door opened and another Indian slipped inside. His sharp eyes assessed her. "Woman, we mean you no harm. I am Running Beaver, the chief's son. We will not hurt you if you come quietly."

In answer, Noelle tried to bite the clamped fingers across her mouth, but the Indian who held her was prepared. Instead, she quit struggling, saving her strength for a moment when they might drop their guard.

Running Beaver glanced out the window. He looked back at the Indian who held her. "Hurry, White Cloud. Tie her up and gag her. Then bring her outside." He slowly opened the door, then raised his hand in warning.

Noelle heard nothing, but in the seconds that followed, a horse nickered. She held her breath. Maybe someone had noticed the Indians break in and alerted Sheriff Wade.

The door partly opened and through the crack she saw a third Indian holding the reins of three ponies and a horse. Her heart sank. How many more Indians were there?

"Wait!" the third Indian called from the shadows. "Protect yourself from her magic."

Noelle stared at him. Magic? What did he mean?

White Cloud tied her wrists behind her while Running Beaver stuffed a gag into her mouth before she could scream. She knew struggling was futile.

After she was bound and gagged, White Cloud released his grip. "We need your help," he said, facing her. "You must come to our camp," he said in surprisingly good English. Then he crossed his arms; the silent message told her that she had no choice but to leave with them.

She shook her head in violent refusal.

"You are coming. Little Henry needs your magic."

No doubt they had seen her performance and believed she possessed special magical powers. She struggled to tell them she had no magic, but the gag smothered her words. She fought down her panic, forcing herself to keep her wits.

What had Luke told her about the Indians? The chief was Luke's friend, and they respected courage. Most of the Paiutes were peaceful, Luke had mentioned. She knew that her one experience with Little Henry and his friends had been provoked more by their curiosity than ill will. Besides, if these men had wanted to harm her, they would have already done so.

Noelle knew if they kidnapped her, she might never find her way back. Once they left town with her, any chance to escape them would diminish. But what could she do?

Running Beaver grabbed her by the arm and held her against the door while the other two Indians brought the ponies and horse. Her fingers were damp with fear as she tried to wiggle her wrists free against the outside doorknob, rattling the door's window pane, but the ropes that bound her were too tight.

She had an idea. She rubbed her finger along the dusty pane of glass, remembering Ike's constant complaint that Curly never kept the new door's window free of trail dust. The men were continually teasing each other about which man would clean the glass.

Her fingertip traced the name *Luke*, in the dust just before Running Beaver yanked her from the doorway toward the horse.

If only Luke would look for her when he found her missing. Perhaps he'll notice his name printed in the dusty pane.

No, this was wishful thinking! Luke would never notice. No one would notice. And if they did, how would they know what it meant? Alarm, close to panic, rose in her mind.

Running Beaver brought her to the horse and motioned for her to mount. Something was decidedly familiar about the animal. She placed her left foot in the stirrup while Running Beaver hoisted her onto the saddle. Although an Indian blanket lay beneath the tan, hand-tooled leather seat, Noelle suddenly remembered where she had seen the horse. Dear God, but the chestnut gelding had belonged to her trail guide, Mr. Douglas. The beast had been with Little Henry and his friends when they'd ransacked her covered wagon.

Running Beaver and White Cloud mounted their ponies, while the third mounted Indian grabbed her horse's reins as they moved along the deserted alleyway at a slow pace.

How long would it take for anyone to notice she was missing? Who would come for her with Luke away and Mike O'Shea feeling jilted? And what would become of her when they arrived at the Indian camp?

Nothing unusual would cause a person to give a second look to the two riders who cantered along the hilly trail toward Crooked Creek. In fact, Luke thought that at first sight, he and Blackjack might be considered to be two decent citizens—a schoolmaster, merchant, or undertaker, instead of a deputized citizen with his prisoner.

"I should have known I couldn't fool you, Luke,"

Blackjack said, scratching his newly grown beard. "But why the hell did you come after me? What's in it for you?"

"The two hundred dollars you stole from me before you staged your drowning in the river—which I never believed for a minute." Luke's gaze never left the trail. "But mostly the gratification I'll get from knowing that the townsfolk of Crooked Creek will learn what a sorry lot you really are."

"There was a time, Luke, when we were good friends. I took you in as though you were my own son."

Luke felt a sudden anger that surprised him. "Like hell you did." He ground out the words. "I brought a sound business investment to your broken-down saloon. With gambling tables that men could trust to be run honestly, your business tripled, and you know it." Luke frowned, stealing a glance at the man riding beside him. "Besides, I don't like to see people take advantage of others, and when they do, I think they should pay."

"Now, now, Luke. I think it's more than money. You feel betrayed by what I did, like you did when your brother died, and when your fiancée ran off and married your best friend while you were away at war."

"That's bull, Luke snarled. "No one cheats me out of money."

"Money, hell! What's two hundred dollars? Be realistic. You'll lose more money by bringing me in. Most of the proceeds of the saloon come from gambling, and they're yours, anyway. Besides, with me out of the way, you can keep the entire profit yourself." Blackjack smiled. "Now that you've proven that you've caught me, let's say you unlock these handcuffs and let me go."

Luke huffed. "Blackjack, you can talk all night, but

you're coming back with me to Crooked Creek." He leaned back in his saddle, the horse taking the lead. "Besides, while you were gone, your niece arrived."

Blackjack stared at Luke. "Noelle?"

"Yeah, your brother's daughter. She arrived in town shortly after your drowning. She's grieving for you as we speak. I think a nice family reunion is in order, don't you?"

Blackjack's face paled and he glanced away. After a long pause, he said in a flat voice, "My brother must be..."

"Yeah. Noelle said that her parents had died. That's why she came West, Blackjack. To be with her wealthy, wonderfully successful Uncle Marcel."

Blackjack's eyes snapped defensively. "Dammit, Luke. What would you expect me to tell my brother? That I lost my grubstake mining?" He shifted uneasily in the saddle. "She was only a baby when..." He snorted, then sat up straighter. "Well, I've got nothing to give the girl. Better she goes back to where she came from."

Luke tried not to think of Noelle and the pain he'd bring her when she finally met her uncle. "In a few hours, you'll have your chance to tell her." He tightened his fists on the reins to keep himself from punching Blackjack.

For the next few hours, they rode in silence, each man to his own thoughts. All Luke could think about was Noelle and how she'd come to hate him when she found out that her revered Uncle Marcel was really a two-bit chiseler who didn't want her.

But it might help her see that she should forget all about a two-bit gambler like himself and marry Mike

O'Shea. Luke bit back the haunting details, concentrating instead on the new life she'd have in Carson City.

He'd heard talk that the state might build a governor's mansion, and Luke was certain of it, if O'Shea got elected. He ground his teeth, thinking of O'Shea's hands on her.

Luke forced the thought from his mind with the image of Noelle, sitting on the veranda of the governor's mansion, baskets of lacy Boston ferns swaying in the breeze as she watched their happy children playing in the shady gardens.

But it was Luke who came to meet her, draw her into his arms. She would be radiant, a dazzling smile for him that would light his soul. Their children's laughter, much like their mother's, filling his heart with incredible happiness.

Blackjack coughed, the sound whirling Luke back to earth. Luke cursed under his breath. God help him, but he had to find the strength to walk out of Noelle's life before he destroyed them both.

When they finally arrived in front of the Crooked Creek jailhouse, it was Luke who alighted first.

The door opened and Sheriff Wade strolled out to greet them. He took one look at Blackjack. "Well, I'll be damned!"

Blackjack said nothing as Luke helped him dismount and led him inside the building.

"I'm turning him over to you, Sam," Luke said, tossing the handcuff keys to the sheriff. "I'll be back for the trial when the district judge gets here." He grinned. "Let's hope it's Hangin' Harry."

Sam chuckled as he smiled at Blackjack. "Well you

ol' sidewinder. Runnin' out on your debts, huh? Wait till the boys hear that you're back.''

Luke unfastened the deputy badge from his vest and tossed it on the sheriff's desk. "Keep the womenfolk away from him, Sam. Especially Hilda. Don't want Blackjack sweet-talking any of them to unlock his way to freedom.''

Sam laughed. "Don't worry, Luke.''

Luke kept his eyes straight ahead as he walked out the door. There was no putting off what he must do next. Blackjack was alive, and Noelle had to be told.

Luke mounted his horse and rode along the street until he came to the Silver Hearts Saloon. A banner stretched across the street, announced the Silver Hearts' Grand Opening. As he rode, his mind was on Noelle. What if she refused to see him? He couldn't blame her if she did.

No doubt she was hurt to read the note he'd left for her. She might think he was a coward.

But when the cowboy had told him that Marcel Bell was staying at his mother's boardinghouse, and that the man's description fitted so closely to Blackjack's, well, Luke couldn't wait.

Luke tied his horse to the rail in front of the saloon, then went inside.

Ike looked up from sweeping the wooden floor. "Evenin' Luke. Have you heard from Noelle?''

"Noelle?'' Luke glanced around the near empty saloon. "I thought she was here.''

Ike put down the broom and came beside him. "No, in fact, me and Curly haven't seen her since last night.'' His forehead wrinkled, and he looped his thumbs under his suspenders. "I got here at dawn. Not like her to go off and not tell anybody,'' he added.

"Where's Curly?"

"I sent Curly to Emily and Daniel's place. We thought that maybe Miss Noelle went to stay out there for a while. But later, I asked Shep, and he said that Miss Noelle hadn't been in the livery, and no wagon or horse was missing."

"You've searched everywhere?" Luke asked. Worry and concern built within him. He crossed the saloon and headed toward the stairway.

"We searched every place we could think of," Ike called out.

Luke took the stairs two at a time. He opened the door to her bedroom, the faint aroma of lilacs reminding him of her. He glanced about the room.

The bed had been slept in, yet remained unmade. A white nightdress lay sprawled across the covers. The kerosene lamp, unlit, remained on the night table. The empty water pitcher and bowl stood untouched on the dresser.

Luke glanced around the room. Noelle's innate sense of neatness wouldn't allow her to leave without making her bed or hanging up her clothes. By all accounts, Noelle had probably left while it was still dark.

Luke's anxiety kicked into high gear. When Noelle left this room, she was in a hurry. *Or left, under duress.*

He shook off the niggling thought. There was no evidence of foul play, he reminded himself. But the logic did nothing to steady his nerves.

He glanced into her closet and the small clothespress where she kept her things. Her leather boots were there. If she had planned to travel, she would have worn her boots. The Hawken rifle hung above the door.

Nothing appeared as though she had planned to leave. Then where was she?

Luke went downstairs and asked Ike, "When was the last time you saw her?"

Ike told Luke everything that happened during the grand opening, and the events of Noelle's performance.

"After you locked up, did you hear anything strange during the night? Riders? Strange noises?"

Ike shook his head, his long face clearly worried. "Where can she be, Luke?"

"I don't know, but don't worry, Ike. I'll find her."

Luke strode from the saloon and headed across the street to see if Shep remembered any strangers in town. As he walked, he went over the few facts that he knew.

After the performance, she'd turned in early, with a headache. Could something have awoken her? She had removed her nightgown, then dressed, yet she hadn't taken the lamp. Why?

Maybe it was already light?

No, Ike said he had arrived at dawn.

Luke started again, trying to retrace his thoughts.

Maybe she heard something, and in the darkness, she turned out the light in order to see...

Something might have awakened her or somebody called to her. Yes, that was it. Noelle had gone searching for something, by all indications. She hadn't been abducted. He felt a momentary sense of relief.

Luke stopped. He hadn't looked in the back alley. Maybe he could find her footprints. He went back inside to the rear of the saloon, his mind deep in thought.

He glanced on the stoop, looking for anything that might piece together some clue. He kneeled, searching for any threads or fibers along the floor or wainscoting.

As he approached the back door and the bright sunlight outside, the window glass above the doorknob caught his eye. From the shadowy hall, Luke stared at the word *Luke* written across the dusty windowpane. He dashed for it like a parched man runs to a well.

Mixed emotions engulfed him as he stared at his name imprinted in the dust. Who else but Noelle would have written it? Why? What did it mean?

Luke glanced out at the dusty yard beyond the rear steps of the saloon. Wooden crates and a rain barrel stood on one side of the building. The horse rail stood beneath the window. Luke pressed his hands together, trying to piece together what might have happened.

He strained against the overhead sunlight for some clue. In the shuffle of footprints, he had no idea how old most of them were. Mens' bootprints covered the area. He leaned down on one knee, studying the ground. Among the blanket of prints, Luke noticed a woman's small sole and heel print. Noelle's.

Consumed with a need for answers, Luke tracked the few imprints, then the recent traffic marks obscured the trail.

Without giving up, Luke studied the ground. Among the horse prints, Luke spied the unshod pony tracks. *Indians.*

Logic pushed back his imagination as he followed the clues, which led away from town. His eyes followed the marks. One shod hoofprint—a nicked horseshoe— just like Noelle's driver, Mr. Douglas's horse. Luke would never forget that nick. He'd tracked that animal's marks back to Noelle's prairie schooner.

Luke stared at the hoofprint. Yes, it was the same horse. The same animal that Luke had given to Little Henry as a gift to the chief from Noelle.

Ike stuck his head out from the doorway. "Curly just came back from Miss Emily's place, Luke." He shook his head. "They ain't see Miss Noelle."

Luke wasn't surprised, but he didn't let on to Ike. He kept his head down, studying the ground.

Ike stepped on to the stoop. "Find anything?"

"No," Luke said, not wanting to alert Ike to his suspicions. "Nothing out here," he lied. Damn, unless he had proof that the Indians had something to do with Noelle's disappearance, it was best not to suggest anything. The townsfolk were nervous enough about Indians without adding unproven allegations to their fears.

"I'll be gone for a few days, Ike," Luke said, heading for the back door.

"When you leavin', Luke?"

"Right after I talk to Curly. Look after things for me," he said, without looking back.

Chapter Fifteen

A sliver of moon hung above the craggy purple mountain ridge behind the Indian camp. From the door of the chief's lodge, Noelle shivered against the cold night and watched the Indian men hop and shuffle in frenzied circles around the blazing fire. Drums pounded to their cries, which penetrated her nerves like piercing arrows. The shaman, wrapped in a coyote skin, the animal's head perched upon his head, stabbed at the night sky with his long plumbed staff. Clusters of bound feathers waved wildly in the air.

Noelle glanced over her shoulder. Through the open tent flap, she stood and watched the tribal women gathered around the mound of fur robes where the chief's son lay in the center of the shelter. Mercifully, he had drifted into unconsciousness.

Yesterday, when the chief had first brought her to see his son shortly after her arrival, Noelle recognized the young man as Little Henry, the leader of the young savages who had broken into her wagon when she had first arrived in Nevada.

Now, so deathly ill with fever, Little Henry appeared

to be as any beloved son, surrounded by a worried family who loved him.

The women of his family leaned against each other in shared anguish, their low, mournful keening like wind through the pines.

Memories of when she and her father had hovered over her mother's sickbed came back to haunt her. Then later, Noelle had been alone when she kept the final midnight vigil at her father's sickbed.

Tears stung her eyes, and her throat tightened. She fought them back with another whispered prayer. Last night, she had prayed for a miracle. If only Little Henry would recover. But this morning, she could see by his hot, parched face that the young brave's condition grew worse, and her prayers were for a peaceful end to his suffering.

She shivered against the mountain's cold. Or was it her own dreaded thoughts bubbling up from the fearful recesses of her mind that chilled her to the bone?

What would happen if Little Henry died? She drew the soft rabbit-hide blanket around her and braced herself for her answer. They might kill her if she was lucky. They would torture her first, before killing her for failing to save Little Henry.

What other reason would the Indians have for bringing her here? Somehow, they believed she could use her magic to save the chief's son. But in the short time she had been here, Little Henry had grown worse, a fact the shaman wouldn't overlook. His resentment of her was evident, and he'd enjoy seeing her fail.

A high-pitched scream caused her to stare back at the shaman. He cavorted toward her, his arms flailing above his head. Instead of retreating, as he'd hoped, Noelle stepped forward and drew the blanket tightly around her shoulders. When he was a few inches from her, he pounced, shaking the rope of rattlesnakes' tails strung around his neck into her face.

Noelle glared in defiance. She remembered what Luke had said when the young braves had ransacked her prairie schooner. Indians respected a show of bravery. She'd be damned if she'd show her fear.

Through the slits in the coyote head, Noelle saw the shaman's black eyes glitter dangerously. No doubt he took her presence in the camp as a personal insult against his power. He wanted his magic to be more powerful than hers.

But Noelle also sensed that if the chief had wanted her harmed, the Indians would have done so immediately when White Cloud and Running Beaver had first brought her to their camp. They wanted her magic, not her life. And as long as Little Henry remained alive, her own life might be safe.

The drumbeat grew louder as she faced the shaman. With shoulders back, she stood her ground.

This time, he didn't dance past, but raised the sharpened pole into the air. He lunged, throwing the war lance at her.

She froze. The quivering rod hit its mark with a cloud of dust, just missing her feet by inches.

Anger charged through her veins, dissolving her fear. Omnipotent hatred as old as time raged behind the coyote's mask. She drew her blanket tighter, refusing to flinch at this bully.

How long the Indians' dance ritual had quieted, she didn't know. Only the tom-tom's frenzied beating pulsated her senses.

The shaman hesitated, then shook his coyote head from side to side, shaking the string of bones and teeth from his waist. Despite the cold, he wore nothing below his leather clout. Noelle met his stare. She tried not to gag from the pungent animal scents with which he had adorned himself.

The man paused, then yanked off the coyote head, revealing his painted, ferocious face. The scream died in her throat. The shaman hovered, wild-eyed. Unlike the other males, his head was shaved, except for a square patch of hair on the back of his head. Black-and-red zigzags were painted across his shiny scalp.

Leaning into her face, he shouted what she thought must be curses. Then he shook his feathered stake and threw it at her. The stave landed between her shoes.

"Aaugg!" he yelled, waving his hands in mocking gestures.

Noelle grabbed the stake from between her feet and shook it at him. The rod was lighter than she expected. His black eyes widened. A low hush rose from the crowd.

Noelle shook the evil-looking thing, then broke it over her knee and threw it toward the fire.

A roar rose from the other Indians. The shaman's jaw fell, but he quickly recovered. He yelled something she didn't understand, then he stepped back, as though waiting for her next move.

He was a brave man, but he faced a woman—a woman whom he had heard had brought back a man from the darkness. He must be afraid of her, yet he gave no sign. The thought made her respect his courage in the face of fear.

Noelle stood, watching him. She remained still as the others studied her. She refused to show fear. She knew she was at their mercy. She was outnumbered and unarmed. They could do anything they wished to her. But she wouldn't beg for mercy or show weakness; it was the only defense she had.

For a long time, the Indians watched her. Their silence was more frightening than their earlier yelling. What retaliation would she have to face for her act of defiance? She didn't know. Now, all that was important to her was that Little Henry was very ill.

She turned and marched back into Little Henry's hut.

All that night and the following morning, the Indian women allowed Noelle to assist them with Little Henry's care. She had sponged his pale, feverish body, and helped him drink the bowls of steeped herbs the women had prepared. When he finally slept, Noelle curled up in a soft cushion of rabbit skins, and slept.

She awoke to the delicious aroma of cooked meat, sage and mesquite. Several women smiled at her as they turned the roasted rabbits over the open fires. Noelle glanced at Little Henry. His fever had lessened, and he rested comfortably for the time being.

Noelle gratefully accepted the small bowl of food from one of the tribal women. Small cakes, made from the flour of ground pine nuts and various seeds filled the earthenware. After Noelle had finished eating, she gestured with her hands, indicating that she wished a soft chamois and an antelope horn filled with water.

The Indian woman nodded her understanding. With the exception of the open hostility of the shaman, the Indian women treated Noelle with respect and kindness. Perhaps they sensed Noelle's sincere wish to heal Little Henry.

During the past two days, the women had helped her learn many words, and sign language aided her communication easily.

Noelle thought back to the shaman and the other braves who avoided her whenever she left Little Henry's lodge. Relieved, Noelle knew that much of their feigned indifference was due to the reduction in Little Henry's fever. Although far from well, Little Henry had regained consciousness, kept water down, and although he was still in pain, Noelle believed he might recover.

If only she knew what caused the pain in his lower abdomen, which made him cup his arms at his sides and draw his knees up in pain.

She brushed Little Henry's forehead with the cool chamois. His large brown eyes watched her warily, but he gave no sign of fear. Noelle smiled and talked soothingly. Whether he understood her or not, she hoped he'd find the sound of her voice soothing. How she longed to do more, but she could only try to keep him comfortable until help came.

If help came. What did she expect would happen? Nothing would keep Luke away, *if* he knew that she'd been kidnapped. Surely Ike and Curly must be worried. But even if they'd alerted Sheriff Wade, what could any of them do if they didn't know where she was?

She glanced back at Little Henry. He suddenly seemed to be worse. His face twisted in pain when his hand gripped his side. He'd been favoring the right side of his belly. An uneasy feeling gripped her as she remembered the agonized death of the young mother who had joined the wagon train at Kansas City. She had experienced similar pain in her right abdomen, too.

Noelle shut away the sad memory. Little Henry would recover. That's all she would think about.

Later that afternoon, Noelle stepped from the lodge, carrying several empty antelope's horns. Dogs barked as a scattering of young boys and girls raced excitedly, bringing Noelle's attention to the growing commotion. Two women, who sat outside the lodge, pounding seeds into flour, got to their feet and hurried in the direction of the activity.

Noelle kept in the shadows as she tried to see what was causing the disturbance. The lone figure of a man rode into the camp.

Luke!

Tears of joy stung her eyes, and her breath caught at the sight of him. But her relief was short-lived when she realized the danger she had brought to him.

Several of the Indian men who had greeted Noelle when she'd first arrived were standing, waiting for Luke. It seemed to take hours for Luke to ride close enough for her to see his face. Remembering how careful he had been of the young Indian braves when they had attacked her wagon, she knew that he would be extremely careful to placate the tribe, now.

But where was Sheriff Wade and the others? Surely Luke wasn't planning to rescue her by himself?

Luke dismounted and walked to the chief, Captain Henry, and the Indian known as Lone Elk. He so resembled the chief in size and bearing that she thought he and Captain Henry might be brothers. When she had first arrived in the camp and Lone Elk had listened to White Cloud and Running Beaver explain why they had brought her to their camp, Lone Elk had seem very displeased. Running Beaver had been scolded, and she wondered then if kidnapping her had been the young braves' idea and not a plan by the chief or the Council of Elders. If that were so, maybe the Indians would release her, and she and Luke might be spared torture and death.

Luke glanced toward her, and in that brief instant when their gazes met, she saw a mixture of raw fury and fear in his eyes. Every muscle of his body was tensed, as if ready to spring to her defense.

Her heart soared. She lifted a trembling hand to her mouth, and nodded to him, assuring him that she was all right.

Luke's dark gaze answered that he understood, but the concern and love she saw that reached out to her in the hungry yearning of his expression almost took her breath away.

The chief puffed on the calumet, or smoking pipe, then raised it in the air, as if an offering to his God, Noelle thought. Then he raised the pipe to the east, south, west and north, then to Luke. Just then, several Indians moved in front of her, blocking her line of vision. Before Noelle was able to move around them, she heard a piercing scream from Little Henry's lodge.

Noelle dashed to his tent, tore back the animal flap and rushed to where Little Henry lay moaning. His body stiffened in pain, his arms cupped to his sides.

Noelle moved beside him and pressed her cheek against his. His body was burning with fever. Thank God Luke was here. He'd think of something to save him. She pressed her lips together. "Little Henry, lie still and don't move—"

Two Indians threw back the tent flaps and strode beside her. Noelle drew back. Against the blinding sunlight, another dark shadow filled the entrance.

"Luke!" she shouted, running to him.

"Are you all right?" he said as she flew to his waiting arms.

"Y-yes…" She snuggled against his hard chest. She pulled back and let her eyes fill with the glorious sight of him. His dark, possessive gaze swept her with a profound look of relief.

"Luke, Little Henry is terribly sick. You must help him—"

"I know. I've just spoken with Lone Elk, the brother of the chief. White Cloud, Lone Elk's son, and Little Henry's brother, Running Beaver, saw your magic act in town. They believe you have the power to save Little Henry's life. They told Lone Elk that you brought back a man from the dead."

"Oh, Luke. I was afraid of that." Noelle shook her head. "How can I explain to them that it's only a trick. Sleight-of-hand. I have no power. I feel just awful, Luke."

He brushed back a tendril of hair from her cheek. Just being here with Luke filled her with hope. "I've explained to Captain Henry that I'm your partner in magic. I'm not sure I've convinced them, but it was worth a try." He grinned that crooked smile that gave her a rush of confidence.

Luke moved to Little Henry's side. He glanced at Lone Elk and said something to him in the Paviosto language. In the short exchange that followed, Noelle sensed that Luke was trying to persuade the Indians to do something they weren't eager to follow.

Noelle moved to Luke's side. "What did you say to them?"

"I was trying to convince them that I held all the powerful magic. I wanted them to let you go." He frowned. "He wouldn't have any of it. The old chief believes I'm trying to save my woman!"

The thought sent a thrill along her spine. "I'm not leaving you, but thanks for trying."

She watched as Luke palpated Little Henry's belly.

The young man moaned as Luke's fingers gently touched his side. After a few minutes, Luke turned to her. "I've seen these symptoms before, Noelle. Once, in the field during the war, one of the German surgeons operated on a young man who had similar symptoms." Luke's eyes narrowed, and he shook his head. "There's not much we can do for him."

"How can you say that? You haven't even tried?"

Luke took a deep breath. "Little Henry needs an operation. There's an infection growing in the lad's intestines that will rupture unless it's removed." He drew a ragged breath. "Noelle, there's nothing I can do for Little Henry."

Her eyes rounded in disbelief. "You must try."

Luke looked at her as if she had asked him to fly.

"Noelle," he said, his voice warm with concern. "You're asking the impossible. Under these primitive conditions, Little Henry will surely die. Besides, I haven't held a scalpel in three years—not since the war." Luke tightened his fists at his sides. "You don't know what you're asking of me, Noelle."

"Little Henry will die if you don't operate."

"And he'll die if I do." In the lengthening pause, Noelle realized something else...when Little Henry died, her life and Luke's would be payment for their failure.

She glanced up at Luke and that thought was clearly in Luke's dark eyes, as well.

"Luke, please. We have nothing to lose—"

"I watched that German physician operate on a private at Chancellorsville. He opened up the patient and remove the inflamed appendage. In their country, it's still considered experimental surgery."

"Did the surgeon save the young private?"

Luke hesitated a long time. "No," he said finally.

"But that doesn't mean you would fail!"

"Noelle, you're not facing the facts."

"It always comes back to that, doesn't it, Luke." Noelle took a deep breath. "How do you know if you're unwilling to take a chance on what's important in life? Yet you'd ride off in a minute to take a chance on a high-stakes game of poker, but when it's something that's really important in your life, you want a written guarantee that you won't fail!" She brushed a stray hair from her face. "Well, life isn't simple, Luke Savage. There are no guarantees in this world. All we have is the opportunity to do whatever we must, then pray it's good enough.

"Noelle," he murmured, his dark eyes gentling. "The last time I held a scalpel, it was at the battle of Chancellorsville. I was trying to save my brother's life. I failed, Noelle. Chad trusted me, and I failed…"

His voice broke, and Noelle watched his eyes fill with the painful memories.

"I'm sorry your brother died, Luke. But knowing you, I'm certain that when you operated on him, you did everything in your power to save him." Tears sprang to her eyes, and she did nothing to stop them. "You're only human, Luke. But at least you tried to save Chad. Other surgeons might have given up, but you tried. That's the difference. And that's what's important."

She tore from the shelter and ran along the outskirts of the camp. The two Indian women, sitting outside the wikiup glanced up from their work, and called to her.

Noelle didn't care. She needed to be alone.

Chapter Sixteen

Luke wanted to follow her, but what good would that do either of them? He glanced back at the figure of Little Henry, lying so still.

Damn, how could he explain to Captain Henry that nothing could be done to help his son—that the infected area deep inside Little Henry's belly would never get any better. Finally, it would burst, the lethal toxin spreading throughout his system until death put the young man out of his misery.

Luke had grown to know these people since that first year he'd come West. He'd worked with the army to bring together the small bands of Indians, helping them find food during the harsh winter. During that time, Luke had lived with the tribe, hunted elk in the mountains during the severe winter, and fished the streams in summer. He'd learned their language, and they trusted him. Although he and Captain Henry respected each other, how could the chief understand such a notion? Besides, if Little Henry died, more than personal friendship would be severed. Any hope for a lasting peace treaty from the Indians would splinter like broken shards of glass.

Outside, children's laughter rose amid the dogs' barking, and old women's chatter. Life went on, regardless of the drama as one small life struggles within its darkness. Luke had learned that lesson in the wounded soldiers' tents during the war.

The silent form of Little Henry, so still, so rigid, reminded him of all the poor devils he'd seen, laid out in the fields at Chancellorsville. The sweet cloying smell of blood, putrefaction and death. The endless screams, moans and cries. So much to do and so little that could be done.

Chad. His brother's dark brown eyes, so trusting. *"It's all right, Luke. I'm not afraid to die."*

The tight knot in his throat nearly choked him as Luke fought back the painful memory of his younger brother's eyes, so full of trust and acceptance. He'd seen that same look in Captain Henry and his wife's expectant faces—that eternal hope that every parent holds for the safety and well-being of their child.

Hope. Trust. Dear God, he didn't want anybody's trust. Trust meant responsibility and promises that were meant to be kept.

Little Henry moaned, and Luke wondered if the lad would ever live to kiss his future bride. Would he ever hold his firstborn? Would he live to claim his inherited right to wave the tribal council's staff?

Another sharp pain tore through Little Henry, and Luke grimaced silently. *Help me,* the almond eyes pleaded, and he grabbed Luke's hand and squeezed with a strength that surprised him.

Luke closed his eyes. *But there's nothing I can do,* he wanted to say. Luke's eyes stung with frustration and pain. *Dear God, I wish it weren't so.*

"You're a brave son of a noble chief, Little Henry,"

Luke whispered in the Paiute tongue. "And your silence bears witness to your courage, but…"

The final words hung unspoken in the growing silence. The tight fingers clung to Luke's hand, speaking an urgency that couldn't go unanswered.

Dear God, maybe Noelle was right. Maybe he should try. One thing was certain, he couldn't stand by and not do anything.

After Luke met with Captain Henry and explained what he was going to do, he gave orders to the women, who immediately scattered to carry out his commands. Then Luke searched the camp for Noelle. He found her sitting beside the small stream. When he took a seat beside her on the stone outcropping, she lifted her head at the sound of his footsteps.

God, how beautiful she was. He knew she must be exhausted and emotionally drained, yet the fine shadows beneath her eyes gave her complexion a delicate hue. Her eyes were large and questioning. She had been crying, and he cursed himself silently.

A fresh well of tears brimmed her bright blue eyes. "Oh, Luke. I had no right to tell you what to do or to make you feel guilty." Noelle hesitated, her breath catching. "Please forgive me."

He moved a hand to touch her face, then pressed her head against his chest. "I went crazy when I realized you were missing," he whispered into her ear. "I feared I'd lost you, and…" He took a deep breath and held her close. "All I could think of was you…. When I saw my name printed on the dusty windowpane, I sensed you'd written my name as some kind of message, but I didn't know…"

She closed her eyes. "I couldn't think of anything

else to do. How did you know I was here, in the Indian camp?''

''Along the ground from the back steps of the saloon, I saw the signs of a struggle. Among the ponies' tracks were the shod prints of a horse. When I recognized the nick in the horseshoe as the same as the one in your driver's horse, I knew it had to be the same animal that I'd given to Little Henry. You were nowhere else, so I took a chance that you were here.''

A rush of fresh tears moistened her eyes. ''All my plan did was to endanger you.''

He put both arms around her and held her close. ''I'd have found you regardless...''

''Oh, Luke. I'm so sorry I got you into this.'' She squeezed her eyes shut. ''Did you tell anyone? Will help be coming?''

He shook his head. ''At the time, all I could think of was to find you. Captain Henry is my friend, and I thought whatever the trouble was, I could settle it peacefully.'' His gaze fell to the distant snow-capped mountains. ''If the townsfolk hear that you've been kidnapped by Indians, who knows what might happen. The only certainty is that there'll be bloodshed on both sides.''

She raised her head and flicked her gaze quickly to his face. ''But Captain Henry will kill us if his son dies.''

''You're not giving up are you, Sunshine?'' His eyes twinkled as he looked into her eyes.

''What do you mean?''

''I thought about what you'd said about my brother. I finally realized that if I hadn't tried to save Chad's life, I would have spent the rest of my life wondering if I might have done something to prevent it. You were right. I did all that anyone could do. I'd never realized before how lucky I was to have been with him. He didn't die alone, he knew I was there.

"Just now, I saw that same look in Little Henry's face that I'd seen in Chad's eyes. Before, I've always thought that I'd failed him. But I see now that if I hadn't tried to save my brother, then that would have been my greater burden."

Noelle drew back and studied him. "Are you saying that you're going to operate on Little Henry?"

"Yes." He took her small hand in his. "I mean, Noelle, that if you're willing to assist me, I'm willing to try to save Little Henry's life."

Her dazzling smile was his reward. "Luke, do you think there's a chance you can save him?"

"I haven't touched a scalpel in nearly three years, Noelle. But I remember a German surgeon, who had volunteered during the war. I watched him use a new surgical procedure that had been used in Europe with such cases as Little Henry's. It's experimental, and under these primitive conditions, I can't promise anything, but..." His voice held a tone of finality. "I know Little Henry will die unless we try.

"I'll need you to help me, Noelle."

"Oh, Luke. Of course I'll do whatever you ask."

"I just came from talking to the chief. I tried to explain what's at stake. I can only hope he'll understand if..." He drew her close. "But for the first time in a long while, I've felt my confidence returning."

"Oh, Luke." She brushed her lips against his. "Tell me what I need to do."

Luke stood and pulled her to her feet. "Come. I've already asked for the tribal women's help, too. We need boiling water and clean materials."

They clasped hands and hurried toward the crowd growing outside Little Henry's lodge.

Noelle patted away the beads of sweat along Luke's forehead with the cloth made from her discarded cotton petticoat. Earlier, she had cut strips and boiled the material as Luke had instructed. Although he had warned her that the procedure could take only a minute or two, each minute dragged on like hours.

She forced herself to gaze at the open incision that Luke had cut along the right side of Little Henry's abdomen. She watched as Luke's fingers began to tie off the cherry red appendage that looked like an angry, accusing finger.

"Cut me another strip of tendon," Luke said. "Hurry."

Noelle's fingers shook as she pulled out another of the strips of antelope tendons the squaws had prepared for her and quickly placed one between Luke's fingers.

"Hold this," he ordered. Noelle held one end firmly as Luke's hands worked deftly to sew up the wound. The next few seconds seemed like an eternity.

Noelle glanced back at the patient's face. Although the strongest men in the tribe had offered to help hold down Little Henry, Luke knew their good intentions might pale when they came to realize the enormity of the procedure.

Luke's decision to knock the patient out by a swift right hook to the jaw was the easiest solution, Noelle realized now. Little Henry had managed to remain unconscious, with the added help of the mixture of whiskey Luke had in his saddlebags, and the medicine man's elixir to numb pain.

The only sounds were the far-off children's laughter

as they played in the still afternoon. Noelle knew Captain Henry and his counsel waited outside. In the distance, the drums were quiet for the moment. But inside the lodge, she felt the strain, like a separate being, span between Luke, Little Henry and herself. Luke appeared too riveted to notice.

Luke grasped the tiny needle made of bone and strung with a fine strip of antelope tendon, and he began to stitch the wound. Noelle patted his forehead again. Steam from the boiling water made the air inside the wikiup feel even hotter than usual. Her back ached, and she wondered what Luke must be feeling.

Finally, Luke glanced at her. "That's it. Now he's in God's hands."

Noelle watched as Luke gently wiped around the wound area and applied a loose dressing across the right side of Little Henry's belly. When he had finished, he took what remained of the cotton strips and wiped his hands on them. Dark circles ringed his eyes, his face bore the strain she knew he felt. Yet he never had looked as magnificent as he did now.

Their eyes met, his look of tenderness warmed her. "Go and rest, Noelle. I'll take the first watch."

"Please, let me watch him. I'm not sleepy, besides, I know you've had little rest. I'll wake you if his condition should change." She brushed back a lock of hair that had fallen over his forehead.

"But—"

"No buts."

"Very well. Come with me while I speak to Captain Henry. I want him to send a message back to Sheriff Wade that we're here. By now, the town must be in a fever's pitch that you're missing. I'll tell them that we've come to help the chief's son."

"I know Curly and Ike will be worried."

"Then I'll explain what you need to watch for in Little Henry's condition." He pulled back the deerskin flap of the lodge as Noelle stepped outside.

A low murmur fell among the waiting crowd. Luke and Noelle strode toward the chief's lodge while the Indian women and men joined them. Lone Elk walked toward them, his face grave.

Luke was silent while they were escorted inside the great lodge. The chief, smoking his pipe, nodded his approval to his braves, allowing Noelle and Luke to be seated. Accepting the calumet from the chief, Luke took several puffs. White smoke laced through the warm air of the lodge, drifting heavenward through the center opening.

Although Noelle understood none of the words the men exchanged, she could sense by the Indians' intense expressions that Luke explained that the surgery might not be successful.

Would they understand if Little Henry didn't survive? Would she and Luke be punished in retaliation? Would their vengeance be turned on the innocent people of Crooked Creek? Noelle held her shoulders back and refused to show fear. She and Luke had done everything humanly possible. Now, the life of Little Henry and the future peace between the Paiutes and Crooked Creek were in greater hands.

While Luke dozed beside her, Noelle sponged Little Henry's parched skin with water. Although she could see that the chief's son was still feverish, Luke had warned her that it might take days before they saw any improvement in Little Henry.

Several times in the night, he had moaned, almost

coming fully awake, but he had been well enough to take the dark elixir from her as Luke had prescribed. When she had finished helping him drink the mixture of herbs, she sat beside Luke and waited. All anyone could do now was wait.

For the next day and night, Little Henry's fever raged, but Luke and Noelle were constantly at his side. They administered cool baths and gave the herb elixirs, aided by several of the older women when they took short periods of sleep.

Despite the demands of their constant vigil, the challenge heartened Noelle. Although she and Luke were absorbed in their work, they were absorbed in each other, as well. They were a team, creating a healing energy between them. When their eyes met, she felt her heart sing with that brief, wordless exchange between them that said it all.

Never had Noelle ever had the opportunity to watch a doctor tend a patient with such constant vigilance as she had experienced watching Luke and Little Henry. Luke's beautiful hands, so capable, so talented, had a much higher calling. She would never forget the carefully precise skill that Luke used to operate on Little Henry. How could he just throw away such a gift that can help others and save lives?

Later that evening, before the fires were lit and the camp began preparing for the night, Noelle glanced out of Little Henry's wikiup to see Lone Elk and Luke standing in front of a new hut, which had been hastily erected from willow branches by several of the younger women.

When Luke returned to Little Henry's lodge, the strange look on Luke's face increased her curiosity. "What did Lone Elk say to you?"

Luke smiled. "The new lodge is for us. Lone Elk told the women to allow us privacy, that you are my woman."

Luke's woman. The words brought feelings in her that she'd tried to deny, but now the thought stirred her blood. Their eyes met. One look into his smouldering gaze and any lingering hint of protest died in her throat.

I am your woman, Luke. I'll always be your woman, she wanted to cry. *You'll always be in my heart.*

Luke stepped toward her and took her hand. "Come, the women will watch Little Henry while we see our new shelter."

When they arrived at the wikiup, Luke pulled back the flap and allowed her to enter. The fresh, green fragrance of willow delighted her. Luke's firm hands circled her waist. "Noelle," he whispered, the word spoken as though it were a song. His strong arms wrapped around her. "There are so many things I want to tell you, but..." His voice broke, and he stared down at her. "I shouldn't be talking to you like this." He drew back slightly. "Emily said that you were going to give O'Shea your answer to his marriage proposal."

Noelle saw the raw look of torment on Luke's face, and her need to comfort him pushed away any remaining threads of shyness. She averted her gaze to the curling black whorls of hair that escaped through the unbuttoned V of his shirt. "Yes, I spoke to him." She rubbed her finger across the springy mat covering his chest. "I told Mike I couldn't marry him."

Luke's hand cupped her chin and tilted her face to his. "You're not marrying O'Shea?"

Instead of the relief she had expected to see in Luke's eyes, his expression remained unchanged.

"You should have accepted him, Noelle."

For one startled moment, she stared at him. "Why…? You know I don't love Mike O'Shea."

"Because he's the kind of man you should marry, Noelle. Successful, committed, stable. You know that as well as I do."

Her hands fell to her sides as she glared at him. She couldn't believe what she was hearing. "How can you expect me to marry someone I don't love? Besides…" *Besides she loved Luke, didn't he realize that?*

"You can learn to love him. O'Shea can take you away from here. He wants to be governor of Nevada. And with you by his side, he will—"

"Stop this!" She wrenched free from his grasp. "How dare you stand there and tell me what I should want!"

"I know what you need—"

"You don't know what I need." The heated words broke with huskiness. Standing there, Luke Savage was everything she wanted. Untamed. Passionate. Magnificent. For as long as she lived, he would be in her blood. She would love this man, desire this man, forever. And for now, she couldn't think of anything that mattered more. She took a step toward him. "Let me show you what I need."

Her fingertips touched the strong angle of his jaw, tracing the jutting corners of his face. She leaned against him, gently at first, until the tips of her breasts pressed against his hard chest.

"Noelle, don't—"

The hot stirring of his breath feathered her skin. "Yes, Luke. Yes. I want to show you, and you're the only man who can give me—"

"Noelle, don't tempt me like this. I'm just a man, for Christsake."

She placed her hands against his shoulder blades, and she felt the muscles tighten beneath her touch. "Hold me, Luke. I need to feel your arms around me." She brushed her lips against his. "Please, I'm not afraid."

Luke groaned, shutting his eyes. "You should be afraid. You should order me out of here and—"

"You don't mean that—" Her warm breath mingled with his, and his heavy-lidded gaze locked with hers.

"You don't know what you're doing to me, my love."

"Then show me what I do to you," she said, the words barely above a whisper. He began to turn away, but she pressed her lips lightly against his firm mouth. He released a breath, then his eyes closed, and she felt his hard, callused hands roam along her waist and hips. His beautiful hands, the healing hands of a doctor, the healing hands of a lover. Yes, his love healed her, made her whole as a woman. *His woman.*

His mouth took hers in a rush of desire, so swift, so hard that she thought for the briefest of moments to pull away. But as his arms pressed her against the hard contours of his length, a rush of fresh excitement drove her back to consciousness as she clung to him.

His heartbeat drummed against hers as her mouth opened with his. A jolt slammed through her as his tongue possessively sought each tender contour of her mouth, drawing her deeper into the magic of his experienced coaxing.

She was tasting and being tasted. He tasted like what she imagined a rare, vintage wine might taste like—full and inviting. He slanted his head, she tilted hers, caught up in the powerful rhythm as their tongues plunged and darted, savoring each other's sweetness.

Far off, an animal howled to its mate. The smoke

from the low-burning campfires wafted the aromatic scent of burning pine and sagebrush into the crisp night air. Yet despite the cool evening, her skin felt warm and flushed with desire as their kiss deepened.

His fingers twined into her unbound hair, and she let herself go as the pleasure of him filled her senses. Then suddenly he pulled his mouth from hers. Lost in the moment, she heard a cry of regret rise from her throat. Her eyelids fluttered open as she felt his fingers tug at the front laces of her gown. Releasing her arms from his neck, Noelle sat back on her haunches and watched him. In that fleeting exchange of glances, she knew that she had led him almost to the brink of no return.

He waited. In his eyes she saw the hunger, and took pleasure in his wanting her. Yet she needed to show him that she would make her own decisions. Without words, she knew he understood—that regardless of the consequences, she would meet them head-on, and take responsibility for whatever comes.

She raised her arms to him in complete surrender. His heated gaze smouldered in answer. A ray of moonlight beamed down from the center of the wikiup, encompassing them in silvery light. Luke gathered the hem of her soft, rabbit-skin gown and lifted the garment over her hips, waist, shoulders and head. The fur brushed across her sensitive skin, causing shivers of pleasure along her body.

His gaze lowered to her bare breasts rising and falling rapidly as he drank in his fill. ''You're so beautiful, Noelle.'' His breath, only inches from her, was warm and moist on her skin, and never had she felt so beloved.

She nestled against the fur pillows as he leaned closer, stripping the shirt from his body. Gone was the reluctant lover, and in his place was this man who wanted her, this man who would enter her soul.

Luke lifted her and carried her to the corner of the wikiup. He laid her upon the soft mound of blankets woven from strips of rabbit pelts. In the moonlight, she studied his face, trying to memorize each ruggedly handsome feature: his deep brown eyes shaded with thick, straight jet lashes, his black, wing-shaped eyebrows, his small, dimpled scar under his cheekbone, his beard-shadowed jaw, even the fine sheen upon his sun-bronzed forehead.

His hands trembled when his fingers cupped her breasts, and when he took her tight bud into his mouth, she was filled with incredible yearning.

Hovering over her, his long legs alongside hers, Luke caressed her breasts, brushing his thumbs over each bud. When she thought she might cry out, he flicked the erect nipple with his tongue, teasing her ache into a demanding need. She groaned, tossing her head back against the soft rabbit fur. A sensation close to near frenzy drove her as he suckled the sensitive tips, first one then the other.

Her fingers twined into his thick hair, silvery jet-black in the beams of moonlight. She pulled his head up, his eyes heavy-lidded with desire.

"I want to pleasure you as you did me that first night," she whispered, fighting against her trembling need.

"Not yet, my darling. There's much much more I want to show you."

Shyly, she moved her fingers down to the side of his waistband, her fingers lingering against the smooth leather. Luke's dark eyes raged with desire. He shifted his weight, allowing her hand to explore, but when she felt his enlarged hardness, her boldness suddenly fled.

"Don't be afraid," he said, his words thick as he undid the trouser fasteners at his waist. When he removed his clothing, he knelt between her legs. His body was truly beautiful. She was reminded of the marble statue of the two lovers she had first seen in her uncle's office. At the time, she didn't understand, but now, she saw the beauty of the man and woman, their bodies naked and entwined with glorious need.

Her fingers raked through his long hair curled with dampness, and he sighed as his hands slid across her soft skin.

He touched her long, silky hair, shining gold in the moonlight. The faint whiff of lilacs touched his senses as he breathed in the scent of her hair. With almost a reverence, he began the slow, teasing strokes that traced each beautiful, sensitive valley and crest—from her forehead, across her eyelids, along her delicate cheekbone to the responsive hollow beneath her jaw. His fingers and lips played her trembling body with the reverence and artistry of a concert maestro playing a Stradivarius violin.

As his hands and mouth moved along the warm curves of her breasts, his stroking increased, caressing her sensitive skin as she lifted and writhed beneath his fingers and tongue. Despite his growing need that burned within him like an inner fire, he forced back his desire to bury himself in her as he watched her writhe and moan in wild abandon. She made a tiny sound at the back of her throat. "Please...I want to pleasure you." Her voice was a mere whisper as she clutched her fingers into his shoulders.

He couldn't help but smile at the wild, passionate

woman beneath him. "To gaze at you is my pleasure, my darling. To touch you is my pleasure. I want you ready. I want you so much, I'm afraid I'll hurt you unless you're ready—"

"No more, now...please." She arched, gasping, her heart pounding. "I'm ready."

He lowered his head, trailing kisses along her quivering belly, then capturing the damp nest at the apex of her thighs.

She arched convulsively, then her silky legs curled around him, drawing herself against his hardness. He shifted, parting her with his fingers as he pressed her down into the soft pillows.

He took her mouth again, craving her kisses, but this time, he entered her. She cried out, and her answering need almost left him speechless.

"It's time, my darling." He said, his voice, husky and low. He thrust into her with an urgency he never knew possible, then hesitated a moment, waiting for her to adapt to him before plunging deeper. But in that brief second, he felt her clench with incredible need, and he found himself overwhelmed with her sweet loving. With this incredible woman, it was as if it were his first time.

She matched his thrusts, curling her body into him. Buried within her, tight and swollen, cresting each wave as their bodies joined in the ancient way since the Garden of Eden.

Wave upon wave of incredible sensation exploded into his mind, fragmenting all reason and thought into extraordinary shards of pleasure.

"*Noelle...*" he sighed her name, his ragged voice sounding far away.

How long they held, he didn't know.

Far off, he heard her cry, felt her wild quivering as she arched beneath him with satisfied pleasure. He met her, filling her to the very core with the same exploding sensations of ecstasy until he thought he would die.

All reason whirled away as she lay there, listening to him gasp out her name. Never had she known such complete happiness. Complete. Yes, with Luke, she felt complete. She closed her eyes, holding him as he stilled, in awe of the intimacy they had just shared.

He lifted his head and smiled crookedly. His black hair was tousled in a way she had never seen before; he looked vulnerable, endearing. He raked his hair back with his fingers, gave her a lingering kiss, then lifted off her, moving the blanket to cover her nakedness.

She watched him, his eyelids closed, his strong profile shadowed in the moonlight. He turned toward her, his arm slipped beneath the blanket and curled around her breast as he buried his face into her hair.

His soft, even breathing feathered the back of her neck. Dear God, she even found the sound of his breathing enticing. Her cheeks blushed with the outward joy of her newfound sensual nature.

''Luke?''

''Mmm.''

''Do you think Amelia Bloomer knows about this thing between a man and a woman?''

She heard him chuckle. He nuzzled the sensitive spot behind her ear with his tongue. ''Don't rightly know.''

She smiled, cuddling up to his hairy warmth. ''I don't know either, but I'd like to think that one day, she'll find out.''

''Why?''

She stretched, feeling the delirious pleasure of laying

beside the man she loved. "Because I think every woman should feel the way I do right now."

He pressed up against her, and she felt his hardened arousal. His warm hand caressed her hardened nipple as he began to rain kisses along the shell of her ear. "And how do you feel?"

She turned to him, and in the darkness, his lips captured hers. Her answer was a soft sigh as desire spiraled deep within her. As their kiss deepened, all thoughts flittered away, except of the man she would love until eternity.

Chapter Seventeen

Women and children's voices drifted inside the hut and broke Noelle's erotic dream. She snuggled deeper into the soft rabbit-pelt blankets, hoping to coax back the pleasurable fantasy of lying on top of Luke, their legs twined around each other. Her face nuzzled the soft, springy hair covering Luke's chest, her nostrils took in the glorious scent of him—wood smoke, prairie sage, and piñon pine.

Noelle bolted instantly awake.

Luke watched her, a slow, lazy smile highlighted the dimpled scar under his cheek. "Mornin', Sunshine."

Noelle pulled back her unbound hair, which streamed across his chest, her eyes flicking nervously over his nakedness.

She wasn't dreaming. Their incredible lovemaking last night had been real. His hand still caressed her left breast. She glanced down at her rosy nipple held captive between his two sun-browned fingers. Self-consciously, she started to draw the rabbit skin over her breasts, but he held the soft fur pelt in protest.

"Sweet, sweet Noelle. Don't pull away from me. Let me look at you."

He enjoyed looking at her! She smiled, surprised and delighted at the joy his bold perusal gave her. She wanted to stare at him, too, she realized with a start. In fact, she wanted to look at him forever.

The thought filled her with giddiness. Her eyes closed and she leaned back, enjoying the provocative sensation of his touch. How she wanted to remain in this wonder of their intimate silence, but one question kept intruding: "Would Little Henry recover?"

Luke's smile gave her instant hope. "He's still feverish, but he's much improved. It's too soon to tell, but he made it through the night. The shaman is with him."

Noelle frowned. "Oh, Luke. Do you trust him? Before you came, the shaman was frightfully angry with me. I remembered what you said about not showing fear, and I threw his stick into the fire." She winced. "I'm sorry I did that. Now, I see that I might have embarrassed him in front of his people."

Luke's grin widened, and he shook his head. "Lone Elk told me what had happened. The shaman knew that his people recognized his bravery in facing the woman who could make men vanish in thin air. But he was also testing you."

"Testing me?"

"Yes. The Indians believe that evil spirits can be tricksters, taking on the qualities of good for their own evil doings. The shaman saved face because he told his people that he was testing your power. Because you courageously stood up to him, you proved that you were truly a good spirit, and worthy of helping Little Henry."

Noelle scowled. "Why that charlatan! He had it all planned that he'd win, regardless of what happened."

Luke laughed. "Come with me while I check on Little Henry."

Noelle put the rabbit-skin gown over her head and pulled it down over her hips. She was dressed by the time Luke finished pulling on his boots. When they were ready, Luke pulled back the skins from the shelter's opening. She took his hand as they followed the hard-packed trail to the willow hut.

Inside, steam, scented with sage, rose from the hot rocks. Several of the native women were spreading fresh boughs along the heated stones. Sunlight filtered through the ceiling, where loosely draped skins and brush covered the center poles. Little Henry was awake, and the broad smile on his handsome face made Noelle's heart sing.

He was naked except for the leather breech cloth, which held the bandages from the operation in place. Noelle hesitated by the entrance as she watched Luke examine Little Henry. The Indian's dark eyed gaze fixed upon Luke with an expression of deep admiration. Noelle wondered if the shaman knew how much the younger braves respected Luke.

The thought troubled her as she watched Luke change the dressing. She remembered the shaman's outrage that she—a woman—had been brought into camp. Even though he'd offered an explanation to his people why she challenged him, what did the shaman really think about an outsider—Luke—healing the chief's son?

"His fever has come down considerably and the incision looks as well as can be expected," Luke said, examining the wound. "I'd say if Little Henry can continue to improve, he might make a full recovery."

Hope filled her with happiness.

When Luke had finished applying the fresh dressing,

a wobbly smile spread across Little Henry's face. Luke felt the side of the Indian's jaw. "Sorry about that, son, but it was for your own good."

Little Henry cast a shy glance every now and then at Noelle. He whispered something that caused Luke to grin.

"What is he saying?" Noelle asked.

Luke smiled. "He is offering you his thanks."

She moved to Little Henry's side. "I'm so glad you're better," she said, wondering how much the young man understood.

"Th-ank you," he said weakly.

Noelle's eyes widened with surprise. "You speak English?"

The Indian nodded, a wry smile on his lips.

So he had understood her when she offered words of comfort. Without warning, hot tears sprang to Noelle's eyes. "I wish I could have done more for you, Little Henry. I'm so happy that you're going to be well."

"Get some rest, Little Henry." Luke took Noelle's arm as they made their way outside.

"It's to you that Little Henry owes his life, Luke."

Luke watched her for a long time before he spoke. The four-day stubble of beard outlined the dark planes of his face; the scar more pronounced, in no way diminished his rugged good looks.

"No, Noelle. You were the one who gave me the courage to try. You believed in me. Without you, I..." He hesitated, then took her hand and squeezed it.

Words weren't necessary in the silence that enveloped them. She understood his gratitude. She felt overwhelmed by his compliment, yet she didn't trust herself to say more. For some reason, she felt like crying. Relief from the worry and fear of these past days, no doubt.

"I don't understand," Noelle said when they had reached a small stand of willows beyond the hut. "I thought you said that most of the Indians didn't speak English."

"Most of the tribes speak English as well as other Indian dialects. But when you came to their village, they feared your magic. They still do. In their way, they believed if they spoke to you in English, it would give you more power over them." He smiled. "After all, you are the sorceress who can make men disappear."

She grimaced at the reminder. "Who taught them?"

"The priests from the missions taught many of them—the Indians are avid learners." He took a few steps to stand beneath the willow's umbrella. "They're very perceptive, too." He grinned, glancing at the native women nearby.

"I think the women who watched us care for Little Henry also can see how very important you are to me." He motioned to the small circle of Indian women pounding seeds into flour.

Noelle blushed, swallowing the tight lump in her throat.

"Oh, Luke, I'm so proud of you. I was sure that Little Henry would be all right." Her thoughts hung on this extraordinary man by her side.

She closed her eyes, clinging to him. "I can't wait until we can tell the chief that Little Henry will recover."

"I'm certain he already knows," he whispered, "but I need to explain to him that these next few days are still critical. Little Henry has made it this far. The lad is young and strong, with an eager spirit." He took her small hand in his. "Come, I'll walk you back to our lodge. Wait for me while I speak to the chief. I'll tell him that it's time you should be leaving."

Surprised, she glanced up at him. "Aren't you leaving, too?"

Luke shook his head. "I'll return with you to town. But once you're home, I'll come back here to remain with Little Henry until he's fully recovered.

"Then let me stay here, with you. We'll return to Crooked Creek together."

Luke remained silent a moment while he contemplated his answer. "We've been here four days, already, Noelle. Even though I sent a message to Sheriff Wade assuring him that we're safe, I'm not so certain that O'Shea won't come charging down on us with the calvary to save you."

"But Mike knows that Captain Henry's Indians wouldn't harm us."

Luke chuckled. "I don't think it's the Indians that O'Shea is worried about," he added with a lazy smile.

Noelle blushed. "When should we leave?"

"We'll get a fresh start at dawn."

Noelle strode beside Luke as they made their way along the hard-packed earth toward the hut that she and Luke shared. The sun warmed her back as she inhaled the crisp mountain air. Along the sun-parched ground, their shadows contrasted sharply with one another— Luke's broad-shouldered build and her smaller stature.

Overhead, an eagle and its mate soared. Exhilaration thrilled her senses as she strode beside the man she loved. How she wished this moment could last forever. She glanced down as their shadows swayed with their even steps, and she was reminded of the natural order of male and female in this wild, rugged and beautiful land. She remembered a fairy story her mother told, of an old couple who had loved one another with such passion, when they died, their souls became shadows locked within the forest's glen, together for all eternity.

Luke motioned to the curve of a stream up ahead. Several women sat beneath the shade of a pine grove, their deft fingers coiling the long grasses into baskets while they watched their small children giggle and splash in a shallow stream nearby.

The women glanced up from their basket weaving and smiled broadly. Suddenly embarrassed, Noelle wondered if they guessed her happiness and knew of her and Luke's recent lovemaking. A warm blush warmed her cheeks. But she didn't care. All that was important was this powerful man at her side, and for now, she could hardly wait until they could be together again.

After Luke left her to return to the chief's lodge, Noelle gathered the seeds and nuts the tribal woman had given her and prepared their meal. A deep yearning came over her. If only Luke could settle down. If only he would want to. Fresh tears welled in her eyes, and she brushed them back. She'd not ruin these few precious hours they had together. For now, they were together, and that was what was important.

When Luke finally returned, it was almost dusk. While Noelle had waited for him, she had bathed and slipped beneath the downy rabbit-blanket. She had drifted off to sleep, because now, the fire in the center of the hut had burned down to glowing embers.

Her flaxen head fit snugly beneath the downy white fur pillow. The soft firelight bathed her skin with a golden hue. He felt a catch in his heart as he watched her sleep. Her small hand, palm up, peeked outside of the rabbit-skin blanket. How he wanted to join her soft, warm body beneath the fur. The thought made him groan with desire.

But he came for a purpose, and he couldn't put it off any longer. It was time to tell her that he'd found Black-jack.

Dear God, had he made a mistake in bringing her uncle back into her life? What kind of a life would Blackjack provide if she had to rely on him? Luke couldn't say he didn't care, for there was no going back, now. He loved her, and he always would.

I told Mike I couldn't marry him. How Luke had longed to hear those words, yet his joy only proved his selfishness.

He leaned over and brushed the delicate tendrils of hair from her forehead. Her eyelashes fluttered open.

"Luke," she said, rubbing her eyes. She clutched the rabbit-skin blanket around her nakedness. "What kept you?"

"I'll not be sleeping with you, tonight, Noelle." His gaze remained on the fresh wood he added to the fire.

"Why not?"

He hesitated, and in that brief pause, it was as though she could read his thoughts. Tomorrow, they would return to their real world, and to the roles they each played. He was the gambler, she was the lady. And regardless of what they wanted, or how much they desired each other, Luke was going to show her that their lovemaking had been a mistake.

She swallowed. "Very well," she said, pride keeping the angry, stinging word she longed to toss out at him at bay. If he could control his emotions, so could she.

"There's something I haven't told you." His voice

held a seriousness that filled her with foreboding. She watched him throw the last piece of pine in the greedy flames.

She lifted her chin, prepared.

"I've found your uncle, Noelle." He met her eyes. "I brought him back to Crooked Creek. He's there, waiting for you."

A fresh wash of disbelief, then joy coursed through her. She threw her hands to her face. "Uncle Marcel is alive?"

"Yes." He swallowed. "He claims that he was hit on the head and suffered amnesia after the loaded wagon he was driving went over the cliff and tumbled into the river. He said he wandered along the trail until someone found him. Blackjack said he didn't know who he was until he saw me walk into the saloon, where I found him."

"Luke. What can I say?" She ran to him and put her head on his chest. "Oh Luke, I owe you so much. And here I was all this time, angry at you for insisting my uncle was alive. Dear God, you've given me back my family." She pulled back and gazed into his eyes with such love that he couldn't bear it. He glanced away, remembering Blackjack's angry words when Luke told him that his niece had come West to stay with him.

"Luke, what's the matter? You should be as happy as I am." She studied him, her smile fading. "What's wrong? What did my uncle say when you told him that I had arrived?"

He let out a breath in a stifled curse, then forced himself to meet her gaze. She stared at him, her morning glory blue eyes round and trusting. God, she was beautiful. He traced his unsteady fingers along her satiny cheek. "Your uncle was very surprised, naturally," he added, wishing now that he'd never laid eyes on Blackjack. "He was saddened to hear of your parents' deaths, but…"

Her delicate brows furrowed with concern. *Dear God, how could Blackjack deny this sweet woman—his niece, his own flesh and blood—anything?* When Blackjack saw her, his heart would melt, and he'd be charmed by her, just as she's charmed everyone else in Crooked Creek.

"Your uncle was very happy," Luke lied, hoping that a small miracle might happen to change Blackjack's mind. "Very happy."

She squeezed her eyes and buried her flaxen head against him.

He held her, his gaze on the mound of rabbit skins where only a few hours ago, they had lain together, making love throughout the night and most of the morning. A wild rush of hunger and need overtook him. "My sweet, sweet Sunshine…"

She tilted her head back and gave him a dazzling smile. "Please don't leave me.…"

He groaned. "I—I must. I've told the chief that we'll leave at dawn.…" His voice was a hoarse whisper.

She pulled his hand down along the soft chamois of her Indian gown and rested it upon her breast. He felt himself harden and his resolve melt.

"God, I want to, but…"

"Don't you want me?" She pressed his hand against her softness.

"Of course I want you. God knows how I hunger for you, but…I'm not the man for you, Noelle. I know it, and I'm damned if I will take you again."

"But it is I who wants you, Luke." Her voice was a husky whisper in his ear.

"I'm only a man, my sweet Sunshine. You don't know what you're doing to me."

"Show me what I'm doing—"

"No!" Luke forced himself to let go of her. Damn his soul, if he didn't leave right this minute, he'd never be able to leave her.

Noelle opened her eyes in time to see Luke toss back the animal skins and slip into the shadows.

Throughout the night, dreams of the shaman's painted face tore through her mind, waking her from a fitful sleep. Noelle sat up and rubbed her temples. Far off, the drums sounded a steady beat against the stillness. She shivered, unable to push back her concern.

What if the shaman was jealous of Luke and her magic? Might he harm Little Henry in some way to get back at them? She knew the shaman held a powerful position in the tribe, and due to no fault of his, she and Luke had been drawn into his world.

Noelle remembered his shattered outrage when she challenged him. He had avoided her completely since then. How could he not feel cast aside by a woman who could make men disappear? Little Henry's recovery might make the shaman fear that his power might be looked upon as weak compared to hers. If only there was something she could do.

Noelle laid back upon the rabbit skins, pondering. Suddenly, she had an idea. She sat up and searched the small deerskin bag of supplies that Luke had left her. Inside, she found his sharp knife.

The next morning, Noelle braided her hair into a single plait, then dressed into the percale dress she had worn when she had been kidnapped and brought to the Indian camp. When she had finished, she followed the

Indian women who waited outside her shelter, and followed them to Captain Henry's lodge, the largest wikiup in the village.

Outside, Luke waited, along with White Cloud and his cousin, Running Beaver. The Indians lowered their heads shyly as Noelle moved past them. She took Luke's offered hand and as he pulled back the antelope hide, she entered the chief's lodge.

"Do exactly as I do," Luke coached. "There's nothing to fear."

The chief and three men—the tribal council—sat cross-legged in a row, smoking pipes. Noelle recognized the last Indian as the shaman, who had tried to intimidate her. He wore the same coyote headpiece as he had then. When she first saw him, he had appeared feral and uncivilized. Now, the painted zigzags were gone from his face. She wondered if he had been forced to remove the bizarre markings. He refused to meet her gaze.

Luke made some signs, then took a seat in front of the fire. Noelle followed Luke's actions, finally taking a seat on the raised rabbit fur pillows at Luke's left side.

The chief, Captain Henry, spoke in his own tongue. When he had finished, Luke turned to her and said, "He praises your bravery."

"Tell him it is an honor to meet him." Luke turned and said something to the chief, who nodded, puffing on his pipe. Then he spoke again.

"Captain Henry says if you ever need the help of his people, they will be at your side as swiftly as the sun melts the valley snow."

"Thank him for me," she said, moved by the thoughtful gesture.

"I already have. I also told him you thought he was a good leader who had brave sons."

She lifted a brow. "Does that mean that I condone Running Beaver's kidnapping me?" She smiled, noticing that Running Beaver, the younger brother of Little Henry, was seated within hearing distance. Noelle noticed, for the first time, how very young he was. She couldn't help admire the courage, if not foolhardiness, it had taken the young man to plan to bring her to the Indian camp in order to help his older brother.

"The chiefs speak of their great respect for the woman with magic hands," Luke said.

Noelle glanced at the three stern Indian faces studying her. "Tell the chiefs that I have something for their shaman."

At her words, the shaman shifted anxiously. If she had any doubt that the Indians couldn't understand her, all reservation faded from her mind.

Luke glanced at her with curiosity. "What is it?"

"A gift."

Captain Henry stood as Lone Elk, Running Beaver and the shaman got to their feet. A soft murmur rippled around the room.

The shaman stood unflinching, his face unreadable as he clutched his feathered stick. Noelle wondered if he had hastily made a new staff, or if the shaman had an assortment of different clubs, each for a different purpose. It didn't matter, she knew. Not for what she had in mind.

Luke helped her to her feet. She gave him an anxious smile, then took several steps in front of the tribunal.

"Gentlemen," she said, her gaze meeting each of the wise faces. "I pray that Little Henry continues to recover. It is with a happy heart that I leave you and your people, knowing that the good spirits will remain with you and Little Henry.

"I wish to thank your shaman for his part in Little Henry's recovery. Your shaman has great magic, too." She drew from her waistband the braided lock she had cut from her long, blond tresses.

At the sight of the flaxen ribbon of hair, a low murmur rose from the crowd. She moved in front of the shaman. "I give you this token of my magic," she said, tying the braid to the feathered staff that he held in his hands.

The shaman's mouth opened in surprise.

Luke smiled, shaking his head as he clapped in approval.

Captain Henry's face remained stoic, but he nodded slightly as if in approval. He stepped forward and removed a leather cord from his neck, then held it out to Noelle. "To magic woman, a brave shaman. Thank you for returning my son's spirit back to him."

Noelle stepped closer, then the great chief placed the necklace over her head. "Thank you," she said.

Luke took her hand. "We must leave now, Captain Henry. I will return in a few days to see your son."

Luke helped Noelle onto his horse, and they rode from the village, the Indians and children running alongside for as long as they could.

Noelle glanced down at the keepsake the chief had given her. The rattlesnake head was a noble gift, one she would treasure always.

How she had changed in these past four days. Never would she have thought that she might live in an Indian camp and actually enjoy it. Yet these past few days had been filled with some of the most glorious experiences of her life.

She blushed, glancing at Luke by her side, thinking of their divine lovemaking. She sighed, basking in the glow of true happiness. Luke had brought her uncle back into her life. With Luke beside her, what more could she want?

Chapter Eighteen

Luke and Noelle had left the village for Crooked Creek soon after daylight. They rode silently, each with their own thoughts as the buckskin's steady hoofbeats moved them closer on their journey. Noelle felt exhilarated with the hope of Little Henry's full recovery and the joy of finally meeting the only living relative she had. She leaned her head against Luke's chest, thrilling to the feel of his strong, steady heartbeat against her ear.

Luke made all of this possible. Her friend. Her beloved. Her lover.

By the time they reached the Silver Hearts Saloon, it was almost dark. Ike's lively piano rendition of "Turkey in the Straw" filled the air.

"I'll tell Blackjack we're here," Luke said, helping Noelle down from the horse.

"Thank you, Luke. Tell him, again, how happy I am that he's alive and well. Tell him I can't wait to see him." She glanced down at her soiled gown. "But I can't see him like this, Luke. I'll need to bathe and change...." She threw him a smile as she darted inside the Silver Hearts saloon.

Luke wheeled Deuce around and headed back along

the street toward the jailhouse where he had left Blackjack. He hoped Blackjack's case hadn't gone to trial yet. If it had, Blackjack might be locked up in jail at Carson City. If that were the case, Noelle might not see her uncle until she visited him in prison.

A fine way for Noelle to finally meet him—with Luke to blame for putting Blackjack there.

"Luke!" Mike O'Shea called from his second-story office window.

Luke glanced up at the lawyer and frowned. O'Shea waved for Luke to come upstairs, then slid the window shut without waiting for an answer.

Cursing under his breath, Luke dismounted and tied Deuce's reins to the hitching post. A few moments later, he went up the stairs and strode though the open door into O'Shea's small office.

"How is Captain Henry's son?" O'Shea asked, offering Luke a cigar.

"Little Henry is better. I think he'll pull through. All we can do now is hope."

O'Shea nodded, leaned back and put his feet on the desk. "Glad to hear it. Last thing we need in these parts is an Indian uprising." The swivel chair creaked as O'Shea turned toward him.

"Noelle has, I trust, returned with you?" O'Shea's mouth twisted, but his face revealed none of the emotion Luke knew O'Shea must be feeling.

"Yeah, I just left her."

O'Shea's eyebrows lifted. "How is she?"

In the brief silence that spanned between them, Luke sensed that O'Shea was referring to more than Noelle's health. "Noelle's a strong and resourceful woman. She made the best of it." For a reason Luke didn't understand, he didn't want to share any more of the details with O'Shea than was absolutely necessary. "Noelle did tell me that she's not going to marry you," he added.

O'Shea's head shot up and a confident smile touched his lips. "Noelle is a lovely woman, but I don't think she knows her own mind." He steepled his fingers. "And I don't see any other suitable men offering for her."

The challenging statement hung between them, but Luke refused to take the bait. "Why'd you call me up here, O'Shea? I'm in a hurry to see Blackjack—"

"Luke, I wanted to be the first to tell you…" O'Shea cut one end from a long, thick cigar "…the circuit judge has already passed sentence on your charges against my client, Marcel Bell, also known as Blackjack."

Luke rubbed the scar on his cheek. "Your client?"

O'Shea's eyebrows lifted. "Of course. I felt it my duty to Noelle to offer my legal services to her uncle."

Luke swore under his breath. "Spit it out, O'Shea. What are you trying to tell me?"

O'Shea waited until he finished lighting his cigar. Tobacco smoke cloyed into Luke's nostrils as he shifted his weight to one hip.

"Judge Willis was most fair, I thought," O'Shea said between puffs. "My client claimed that all monies owed to you for the unfortunate partnership arrangement you had with my client have been more than compensated from my client's lost revenues during the time of his absence." O'Shea's eyes brightened with delight. "In other words, my good man, you've been paid back the two hundred dollars, plus interest."

Luke folded his arms in front of himself. "But the saloon has been closed down for most of that time."

"Ah, well, that isn't my client's fault. Under the law,

you had every right to the saloon's bar and gambling concessions. If you agreed to Noelle's suggestion to close down the establishment, well, it's not my client's fault.''

''Suggestion, hell. Noelle insisted on closing down the saloon.''

O'Shea shrugged. ''Perhaps, but the lady had no legal right to shut the saloon. You, on the other hand, could have fought the decision in court, and—''

''Yeah, let me guess. You would have represented her.''

O'Shea grinned, puffing on the cigar.

''Well, what about Hilda Mueller's property that Blackjack swindled her out of?''

O'Shea shook his head. ''In court, Blackjack testified, under oath, that he had asked Hilda to marry him. She had only wanted to deed her property to him as a…wedding present. Besides, the deed had never been filed.'' O'Shea's grin widened. ''Case closed.''

''What?'' Luke slammed his fist on the desk. ''That slimy polecat has been sugaring up to poor Hilda for the past year. He never planned to marry her.''

O'Shea threw up his hands. ''The course of true love never runs smoothly, Luke.'' He lifted a brow. ''I thought you knew that,'' he added sarcastically. Without waiting, O'Shea said, ''As of now, Hilda and Blackjack are planning a trip to San Francisco to shop for Hilda's trousseau. Blackjack even invited Judge Willis to the wedding next month.''

''Why that flat-out, no-good, ornery—''

''There's one more thing, Luke.''

Luke strode toward the door, turned and folded his arms across his chest. ''Go on.''

"Blackjack has pressed charges against you and Noelle for damages against his establishment."

"He's what?"

"You heard me."

"You mean Blackjack's going to sue us? For what?"

O'Shea tipped the ash from his cigar into an ashtray. "My client claims that the paint and wallpaper and other changes done to his saloon aren't fitting to the—"

"You can tell that son of a…no, never mind, I'll tell him, myself." Luke took a deep breath. "Where is that no-account?"

"He's residing at Hilda's boardinghouse." O'Shea glanced at the timepiece hanging from his vest. "Most likely, he'll be finishing up his second helping of Hilda's famous wiener schnitzel, right about now."

Luke shoved his hat low over his head, and strode through the door. He was down the stairs and mounting his horse before O'Shea finally stopped laughing.

Lamplight winked from the porch windows of Hilda's two-story frame house when Luke stepped up to the screen door. The wind carried a chill, straight from the mountains, and Luke felt it creep into his bones like a bad dream.

In a way, maybe O'Shea had done Noelle and Luke a favor. Now, when Noelle met her uncle for the first time, Blackjack would be a free man. That was better than having his niece visit him behind bars.

Luke rapped on the porch door. With hat in hand, he smiled when Hilda hobbled to answer his knock.

"Mister Luke, come in, come in."

"Thanks, Hilda." An aroma of incredibly delicious food rushed at him. His mouth watered, and he was reminded that the last meal he had eaten had been at the Indian camp, early that morning.

"I'm here to see Blackjack, Hilda. Is he in?"

Her round face lit with an almost girlish charm. "*Ja,* my Blackjack is here." She threw her ample arms around Luke's neck. "How can I thank you for bringing my *liebschen* back to me alive. I am a lucky woman to have you for my friend."

Luke sucked in a breath. "Th-that's all right, Hilda. Just show me to him, will you?"

"*Ja,* of course. But I'll have a big piece of my apple strudel waiting when you're through." She winked. "I'll just leave the plate on the dining room table."

"Thanks, Hilda."

She showed him to the private study in the rear of the house. Luke decided not to knock. He pushed the door open and went inside the room.

With a brandy snifter in one hand and a newspaper in the other, Blackjack sat alone, in front of the roaring fire in the hearth. He raised his head from the newspaper sprawled across his lap. Luke strode toward him and leaned against the brick mantel.

Blackjack put his brandy down upon the side table and folded the paper. "By that ornery look on your face, Luke, I'd say you've already heard that I'm a free man."

"Yeah, O'Shea told me all about how you hornswoggled the judge into thinking you're one of our town's leading citizens."

Luke crossed his ankles and leaned back against the rough hewn board above the mantel. "You might have gotten off this time, Blackjack, but just remember. You told the judge and other witnesses that you plan to marry Hilda. What that dear woman sees in you is beyond me, but you better not be planning another disappearing act, or—"

"How dare you insinuate that I'd skip out on my own darling Hilda and our wedding." Blackjack's dark bushy brows drew into a V. "I'm the luckiest man alive to have a woman like Hilda. That lump on the head I got when I almost drowned in that river, swollen with the flash flood waters, might have killed me. I might have died an old bachelor."

"Save me all the hogwash, Blackjack. You planned that little show, and you'll never convince me otherwise." Luke wanted to throttle the man, but what good would it do? Besides, he knew there was nothing else to say. "So, best wishes, old partner. When's the lucky day of your wedding?"

Blackjack glanced warily at Luke. "It's up to the little woman." He took a sip of brandy, offering no invitation for Luke to have a glass or to take a seat.

"Well, aren't you going to ask me how your niece is?" Luke asked, barely keeping his temper under control. Why were women always drawn to the wrong man? How could a decent, hardworking woman like Hilda be so blind? Damn, it wasn't any of his business. What really rankled Luke was that he was responsible for bringing this two-bit chiseler back into everyone's lives.

"I told your niece that you've returned. Noelle is overjoyed and wants to know when she can see you."

Blackjack's black brows slashed downward. "I've no wish to see her. I told you that. The girl doesn't belong here, anyway."

"She's a woman, not a girl. A mighty fine woman, too. And I still can't see how someone as lovely and decent as Noelle could be related to you." Luke swore under his breath. "But she believes you're a good, decent man. All she talks about is how remarkable you are, what a great guy you are.'' He felt his control slipping. ''I refuse to tell her that you won't see her.''

Blackjack drained his glass and plopped the snifter on the table with a clank. ''I don't intend to see her, Luke. Her coming here was a mistake.''

''But she said you always told her father that you'd take care of her if—''

''Bah! That's my brother's words, not mine. Clinging vines, the whole lot of them. My brother never could stand on his own two feet without my help.'' Blackjack waved his hand in dismissal. ''I'll pay for her way back as far as Kansas City. She can find work there.''

''Damn you, Blackjack. I won't do your dirty work. If you don't want to see her, then you tell her, yourself.''

Blackjack's blue eyes froze. ''You tell her, or I'll have my lawyer tell her—I want her out of my saloon. She's got until the end of the week, then I want her gone.''

''Mike O'Shea said that you're suing us for damages. Are you out of your mind? The saloon isn't damaged, it's improved. Besides, we thought you were dead.''

''I had amnesia since my unfortunate accident, remember?'' Blackjack's voice was silky. ''How did I know you'd think me dead? Instead of running the business in my absence, like a good partner should, you let my niece close the saloon, frill up the place and sell off my clothing, goods and collections of a lifetime!''

Luke huffed a laugh. Collections, hell. Rubbish was more like it. But nothing he could say would change Blackjack's mind. It was too late. Nothing Luke could say or do would erase the damage that Blackjack's return would cause Noelle. Luke had no one to blame but himself.

Luke sauntered toward the door. "If that's your final word, I might as well leave...."

Blackjack sat up straight and folded his arms. "My final word. Nothing will change my mind."

Luke clenched his jaw in resignation. His palms itched to wipe that smug look from Blackjack's face.

Damn, how was he going to tell Noelle that her uncle didn't want to see her? Didn't want her? She would blame Luke, and rightly so. He'd ruined everything—all she had worked for. Now she had no place to go after this week.

Luke strode from the room. He should have left Blackjack in Virginia City. At least Noelle would have been able to keep her inheritance and her sense of independence.

How was he going to explain these things to her? The question loomed in his mind all the way back to the Silver Hearts Saloon.

Noelle had just finished buttoning her yellow muslin gown when she glanced out of the upstairs window. She noticed Luke crossing the street, a deep scowl across his handsome face.

A thread of worry skittered up her spine. Had Luke received word that Little Henry's condition had worsened?

No, of course not. News couldn't travel from the Indian village to town this fast. So, what could be the matter?

She dashed down the stairs and almost collided with Luke when he brushed past her. "Luke, what's wrong? Did you see my uncle?"

"Let's go someplace where we can talk, Noelle."

Something in his voice sent alarm bells ringing inside

her. She let him guide her into the office, then she took a chair beside the small stove in one corner. She paused, alert to the concerned look in his dark eyes.

"Noelle, your uncle is well. He's staying at Hilda Mueller's boardinghouse. He said that he and Hilda are planning to be married soon."

She clapped her hands. "Oh, Luke. How romantic!" She jumped to her feet. "Hilda is such a wonderful woman. Oh, please, I can't wait any longer to see him and to give him my congratulations."

"Noelle…"

She stopped, catching the pained look in his face. "Luke, something's the matter. What is it?"

"Blackjack…he doesn't want to see you."

She heard the words, but they made no sense. "He doesn't?"

Luke took a deep breath. "Noelle, God, how I wish I could spare you. But he—"

"But he what?" She touched the hard plane of Luke's cheek as she fought a wave of anxiousness. "You're upset. Please, tell me what's wrong. What did my uncle say?"

Luke took a deep breath. "Just what I said—he doesn't want to see you.…"

"But why not?"

"He's…Blackjack is a loner, Noelle. I've known him for almost three years, and I think…" Luke took her hand into his hard callused palm.

"No, I won't make any excuses for him."

Luke began again. "Noelle, he's angry at both of us for making changes in the saloon. He's suing us for damages, as he calls it. He also said he wants you gone by the end of the week. He's offered to pay your way as far as Kansas City."

She shook her head in confusion. But why? She had thought her uncle might find her lacking in deportment. Or he'd be disappointed that she didn't have the Bellencourt dark hair instead of her mother's fair complexion. Maybe her uncle might hope she would be taller, or maybe he'd wish she'd married a wealthy gentleman, or...

Her throat tightened. No, she really believed—with all of her heart—that he'd be as thrilled to have a niece as she was to have an uncle. She never thought he would refuse to see her.

Noelle sat down on the chair, her knees shaky. "I see," she answered finally.

Luke knelt beside her. "I've been saving a little money this past year, Noelle, and I'll see to it that you have a ticket for wherever you want to go."

She stared, unbelieving. "You want me to go, too?"

Luke raked his fingers through his hair. "I want you to be happy, Noelle. I want you to be safe...."

"I see." She pulled away from him. How naive she had been to believe that Luke could want her, too. Want her enough to stand by her. Well, if he didn't want her, then she would somehow survive. She would survive her uncle's rebuff. She'd already proven that she could take care of herself.

But it would take longer to survive Luke's rejection. Noelle rose to her feet and strode toward the door. With all of her inner strength, she forced herself to look at him. "Thank you for bringing me my uncle's message. If y-you'll excuse me..."

"Noelle, wait!"

Tears began to stream down her cheeks. Her throat tightened as she dashed out of the office and bolted toward the stairs, almost knocking into Curly, who came from behind the bar, a tray full of empty mugs in his hands.

Noelle hiked up her skirts and ran up the stairs, not stopping until she entered her bedroom, bolted the door, and threw herself upon the bed.

Chapter Nineteen

Boisterous laughter shattered Noelle's dream. Bolting upright from the bed, she shook the cobwebs from her mind, then glanced out the window. Across the street, several miners sprawled drunkenly against the Red Garter dance hall steps, singing in off-key revelry.

Ordinarily such a sight would bring a smile to her lips and a thought that maybe the miners were celebrating a rich claim. But now, their laughter made her own misery all the more painful.

Noelle rubbed her throbbing temples. How long had she slept? She glanced at the deep violet cast along the horizon—several hours must have lapsed since Luke's visit.

The memory brought back a bitter reality. No, she hadn't dreamed that her uncle refused to see her. He didn't know her, after all. Maybe he felt she was a dependent relative, wanting him to take care of her. Still, that didn't account for why he wouldn't even grant her a visit.

Luke. Dear God, how could she accept the fact that the man she loved didn't want her, either. *I'll see to it you'll have a ticket for wherever you want to go.* A shudder tore through her. Dear God, it was as if he were buying her off, sending her out of his sight. She felt hurt, confused and angry.

Shock, disillusionment and grief engulfed her. She had been betrayed by the only two people on earth who mattered to her. Inside, a raw sense of vulnerability threatened to overtake her.

But she would survive, there was no doubt in her mind about that. In her heart, she truly had believed that Luke would settle down. He loved her, she was certain. But apparently loving her wasn't enough for him.

Noelle went to the bureau and poured water from the pitcher into the basin. Staring in the mirror, Noelle splashed her cheeks with the chilly water, flushing color to her face.

Anger began to replace the hurt of rejection, the pain of her loss. If her uncle didn't want to see her, at least he could tell her so, in person. *If her uncle had been in Crooked Creek when she first arrived, would he have refused to see her?* Noelle's anger grew. *Why? What threat could she possibly pose to him?*

Noelle had spent months of risking life and limb to travel across the country to honor her promise she'd made to her father—her promise to go to Nevada and seek her uncle. Now that Marcel Bell, or Blackjack— or whatever he chose to call himself—has returned from the dead, she was going to meet him, regardless of what he wanted.

Determination fueled her decision as she unpinned her bound curls and vigorously brushed her hair. Her fingers shook as she unbuttoned her plain, cotton gown. Stepping from the heap of skirts, she dashed to the closet and pulled out the blue silk gown she had worn when she'd first arrived in town.

With grim intent, she hurriedly changed into her best gown and matching bonnet. She was finally going to meet her Uncle Marcel, whether he damned well liked it or not.

Noelle brought the team of horses to a teeth-jarring stop in front of Hilda Mueller's boardinghouse. Ike and Curly jumped down from the wagon and grabbed the horses' reins.

"Curly an' me will carry the chest and boxes onto the porch," Ike said, taking the reins from her and looping them around the brake handle.

Curly hopped to the back of the wagon and began to slide the narrow end of the long, wooden crate containing the full-length mirror toward Ike.

"Thank you, both," Noelle said. She glanced at Curly, whose usually cheery smile turned down into a worried frown. Forcing a grin she didn't feel, Noelle was immediately rewarded with Curly's toothy smile.

"You and Ike take the wagon back to Shep's when you're through unloading the crates."

"We don't mind waitin' for you, Miss Noelle," Ike said.

"You don't want t' walk the streets by yourself," Curly added protectively.

"No, go ahead. I'll be all right. I'll enjoy the walk back to the Silver Hearts when I'm finished."

"We really don't mind waitin', do we Curly?" Ike said with unusual persistence.

"No, Miss Noelle." Curly's dark brows knotted with worry.

Her throat tightened with gratitude as she realized how much these two dear men cared for her. "Don't worry, my friends. I'll be just fine.'' She winked at them.

Noelle sat for a moment, gazing at the two-story frame house before her. The front porch was empty except for George and Rufus, retired prospectors, who rocked away their days, outbragging each other with colorful tales of their past.

She squared her shoulders and set her chin. Stepping down from the wagon, Noelle walked purposefully toward the porch steps. A sudden breeze plucked at her bonnet's blue satin ribbons beneath her chin. Before she reached the front door, George and Rufus unfolded their long, rickety legs, doffed their hats and raced to open the door for her.

Acknowledging them with a smile, Noelle's attention turned to Hilda as the dark-haired woman opened the door. "*Willkommen,* Miss Noelle. What a pleasant surprise.''

"Thank you, Hilda. I'm here to see my uncle. Is he in?''

Hilda's hands clasped in front of her bosom. "*Gut.* I'm glad you've come.'' Wrinkles creased in the corners of her eyes when she smiled. "*Ja,* your uncle has just finished his supper. Come, I show you.''

The aroma of roast chicken wafted through the warm kitchen to greet Noelle's nose as she followed Hilda's minced walk toward the rear of the house. Crocheted rag rugs cushioned the sound of their footfalls as they moved past overstuffed sofas covered with white, starched doilies.

Mike O'Shea had mentioned that Hilda had wanted to give this home to Uncle Marcel as a wedding present. A sharp sense of foreboding gripped her. Had her uncle

really planned to abscond with Hilda's property, as
Luke had said?

Noelle glanced through the open door to a long table,
its wooden chairs waiting for tomorrow's hungry boarders. Hilda's boardinghouse—did Hilda really trust her
uncle with her only source of income? What if he never
planned to marry her? The thought worried Noelle more
than she cared to admit.

At the end of the unlit hall, lamplight glowed cheer-
fully from the rear of the house. Hilda hesitated before
knocking on the study door. She glanced back at Noelle,
her eyes shadowed in the half-light. Her mouth opened,
then closed, as if she wanted to say something but
thought better of it.

Hilda stepped away from the door. "He's inside,"
she offered finally.

A moment of sudden panic rushed through Noelle,
but she fought it back. Biting her lip, she battled the
looming trepidation deep within her. She felt like an
orphan begging for a family.

"Thank you, Hilda," she whispered. "I won't stay
long." Noelle hesitated while Hilda nodded silently,
then left her alone, facing the study door.

Noelle's stomach clenched as she paused, garnering
strength against the rebuff that might come. She tightened her fingers into a fist and rapped softly, hesitated
a moment, then turned the doorknob. She pushed open
the door.

The solitary figure seated in the corner chair lifted
his blue gaze from the newspaper. For an instant, he
looked so like Papa that her breath caught in her throat.
Noelle could only stare at him in amazement.

The Bellencourt blue eyes appraised her from beneath
black thick brows. Heavier than her father, Marcel's

face was fuller, but the same hairline and full head of dark wavy hair was almost identical to her father's. Noelle's stomach tightened and tears stung her eyes. He looked so very much like Papa, that for an instant, she thought to rush into the comfort of his arms.

But something was very different about Marcel, too. As he studied her, those eyes hardened like chips of ice—something she had never seen in her father's eyes.

Marcel's back stiffened, his jaw clenched in growing irritation. This was a man she didn't know.

"Uncle Marcel."

His chin rose in challenge, then he swallowed, his Adam's apple lifting above the stiff white collar of his shirt. His good manners won over his surprise and outrage, and he rose to his feet. The newspaper slipped to the floor.

The silence heightened the charged emotion between them as freak lightning might fuel an autumn thunderstorm. Moments ticked loudly from the clock on the mantel. Steeling herself for the looming rejection she knew was coming, she waited for him to speak.

When it was embarrassingly obvious that he wouldn't, Noelle found her courage again.

"Uncle Marcel, I'm your brother's daughter, Noelle." She took a deep breath as his eyes challenged her. "I promised my father that after…that after he…died, I'd find you and bring you the equipment from the family's illusionist act." She studied her uncle for any sign of emotion, but his face appeared unreadable.

She took a deep breath. The sound of her unwavering voice gave her courage. "My father held you in the highest regard. I think you should know that." She waited for some sign, some recognition of what she had said, but instead, his cold appraisal bored through her.

"Yes, how proud Papa was of his big, successful brother." She could feel her irritation build as he steeled his feelings behind that mask. She lifted her chin an inch, and crossed the room to position herself beside the fringed footstool a few yards from where he stood.

"I don't know why you refused to see me, uncle. At first, I was hurt. Bewildered and hurt. But now, I really don't care. You see, I promised my father that I'd find you, and nothing will keep me from that promise, not even you."

She noticed a flicker of emotion in his eyes, but it faded as quickly as it came. She was glad for some reaction. How could this man be so unfeeling? No mistake—Marcel was as different from his younger brother as an iceberg to a summer's breeze.

She took several steps toward the door, then whirled to face him. "Mr. Bell, or shall I call you, Blackjack?" She couldn't hide the sarcasm in her voice.

"You might be interested to know how much your letters meant to my family. Papa read them aloud, over and over during the years. My favorite letter was when you first arrived in Nevada and filed your claim to one of the biggest silver lodes in the state."

The muscles along his jaw flickered, and she took pleasure in his unease. "How I delighted in your descriptions of the big mansion you built. I could almost feel the polished Italian marble, hear the crystal chandeliers ring and feel the silks and satin cushions of your imported antiques. You dazzled my childlike imagination. I treasured the world you built for yourself. I'd memorized passages of your letters like they were poetry. My favorite was your description of the sunlight through the Gothic stained-glass windows, and how the early morning light would splatter diamond rainbows of color across your white marble hall.''

Her eyes stung with tears. ''What a fool I was. What a fool you made of us all.''

She thought of Luke's skepticism when she first told him of her rich Uncle Marcel who lived in Crooked Creek. The memory fueled her anger. ''I'm glad my father never learned the truth about you!''

Marcel's face remained a mask of chiseled granite behind whatever he was feeling. ''Are you quite through, young woman?''

''Quite through.''

''Good. Who do you think you are to explain my life to me?'' The words were spoken in a violent fury. ''You know nothing of what you speak.'' He motioned to the chair beside him. ''Sit down. It's time for you to learn the truth.''

Noelle caught her breath. ''Whatever do you mean?''

''I suggest you sit down, Miss Bellencourt. There are a few things you should know about your dear father.''

The tension deepened between them. Stiffly, Noelle took a seat beside the footstool and watched Marcel stride to the side table, and splash an inch of amber liquid into a glass.

''It was I who developed The Great Bellencourt into one of the greatest illusionist acts of Europe.'' His gaze lingered on the sparkling brandy. ''When your father came of age, I taught him everything he ever knew. We were famous.

''But when your father married your mother, she wanted him to immigrate to America. Nothing would change her mind. Although I finally agreed to join them, I warned your father that the move would destroy our act. But your father wouldn't listen. As always, he believed your mother, that everything would work out for the best.''

Marcel took a gulp from his drink. "They were wrong, you see." His eyes darkened with memories, and Noelle realized, for the first time, the intense rivalry that had existed between the two brothers.

"The theaters in New York City didn't appreciate our art." He huffed. "The wages they offered were a disgrace. An insult. I pleaded with your father to come West with me, but he wouldn't leave you or your mother. It was your mother who kept him tied to her apron strings. She ruined him. She ruined all of us."

Noelle couldn't believe what she was hearing. Her nails dug into her palms; she unclenched her fingers, aware of her outrage at this man. "How dare you say that about my mother? She loved my papa, worshiped him and believed in him to her dying day."

His mouth quirked. "Love, bah!"

Noelle rose to her feet. "You know nothing of their love."

"You know nothing of us, Noelle." Marcel pointed a finger at her, his jaw clenched. "When I first met your mother, she was a stunning beauty. She could have had any man she chose, but she wanted your father, God knows why."

For a startling instant, Noelle heard something in Marcel's voice that took her breath away. Could it be..?

"My mother was beautiful, yes." She hesitated, groping for the right words. "My father was so proud of her. I remember he'd say that when mother first joined the act, she would walk on the stage and a gasp would rise from the audience. Every man's eyes were upon her. Kings to commoners, no man could resist her charms.''

A chilly, black silence lengthened between them. Noelle watched her uncle's back stiffen. ''Do you remember, uncle? Were your eyes upon her, too? Did you love her? Did she choose my father over you?''

In that brief, shattering moment, the truth lay bare in Marcel's blue eyes. *She had guessed the truth!*

Her mind fought back to remember what her parents had said about those early days in New York City. She remembered Papa's sadness when he spoke of their act breaking up and the day Uncle Marcel left to make his fortune. But Marcel's raw anger at her mother—after all these years?

''You're still in love with her....'' Noelle spoke so softly that she wasn't certain she had said the words aloud.

Although Marcel's features stilled, the spark of rekindled memories spoke the truth from his eyes. ''Yes,'' he said finally. The word hung in the air like a low roll of distant thunder.

Noelle tried to understand, tried to realize what this all meant, but her uncle's admission only added to her confusion. Her gaze fixed on her uncle, and she was shocked at the change in him. It was as though he had finally realized the truth, himself.

For one staggering moment, Noelle realized the price her uncle had paid—not only had he lost the woman he once loved, but that love had cost him his brother, too.

Marcel's gaze broke away, his face suddenly like someone who had been struck in the face. For the first time, Noelle felt almost sorry for him.

''Did my father know?'' she asked gently.

He gazed out the window, his breath uneven. ''I don't

believe so.'' His voice barely rose above a whisper.
''I'd seen her first, you know. God, she was beautiful....'' Marcel glanced back at her. ''You look very
much like her, Noelle. The same features, the fair hair
and ivory skin.'' His mouth lifted in a wistful smile.
''For a moment, when you first walked into this room,
I...''

He closed his eyes and let his breath out slowly.
''That was a long, long time ago. It has nothing to do
with the present.'' He schooled his features, again, into
a controlled mask.

''Crooked Creek is no place for you, Noelle. I'll provide you with a ticket to Kansas City. I have friends
there who'll see to it that you find a decent position
until you marry.''

Noelle held her anger in check. ''I'm staying in
Crooked Creek. I'll find employment, I don't need your
help.''

Marcel's thick eyebrows slanted into a V. ''God for-
bid, you're as stubborn as your mother.''

''I'm as stubborn as I need to be.'' She whirled back
to face him. ''My mind is made up.'' She strode to the
door, then turned around. ''One more thing, Mr. Bell.''
She met his unflinching gaze with one of her own. ''I
don't know why it was so important to my father that
you receive the props for the magic act. I do know that
he worshiped you. You were his older brother, he respected you. Never once did I hear him say an unkind
word about you. He loved you to his dying day, and he
passed down to me the importance of family. Through
my father, I came to worship you, too. I believed in you
when I had nothing left to look forward to. It was that
strength of family that gave me the courage to come
West to find you. Well, now that I have, I'm not going

back. I've learned a great deal, the most important lesson learned is that I don't need you, or Luke Savage, or anyone. So you can forget any responsibility you think you have for your brother's niece. The slate is wiped clean!''

Noelle strode from the room, fighting the tears that threatened. She held her head high as she dashed down the steps and along the dusty road through the main street.

Marcel Bellencourt was a closed chapter on her past. She would begin anew, this time wiser and stronger. Never again would she believe in the perfect man. Luke Savage had told her often enough. *A man was a low-down polecat, only looking to better himself any way he can.* Noelle bit down on her lip. Now, she knew he spoke the truth.

Chapter Twenty

The sound of a hammer pounding on Shep's anvil echoed along the side of his head. Luke opened one eye. No, he wasn't in Shep's stable, and that sound wasn't coming from Shep's anvil, although his head felt like it. Damn, he had the mother lode of all hangovers hammering through his brain.

Luke struggled to raise his head, then thought better of it. Damn, only a fool tries to drown his sorrows in red-eye. But come to think of it, he was a fool in so many ways, he might as well add another way to his growing list.

Luke rolled over and the hammering inside his head grew louder. He staggered to his feet and glanced around. He was in an upstairs bedroom in Hilda's boardinghouse. If memory served him right, Blackjack and old Rufus had helped him up the stairs late last night and thrown a blanket over him.

Blackjack. Luke groaned as his memory slowly returned. He'd ridden back late last night from the Indian camp. Thank God, Little Henry was healing well. If he continued to improve, he'd be all right in a few weeks.

That situation was the only thing that had gone right all week.

Luke rubbed the throbbing ache alongside his head as he tried to remember what had happened last night after he'd returned from the Indian camp to check on Little Henry's condition. He remembered creeping up the hallway stairs, way after midnight, to keep from waking Hilda.

The last person Luke had expected to see was Blackjack, sprawled out at the top of the steps, waiting for him. Blackjack, half soused, waving that brandy bottle like a lucky gambler brandishing four aces. And like a damn fool, Luke had joined him in a drink. At the time, it had seemed like the proper thing to do, as Blackjack had been drinking and waxing poetic about lost love.

Again, Luke remembered what an ever-changing mystery Blackjack was. He'd never known the man to speak of love before. When they had finished that bottle and were polishing off another, Hilda, brandishing a rolling pin, broke up their party.

Luke scratched his two-day beard and forced himself to stare at his reflection in the mirror. He wondered if he could shave without moving his head. Shave or cut his throat. He didn't care which.

An hour later, Luke carefully put one foot in front of the other as he made his way from the public bath. Bright sunlight almost blinded him as he tilted his hat brim low over his aching head. His mouth still felt like wool fleece, and his stomach was barely holding the strong coffee Hilda had forced down his throat and Blackjack's.

He tried not to move his head or body as he strode along Main Street; the galloping hooves of riders clip-clopping past resounded in his head like rifle shots. He put his fingers in his ears, and squinted into the blinding sunlight. His body felt as if a longhorn steer had played toss-the-can with his carcass for a week.

As Luke made his way along the town's business establishments, the familiar melody of Ike's piano rendition of "Marching Through Georgia" grew louder. Luke stopped, then with fresh resolve, he straightened his shoulders and rushed past the shuttered doors of the Silver Hearts Saloon until he was safely down the street.

At the corner, Luke stopped, then glanced back over his shoulder. How he wanted to turn around and march back inside that saloon and explain to Noelle how sorry he was for messing up everything. Yet what good would it do? She'd be busy packing her things; the last person she wanted to see was him. Besides, he had to find the courage to do the one decent thing in his life—he had to muster the courage to leave town for good.

He mustn't see Noelle again. Because if he did, he'd take one look at her and cave in. He'd throw away all reason and beg her to marry him. Damn him, but he couldn't let himself weaken. She deserved a better man than him. And when he was gone for good from Crooked Creek, Noelle would see that marrying Michael O'Shea was best for her.

A cold knot wrenched his gut at the thought of O'Shea and Noelle. Luke brushed away the image and grabbed hold of the hitching post at the end of the street. He adjusted his feet solidly beneath him as he steadied himself, and stared across the street at the bank building. He blinked the blurry image into focus. He was still drunk.

Luke took a deep breath, then started across the street. With luck, maybe he'd be run over by the stage.

Ten minutes later, Luke made his way out of the bank

to the long wooden flight of stairs that led to Mike O'Shea's law office.

Luke blinked, cursing himself at the lingering blurry vision of his drunkenness. He clamped hold of the sturdy stair rail and glanced to the top of the steps.

God, those stairs looked higher than Sun Mountain, and just as steep. His stomach flip-flopped. Closing his eyelids, Luke willed his stomach to be still.

Luke tried again. This time, he held the railing with both hands, and placed his boot on the first narrow step. Gingerly, he lifted his weight, leaning heavily on the rail.

He closed his eyes, all sense of movement making him dizzy. He inched his way up each stair, one at a time, trying with all his might. As he settled his large boot in the middle of each plank, he prayed that he'd judged correctly. The last thing he needed was to fall down and make a bigger fool of himself in front of O'Shea. He could almost imagine the lawyer's loud guffaws.

For what seemed like an eternity, Luke worked his way up until the aroma of Cuban cigar smoke almost made him gag. The wafting smell outside the window told Luke that the lawyer was in. At least Luke hadn't endured climbing this mountain of stairs for nothing.

Luke hung on the doorknob, aimed his boot, and before he could kick the door, O'Shea opened it and stood staring at him.

O'Shea's mouth opened. "If I didn't know better, Luke, I'd say you were drunk!"

"You're right, as usual, O'Shea. Go sit at the head of the class."

O'Shea helped him to a chair, then stepped back, grinning. "Damn, you look like hell." He took a seat behind his desk and picked up the quilled pen he'd been writing with. "You *are* drunk."

"Looking at your ugly face is sobering me up fast." Luke clasped the wooden arms of the chair to keep the room from spinning. "I'm here on business, mister lawyer."

O'Shea quirked his mouth as he watched him. "What kind of business?"

Luke leaned over and poked O'Shea in the vest. "Your kind of business. You and Noelle."

O'Shea steepled his fingers, leaned back and studied Luke. "Go on."

Luke braced himself while he rummaged in his hip pocket for the small leather bag he had withdrawn from his savings account at the bank. "Here, this is for Noelle." He plopped the pouch on the desk. "After I leave town, I want you to give this to her."

O'Shea studied him like a desert owl watched a chipmunk. "Where are you going?"

"Doesn't matter. I'm leaving, that's all that's important. Nothing keeping me here. Besides, with me gone, Noelle will come to her senses and marry you."

O'Shea narrowed his gaze. "Does Noelle know you're leaving?"

"Yeah, I told her."

"Did she say she'd marry me?"

"Why would I talk about you when I was with her?" He rubbed his screaming temples. "But she'll marry you. She has no other choice."

O'Shea leaned forward and propped his elbows on the desk. "Let me get this straight. You've told Noelle that you're leaving town, because you want her to forget about you and marry me?"

Luke started to nod his head, but the room tilted

again. "Noelle's a smart woman. She knows a good man when she sees one."

O'Shea picked up the bag of gold and mentally assessed its value. "Good bit of change, Luke." He twisted his mouth in thought. "Very well, I'll give it to her." He stood up and walked across the room to the safe, dialed the safe's tumbler, then opened the door and placed the bag inside. When he sat down again, he wrote out a receipt and handed the paper to Luke.

Luke tucked the receipt into his shirt pocket without looking at it. "That's what I like about you, O'Shea. You do everything up, nice and tidy."

Mike O'Shea shook his head. "And you're still lit to the gills. Here," he said, getting to his feet. "Let me help you back to the boardinghouse. Hilda's famous snakebite medicine will put the starch back in your spine and bring your eyes back into focus."

Luke shook his head, but the motion sent the room reeling. He waved his hands, trying to push O'Shea away. "No, I'm fine. Besides, Hilda's too busy tending Blackjack's hangover. Compared to him, I'm as sober as a Sunday pulpit thumper."

"What the hell happened to you and Blackjack last night?" O'Shea leaned on the corner of his desk and appraised him. "Did Noelle finally meet her uncle?"

"Yeah, and from watching Blackjack drown his sorrow inside a brandy bottle, it's my guess that Noelle discovered what a louse he really is." Luke rose to his feet. "Now she knows that the two men in her life are made out of the same thin cloth. A sobering thought."

Luke steadied himself against the doorjamb. "Well, I've got packing to do. The sooner I clear out of here, the sooner everyone can get on with their lives."

O'Shea shot him a worried look as Luke clung to the

doorjamb, then he took a step and turned toward the stair railing.

"Let me help you down those stairs, Luke—"

"Save your help for those who need it." Luke lifted his hands from the railing, proving that he didn't need anyone's help—especially Michael O'Shea's. The slam of cold, crisp morning air exhilarated him. "I feel better all ready," Luke said, inhaling a deep breath. He placed his right boot on the top step, misjudged, then before he knew what happened, the ground came up to meet him.

"Luke, you damn fool! Are you all right?" O'Shea's voice sounded very far away. Then Luke heard nothing at all.

"Luke, can you hear me?" Noelle's voice sounded like soft, tinkly bells.

Luke opened one eye and thought he was dreaming. "Noelle?"

She smiled at him in that special way that made him feel as if he were the most important man in the world. "Luke, do you hurt anywhere?"

He smiled crookedly back at her. "Feeling no pain." This must be heaven. He felt her soft, tender hands press across his forehead, and he smelled the faint whiff of lilacs. His eyelids opened, and the face of an angel gazed down at him.

"Noelle…"

"Shh! Hilda said to keep you very quiet. You've had a terrible fall. Do you remember anything, Luke?"

"Mmm." He tried to remember, but his mind was a peaceful blur. "What happened?"

"You fell down Mike O'Shea's stairs." She tenderly brushed a lock of hair from his face. "Curly and Ike carried you here so I could take care of you." She smiled as her fingers lightly caressed his face. "Oh, Luke. The most wonderful thing has happened."

Luke moaned. "I've died and gone to heaven?"

"Oh, Luke, be serious." She laughed softly.

Luke struggled to sit up.

"Here, let me help you," she said, holding his head. Luke glanced around. He was propped up on the blue, lumpy sofa in Blackjack's office. "Where's O'Shea? I thought he'd be here, gloating."

"Mike was here, but he and the others are at the sheriff's office. They called a town meeting after Captain Henry and the Indian council rode into town—"

"Captain Henry?" Luke held his splitting head. "He came here, to Crooked Creek?"

She smiled. "Yes, Luke." She sat back, looking at him. For a moment, he wanted to remember her, just like she was now, gazing at him with so much love in her eyes. God, he felt as if he could do anything when she looked at him like that.

"Captain Henry made a speech and told the sheriff how you helped Little Henry. In gratitude, the chief has promised to sign a new peace treaty with the town for your saving his son." Noelle made a little sound in the back of her throat, and Luke realized that there was more at stake here than Little Henry's life. With a new treaty between Captain Henry's tribe and the town of Crooked Creek, the townsfolk were almost guaranteed safety from other renegade tribes' war parties, as well. The promise of peace between the Indians and the miners was the first step in turning Crooked Creek into a safe town for future settlers' families.

"Luke, isn't it wonderful? Sheriff Wade said that we can begin by building a schoolhouse." She laughed.

"Of course, Ike teased Curly that he could be the first pupil." She chuckled. "Oh, Luke, I'm so proud of you."

"You were a great part in Little Henry's recovery, Noelle. It wouldn't have happened without you."

She smiled, her eyes bright. "What's important is that Little Henry is going to recover." She blinked back a threat of tears. "Come, let me help you to your feet."

Luke leaned on her shoulder and tried to stand. From outside the window, he heard voices yelling and hollering. "What's the commotion about?" he asked.

"I don't know." Noelle ran to the door and glanced down the street. "Luke, it's Sheriff Wade, Emily and Daniel, Shep. Why, all of the townsfolk are marching this way." She turned to stare at him.

Noelle came to his side and helped him to the door. Luke stared as the small mob of people marched along Main street toward them.

"For he's a jolly good fellow," chanted the crowd.

Luke glanced at Noelle, perplexed. "What's going on?"

"Let's go outside and find out," she answered, smiling. He put his arm around her shoulders as they made their way to the front of the saloon.

Emily, with little Naomi in her arms, took her place beside Noelle. "The town had its first meeting, Luke. We've elected Sheriff Wade as our spokesman." She grinned, pointing to the tall, rangy sheriff.

"Quiet, people," the sheriff said, waving his hands for the crowd to quiet. "Quiet. Let's pipe down while Mike O'Shea makes his speech." But the crowd kept on chanting, cheering. Finally, a gun blast pierced through the noise.

Luke glanced at the sound to see Ike holding a smoking revolver at his side. "Quiet!"

Mike climbed up into the wagon bed, raising his hands. "Ladies and gentlemen of Crooked Creek." Hoots and cheers sprang up among the townspeople. "You good people have made one of our town's most illustrious citizens an offer, and it is my duty and pleasure to present that offer—"

"Save all your fancy words for when you're elected governor, O'Shea," Shep hollered from across the street.

"Yeah, just get down to the business at hand," Ike said, his long face serious. The crowd cheered.

"Very well," Mike said, good-naturedly. He turned to face Luke. "Dr. Luke Savage, the people of Crooked Creek offer you the position of their family physician. In exchange for your services, the good citizens will deed you a piece of property at the edge of town, with the promise to build you a new home and office."

Hurrahs and cheers drowned out O'Shea's words. "Please," Mike raised his hands to the thundering applause. "Let's hear what the man has to say."

Noelle drew away, her heart in her mouth. She knew the offer of a house and medical practice for the town of Crooked Creek wasn't the only offer presenting itself to Luke.

Luke stared at her, his face suddenly serious as they gazed into each other's eyes. Amid the crowd's cheering, she knew as well as if Luke had spoken to her that the town's offer meant everything that he had been running away from these past three years. Responsibility, commitment, and...

Noelle glanced away, afraid to reveal the open vulnerability she felt. Luke had never said he wanted to settle down. She had no right to expect him to give up his freedom. Besides, if he was weakened into accepting, could he endure the daily boredom of commitment?

Her glance drifted to Emily and Daniel, their smiling faces fixed upon each other and their baby. A tinge of envy touched her heart as Noelle thought of her friend and the love the small family showered upon each other. How lucky Emily and Daniel were to have found each other.

The crowd chanted Luke's name, and Noelle clapped her hands in rhythm as the people from the Red Garter streamed across the street. Finally, everyone was calling Luke's name as they waited for his answer.

Luke climbed upon the back of the wagon. Ike and Curly sat along the sides, dangling their legs over the rails.

"Fine man, that Luke Savage," the man beside her said.

Noelle turned around to see her uncle, Marcel. On his head, she recognized her father's top hat that had been packed away in the trunks she had brought to her uncle. The hat had been worn by Papa when he performed as the Great Bellencourt.

Her uncle's blue eyes twinkled merrily at her beneath the black felt brim.

"Yes, I think Luke Savage is a fine man, too." She glanced warily at this strange man who was her uncle.

"I've thought a great deal about why your father wanted me to have the contents of those boxes, Noelle." His voice was soft and gentle, and Noelle recognized nothing of the cold, hard man she had met yesterday.

She said nothing, waiting for him to continue.

"I spent most of the night going through those old

things.'' A twinge of sadness crept into his eyes. ''A profusion of memories came back to haunt me.'' He smiled, and a faraway look came into his eyes. ''Your father knew what he was doing when he asked you to bring me those things. He knew the wealth of memories we shared, and in remembering, he knew I'd recall our home and that special blood bond that is family. He knew what a healing balm those memories would give a bitter old man like me.''

Blackjack smiled, the warmth lighting his eyes. ''Nothing can truly sever that blood bond, my dear.'' He touched her hand. ''Ah, Noelle. Can you forgive a very foolish old man?''

Noelle blinked back a well of happiness. ''Oh, Uncle Marcel. I don't know about a foolish old man, but I know I can forgive you.'' She slipped her arms around his neck as he hugged her.

''Welcome home, little one.'' Blackjack's voice choked with emotion.

''Quiet!'' Mike O'Shea yelled from the back of the wagon. ''Luke wants to make a speech.''

''Speech! Speech! Speech!'' The crowd hammered the chorus.

Luke held up his hands, and turned to address the crowd. ''Ladies, gentlemen, and the rest of you.'' A roar of laughter followed. Luke spoke, his deep voice rich with emotion. ''Thank you, good people, from the bottom of my heart. But I can't accept your offer....'' Luke's gaze scanned the hushed crowd, coming to finally rest upon Noelle's face.

Her uncle placed a comforting hand on Noelle's shoulder as she bit back the crush of disappointment.

Luke held out a hand to her. ''I can't accept your offer unless this lovely lady agrees to be my wife.''

Noelle's breath caught as a riot of hoots and hollers filled the air the crowd chanted her name. She gazed at Luke, her vision blurry with tears of joy.

Luke reached out for her and the crowd parted as she felt herself being lifted to the wagon. Moments later, she was standing beside him. His arm slid around her waist.

"Noelle, will you marry me?" Luke whispered in her ear. The rising din rang in her ears.

"Luke, are you certain this is what you want?"

His dark eyes deepened with a smoldering intensity. "Noelle, I've never been surer of anything in my life." He took her in his arms, wanting so much more. "Don't you see, Noelle? You've given me back my belief in myself. Because of your faith in me, I've found my way back to you. I want you for my wife. That is, if you'll have me."

She slipped her arms around his neck, the crowd cheering with delight. "Of course, I'll marry you."

Luke picked her up and whirled her around. Several guns fired in the air and in the background, the rinky-tink piano rendition of "Hear Comes the Bride" echoed above the din.

"And I expect the wedding to be very soon, Luke," Blackjack added, joining Noelle and Luke on the wagon. "And I hope you'll let me have the honor of giving the bride away, my dear."

Noelle laughed. "Of course. Who else, Uncle Marcel?"

Hilda sniffed into her handkerchief. "I love weddings. And I'll bake you the biggest wedding cake. Enough for the whole town."

Daniel lifted Naomi from Emily's arms, then she clambered aboard the wagon. "And I'll help sew your wedding dress, Noelle. You'll be the most fetching bride in all of Nevada.''

Mike O'Shea shook Luke's hand, then gave him a sharp slap on the back. "Guess the best man won," he said, grinning. "Have you decided who'll be your best man at the wedding?"

Luke grinned crookedly. "I was just about to ask you, pal. What about it?"

Mike winked at Noelle, then grinned at Luke. "Of course I'll be your best man, and your stand-in, in case you're late for the wedding."

Luke glanced at Noelle, pulling her close. "Not a chance of letting her out of my sight. This time is forever."

If O'Shea said anything after that, Luke didn't hear him. In fact, all he could do was drink in the sight of his future bride.

Tears of happiness brightened those morning glory eyes, and Luke made a promise to himself that he would spend each precious day of their lives together showing her how very much he loved her.

"Do lilacs grow in Nevada?" Luke asked her.

"Lilacs?" She smiled. "I don't know. Maybe they will. If we keep them watered." She laughed. "Why do you ask?"

"Because I want our home to be surrounded by flowers. Roses in summer, the smell of lilacs in the spring. We'll have babies, and puppies, and all the sissy calves you want." He lifted her into his arms. "Because with you at my side, my darling, anything's possible."

His mouth covered hers, and the crowd exploded in cheers.

"I think it's time we go for a buggy ride," Luke

whispered into her hair. "Let's sneak away and be alone."

She giggled, then nestled into his arms. "I think you're a little late," she said, pointing to the black buggy and the pair of prancing horses that were pulling out of Shep's livery stable.

Luke glanced over his shoulder as his buggy bounded down Main Street toward the stand of pines in the hills beyond the town.

Blackjack waved his black top hat with one hand, his other arm around Hilda, just before the buggy turned the corner out of sight.

"Damn that Blackjack," Luke muttered, then drew Noelle to him.

"I've got another idea," she whispered into Luke's ear. "Let's wallpaper the bedroom closet," she said, not able to stifle the laughter. "We never got around to finishing the job, if you remember."

"Mmm, I remember," Luke said huskily into her ear. He helped her down from the wagon and very quietly, they worked their way through the crowd, into the Silver Hearts Saloon.

"Mighty fine idea, this wallpapering," Luke said, as he carried her up the stairs, the music of her laughter ringing in his ears.

*   *   *   *   *

Anglophile

('an-glə-fil)

One who greatly admires or favors England
and things English.

+

Dreamer

('drē-mər)

One who lives in a world of fancy and
imagination.

=

MY LORD PROTECTOR
by Deborah Hale
England, 1748 (29052-7)

THE BRIDE OF WINDERMERE
by Margo Maguire
England, 1421 (29053-5)

ROBBER BRIDE
by Deborah Simmons
England, 1274 (29055-1)

**Harlequin Historicals
the way the past *should* have been.**

Coming to bookstores in February 1999
and March 1999.
Available at your favorite retail outlet.

Sultry, sensual and ruthless...

THE AUSTRALIANS

Stories of romance Australian-style, guaranteed to fulfill that sense of adventure!

This April 1999 look for
Wildcat Wife
by **Lindsay Armstrong**

As an interior designer, Saffron Shaw was the hottest ticket in Queensland. She could pick and choose her clients, and thought nothing of turning down a commission from Fraser Ross. But Fraser wanted much more from the sultry artist than a new look for his home....

The Wonder from Down Under: where spirited women win the hearts of Australia's most independent men!

Available April 1999
at your favorite retail outlet.

HARLEQUIN®
Makes any time special ™